Praise for V
Cat & Gilley

COACH

"Laurie smoothly mixes eccentric characters and gossipy backstories with sufficient plot complications. This is quick and easy reading for cozy fans."
—*Publishers Weekly*

"Heroine and author both shine in a tale that offers a good time to everyone but the victim."
—*Kirkus Reviews*

TO COACH A KILLER

"Enjoyable . . . Fans of superior cozies will be well satisfied."
—*Publishers Weekly*

"A principled main character; well-drawn secondary characters; satisfying plot twists; and a smattering of humor distinguish this engaging mystery."
—*Booklist*

"A fun read that gets by on its characters' charm."
—*Kirkus Reviews*

Books by Victoria Laurie

COACHED TO DEATH

TO COACH A KILLER

COACHED IN THE ACT

COACHED RED-HANDED

COACHING FIRE

Published by Kensington Publishing Corp.

Coached Red-Handed

VICTORIA
LAURIE

Kensington Publishing Corp.
www.kensingtonbooks.com

KENSINGTON BOOKS are published by

Kensington Publishing Corp.
119 West 40th Street
New York, NY 10018

First Hardcover Edition: August 2022

First Mass Market Edition: December 2023
ISBN: 978-1-4967-3444-0

ISBN: 978-1-4967-3445-7 (ebook)

10 9 8 7 6 5 4 3 2 1

Printed in the United States of America

Chapter 1

I watched through the kitchen window as, across the drive, in the doorway of my guesthouse, Gilley signed for the package brought by certified mail, delivered to him by the postman. I winced when the postwoman turned away and Gilley was left to stare at the large envelope. "The poor love," I whispered.

I knew what was in that package, and I also personally knew how painful it was to receive the documents enclosed. With a tsk I turned away from the window and wrung my hands. I very much wanted to go over to Chez Kitty—my guesthouse—and whisk Gilley off somewhere fun to escape the full force of those dreadfully sad feelings.

But he'd been adamant that today, on the day he knew the papers were coming, he be left alone. He'd told me emphatically the day before that he didn't want any witnesses or attempts at cheer. He simply wanted to read over his divorce papers, sign them, and absorb the fact that the man he'd loved for nearly a decade was no longer his husband. His partner. His one true love in the world.

Trying to busy myself, I moved to the stove, grabbed the kettle, and filled it with water. I then set it on the burner and got down my favorite tea from Harney and Sons. It was called "Paris" in its beautiful blue and white tin and it always lifted my own spirits. Opening the lid I inhaled deeply. Hints of caramel and vanilla hit my nose and I sighed with pleasure. Lifting two of the bags from the tin, I put them in the clay teapot I'd bought on a visit to the UK years before when I'd taken a long, leisurely shopping trip through Harrods.

After setting the teapot aside, waiting for the water to boil in the teakettle already on the burner at the stove, I moved to the fridge and rooted around, looking for some of Gilley's absolutely scrumptious chocolate chip cookie dough.

Gil had taken several pastry and baking classes in years past, and it was my firm belief that he was as good as any professional now. He'd made some especially delicious creations in the past two months in fact, just as his divorce case proceeded through mediation. Gil had used baking to de-stress, and he'd also been donating most of his creations to various shelters and charitable organizations. I was grateful he'd come up with a distraction, because it gave him a little boost to be cheered when he walked through the door at the animal shelter or one of the nursing homes he visited.

After rolling out four balls of cookie dough, I

set them aside while the oven heated and poured the boiling water into the teakettle to steep. Then I was back at the window again, staring out across the drive, willing Gilley to make an appearance so that I could wrap him in a hug and tell him I understood.

"If he doesn't come over by dinnertime, I'll check on him," I whispered.

The beeper on the oven went off, startling me, and I smiled at myself as I put the cookies in the oven to bake. A few minutes later I was pouring myself a cup of tea when I heard the front door open and my AI butler announce, "Good afternoon, Sir Gilley."

"Hey Sebastian," Gilley said, his voice sounding thick and watery. I winced because I knew he'd likely been crying.

"Gil?" I called.

He didn't answer, but the padding of paws on the floor told me that he'd come over with Spooks—the dog he'd adopted from the shelter ten months before.

Before Spooks even rounded the corner, I was reaching for one of the porcelain jars on the counter that was always kept fully stocked with bison chew sticks. Spooks loved them and I loved giving him a treat every time he came to visit. He was a marvelous dog and the perfect, comforting companion to Gilley these past several months.

The silver-coated American Staffordshire terrier greeted me with wagging tail and eager eyes and I bent to kiss the top of his large, bony head after I'd placed the chew in his mouth. This was our ritual. Spooks would always wait for me to kiss his forehead before dashing to the family room just off the kitchen to devour his treat.

Once he'd scampered away, I stood tall again and saw that Gilley had come to the doorway of the kitchen and had settled for leaning against the doorframe, looking heartbroken.

I said nothing; I simply opened my arms and he came in for a hug. "I'm so, so sorry, Gilley," I whispered.

He embraced me tightly and sniffled. "Thanks, Cat."

The bell on the oven went off, but I didn't release Gilley until he was ready to let go first. "What's baking?" he asked, stepping back.

"Your cookies. Can't you smell them?"

He pointed to his nose, sniffling again.

"Ah," I said, handing him a tissue box before I pulled the cookies out of the oven and set them one by one on a large dinner plate to cool. I then got down another teacup and poured Gilley some of the delicious brew.

It sat in front of him while he stared at the countertop, looking forlorn. "Michel wants to swing by late next week to get the rest of his stuff."

"What belongings does he still have at the cottage?" I asked.

"His Nate Clean leather jacket; the art on the wall in the bedroom, the Adirondack chairs, a couple of cameras . . ."—he paused to shrug—"and my heart."

"Oh, Gil," I said, moving back over to him to squeeze his shoulders. He wiped a tear and I asked, "What can I do for you?"

He simply shook his head. "Nothing, sugar." We

were quiet for a moment, leaning into each other when Gilley added, "I don't know that I can take seeing him, Cat. We haven't been together in the same place in over eight months, and I'm so scared that I'll lose it when he shows up to collect his stuff."

"Well then, just come over here, lovey. You can stay with me in the main house and I'll run interference with Michel."

Gilley shook his head sadly. "Thanks, but that won't work, Cat. I won't be able to resist seeing him in person. You know I won't."

I sighed. "I do. What if you went into the City for the day?" New York City was a mere two and a half hours away, and there was plenty for Gilley to do to keep him distracted long enough for Michel to collect his things and leave before Gilley got back.

But Gil merely shook his head again. "That won't work, either. I'll find some excuse to stay in the Hamptons and spy on him while he's here. I think he has a boyfriend, and if he brings him here . . . I'll just . . . I'll . . ."

Gilley's voice trailed off as another tear slid down his cheek. My own eyes watered. I knew this heartbreak all too well. The end of a marriage isn't simply the end of a relationship, it's the end of an identity as the bonded partner of another person, and an end to the dream of the future you carried for the entire length of your marriage.

When my own ex-husband left me for a bartender at our country club, I was absolutely gutted. It was a blow I thought I'd never recover from, and yet, with time, I managed not only to pick myself up, dust myself off, and move on, but also to find love again and a new dream for the future.

But telling all that to Gilley wouldn't take the sting out of what he was feeling or facing right now.

He sniffled again, blew his nose, then reached for his cup of tea. Holding it up to his nose, for the briefest moment his expression changed from heartbreak to inquisitiveness. He sniffed the brew a little harder. "This smells amazing."

"Harney and Sons," I said.

"Not your usual flavor though, right?"

"Correct. This is called 'Paris.' "

Gilley sniffed the steaming liquid deeply for a third time. "My God, that's incredible. Does Paris really smell like this?"

I smiled. "Not quite."

Gilley sighed. "I've never been to Paris."

I stared at him in disbelief. Gilley and his former business partner and still best friend, M.J. Whitefeather, used to be members of a ghost-busting troupe that investigated haunted locations all over Europe. "How is it possible that you've never been to Paris?"

He shrugged. "It was a language thing. None of us spoke French, and M.J. was worried that we'd be dealing with spooks that we couldn't communicate with, so we stuck to the English-speaking places in Europe."

"Ah," I said. And then I had the most magnificent idea. "Gilley!" I said, grabbing him by the shoulders.

"Cat!" he replied, looking slightly alarmed.

I grinned. "What if we went on a European holiday together?"

He blinked. Then blinked again. "When, like this summer?"

"No! Like the day before Michel shows up!"

More blinking followed.

"Okay, maybe two days before he shows up," I said. "We'll want to avoid any risk of bumping into him, and we can tell Sebastian to let him into Chez Kitty and lock up after he leaves."

Gilley added a dropped jaw to the blinking.

I took that to mean he wasn't outright opposed to the idea. "We can start in Paris and make our way anywhere beyond that that you want to go or haven't already been to."

"I've never been to Amsterdam," he said, and I could tell he was starting to warm to the idea.

"Done," I said, so excited I began hopping from foot to foot. "We'll begin in Paris, make our way to Brussels—you'll love Brussels—then to Amsterdam, unless we also want to take in Cologne, which has the most marvelous cathedrals and art museums, not to mention *the* most fabulous Excelsior Hotel Ernst with a restaurant run by a master chef that you will just *die* for!"

Gilley's brows were arched and his eyes were wide. I could see my idea was sparking some appeal. "I'd want to pay my own way," he said.

I cupped his chin gently and said, "You're adorable. The trip's on me, kiddo."

"It's too much, Cat," he said.

"It's not. And it's what you need. If it'll make you feel better, we can set a limit on the amount that I'll spend on you when we go shopping in Paris."

Gilley giggled, and my chest filled with hope. "Please say yes," I said.

Gilley nodded. "Okay. Yes."

At that moment Spooks came over to nudge his way between us, probably to see what all the excitement was about and just like that, Gilley's face fell. "What about Spooks? What do I do with him?"

"We could board him," I suggested.

Gilley scowled, and he got down from his chair to wrap his arms around Spooks's middle. "He'll think I've abandoned him."

I eyed Spooks critically and the sweet pooch leaned against Gilley and closed his eyes for a moment, as if he were relishing his human's affection. "You're right," I said, my heart melting. "There's no way we can put Spooks in a kennel and risk having him experience even one anxious moment."

Gilley nodded and kissed his pup on the forehead half a dozen times. The pair had really bonded. "What if we took him with us?" Gilley asked.

I let out a laugh before I could catch myself. "Sorry," I said, clearing my throat. "That was rude. The truth is, lovey, while appealing, I doubt we could get the necessary paperwork required to travel through three separate countries with a dog in tow cleared in time to make it to Europe and avoid bumping into Michel. We'd probably need a ninety-day head start for something like that."

Gilley's face fell. "I can't leave him behind, Cat."

And then an idea hit me. "What if we ask Sunny if she can puppy sit?"

Sunny D'Angelo—wait, excuse me, she was now

Sunny *Shepherd*—was the twin sister of my main squeeze, Steven Shepherd.

Shep is a detective with the East Hampton PD and had been my significant other for nearly three years, and his sister and I were also now very close. In fact, she'd been the first friend I'd made when I moved to the Hamptons.

Sunny had a young son named Finley who was turning three in a few weeks, and both he and his mother were very big fans of Spooks.

"Do you think Sunny would agree to doggy sit?" Gilley asked, hope once again animating his features.

"There's only one way to find out, lovey," I said, moving away from Gilley to the fridge. "We'll take her over some of your scrumptious cookies to butter her up."

I heard the scraping sound of the barstool being pushed away from the counter and a moment later Gilley was next to me, practically pushing me out of the way as he bent toward the fridge. "We're going to be asking her to puppy sit for the entire length of our vacation, sugar. No *way* are cookies enough to butter her up. This calls for something *big.*"

I laughed and stepped back to my chair at the island to give Gilley some room to create. And create he did. It took nearly an hour and a half but at the end of it was the most delicious-smelling (and probably tasting) chocolate raspberry pudding cake I'd ever gazed upon. Gilley even went to the added detail of cutting out a stencil in the shape of a dog and sprinkling powdered sugar over it, leaving the stenciled shape in relief.

"You amaze me," I said as he turned to me, finished cake in hand.

Gilley blushed. "Aww," he said. "It's nothing. A small effort given the favor we'll be asking."

I nodded and then went over to my pantry and rooted around on the shelf where I kept my teas. "Here," I said, bringing out another tin of Paris that I'd purchased in a two-for-one special. "We'll add a tin of this to sweeten the pot."

"I love that you're willing to part with your favorite tea, Cat."

I walked over to a drawer at the far end of the kitchen where I kept a sampling of tissue paper, ribbon, and gift bags and pulled out some blue ribbon. "Anything for Spooks," I said, tying a bow around the tea tin.

"Let's go before the cake cools down too much. I want Sunny to enjoy it while it's still warm."

Gilley and I drove over to Sunny's house and I was very careful to drive slowly and smoothly so as not to jostle Gilley's creation.

We arrived at Sunny's and we both immediately noticed a sleek new Tesla convertible in the driveway.

"Is that Sunny's?" Gilley asked.

"No," I said. "She got another Range Rover, remember?"

Gilley turned to look at me. "Does she have company over?"

I bit my lip. Gilley and I thought nothing of stopping over at Sunny's unannounced. She was always so happy to see us, but suddenly, I realized that it was likely a habit that was probably a bit intrusive if not downright rude.

"Should we leave?" I asked.

Gilley frowned and glanced at the cake he'd spent the better part of two hours creating. "I really want to give her my cake, Cat."

I eyed the front door to Sunny's house and then Gilley's cake. "Well, if she does have company over, it might be nice if Sunny and her guest had a little cake to nosh on, right?"

"And tea," Gilley reminded me.

"And tea," I agreed. "Okay, let's go ring the bell."

We got out of the car and approached the house, walking up the two steps to the front door. We were about to press the bell when the door opened to reveal Sunny, lip-locked in the embrace of another dear friend of ours, Marcus Brown.

Our reaction was total, stunned silence. Marcus had been my attorney on a couple of occasions, and he'd also represented Sunny at one point. He was an absolutely gorgeous man, and the best criminal defense lawyer in the Hamptons if not in all of Long Island.

I'd always thought of Marcus as a bit of a player where women were concerned. To my knowledge he'd never been married, and I imagined he had a string of women eagerly anticipating a call from him. So to see him holding Sunny so tightly, so protectively and kissing her with such care and passion took me totally by surprise.

And judging by the dropped jaw that Gilley was sporting, the feeling was mutual.

Right around that point, Sunny and Marcus seemed to become aware that they had an audience. They both turned their faces slightly and each of them peeked with one eye at us, standing just on the other side of the storm door.

I waved.

Gilley giggled.

Marcus and Sunny shot apart like water on a hot griddle.

"Gilley!" Sunny said, eyeing him first.

"Cat!" Marcus said, eyeing me first.

"Hello," I sang, allowing the *huge* grin on my lips to spread wide, wide, wide.

"How's things?" Gilley asked, oh, so casually.

Sunny and Marcus cleared their throats in unison and Sunny's face flushed a deep red.

The four of us stood there, staring at each other for a solid ten seconds before Marcus lifted his wrist to eyeball what looked to be a very expensive watch and announce, "I'm late. Busy afternoon. Sorry."

And with that he opened the storm door and eased in between Gilley and me to walk quickly to his car, the whole time pretending to eyeball his watch like the Mad Hatter who just couldn't *believe* how late he was.

We all watched him go and after he'd left her driveway, Gilley and I turned to Sunny with expectant expressions.

In turn, she stared back at us with the innocence of a newborn foal.

Neither one of us was buying it.

"We brought cake!" Gilley announced, holding up his creation, which still smelled heavenly.

Sunny's expression turned pained. "Uh . . ." she said.

Gilley ignored any hesitancy she was projecting to let us in and stepped forward into her foyer, his cake raised high like a shield.

I grinned at Sunny and followed after Gilley.

We all arrived in Sunny's kitchen and for the first time since I could remember I didn't wince upon entering. Something terrible had happened to me here several months before, and it had become nearly impossible to step into Sunny's kitchen since then without bracing for an attack.

But today I realized I hadn't winced or braced myself at all. I'd simply strolled in, happy as a clam to catch two of my favorite people in a romantic embrace.

"I brought tea," I said, wiggling the tin for her to see.

"How nice," Sunny said, but her warmth and her smile were both forced.

Setting down the tin I eyed her curiously and realized why she seemed so tense. "Shepherd doesn't know, does he?"

Sunny grimaced. "No," she whispered.

"And you don't want me to tell him," I said next.

"Definitely not!" she said, and then rushed to add, "It's not because I'm trying to hide anything from him . . . it's just so new, Cat. And I don't want Steve to weigh in on it yet."

"Weigh in?"

Sunny frowned—a rare expression for her. "Every boyfriend I ever had, including Darius, Stevie made sure to point out all their flaws to me over and over like he was trying to protect me from a bad relationship, but all it did was plant the idea in my mind that I continually choose bad men. I don't want to look at Marcus under that spotlight. I *like* him, Cat. A lot. Like a *lot*—a lot."

Gilley and I exchanged a look and then we both spread our arms wide and rushed to hug Sunny, who was caught completely off guard. "Oh, honey!" I sang as we all hugged. "We love Marcus and couldn't be happier for the two of you!"

Sunny laughed and I noticed that her eyes were a little misty. Her recent divorce had been swift but very painful for a number of reasons. She'd had a tough, tough year and deserved a little happiness. "It's not officially a thing yet, though," she said. "I mean, we've been seeing each other only for the past four months."

"*Four months?*" Gilley and I exclaimed together.

"How did we miss that?" I asked.

Gilley shrugged.

"We've been very, very discreet," Sunny admitted. "When we've hung out together, we've mostly stuck to Sag Harbor."

Sag Harbor was on the north side of this section of Long Island, directly across from us here in East Hampton. "That was smart," Gilley said, moving back to his cake and digging through Sunny's drawers, probably looking for a knife to cut it with. "Shepherd has been so loaded down with home improvement projects and work lately, I doubt he gets to Sag Harbor very often."

"Almost never," Sunny said.

"We won't tell him," I promised, holding up my hand in a vow of secrecy, and Gilley promptly mimicked the move. "We'll let you tell him, and if he even thinks about saying anything negative about Marcus, you tell me and I'll set him straight!"

Sunny sighed with relief. "Thanks, you guys."

"Come," Gilley said. "Sit. We'll make you some tea and serve you some cake and have a little chat."

Sunny considered him with a sideways smile. "A little chat? Something tells me you two are up to something."

Gilley and I exchanged another look and I nodded to him so that he could explain on my way to the teakettle by the stove.

"We're not up to something so much as we're embarking on an adventure," he told her.

"Oh?" Sunny said. "What adventure are you two about to have?"

"A European one," I said, setting the burner under the kettle to high.

Gilley finally found a knife and began to cut into the cake. "We're headed to Paris, Brussels, Cologne, and Amsterdam for a grand tour!"

Sunny clapped her hands. "Oh, that sounds wonderful! When do you leave?"

"Next week," Gilley said, bouncing on the balls of his feet.

Watching him excitedly tell Sunny about our plans made me feel so relieved. He would've been so depressed, thinking about Michel coming to Chez Kitty to clear out his belongings. Now he had something to look forward to, and a great deal of planning and packing to occupy his idle time, which is always the worst time when you're struggling with a heartbreak.

"You're leaving so soon?" Sunny asked, and she quickly followed that with, "Do you need someone to look after Spooks while you're away?"

I grinned at Gilley and he smiled wide in return. Our plan had worked perfectly.

A bit later as we were finishing up our tea and cake, Sunny suddenly exclaimed, "Oh! Cat, I almost forgot. I know you're leaving very soon, but do you think you could talk to the friend of a friend of mine?"

I eyed her curiously. "Talk about what?"

"Gabriel Ducey is one of my oldest friends. We go back to elementary school together. Anyway, as I might've mentioned before, Gabby is a published author and she's always said that she owes her success to her mentor, a highly successful author who lives here in the Hamptons. Gabby says that she and her mentor got together for a little chat about a week ago, and Gabby discovered that this magnificent woman is struggling with a few things and could really use some life advice. I told Gabby about you and she spoke to her mentor, who's anxious to meet you. Professionally, of course."

I blinked. "Oh, wow," I said, trying to think through all I had to do to get ready to head to Europe at the spur of the moment and try to fit in a new client.

My gaze traveled to Gilley, who kept my appointment book, and he said, "You do have the afternoon totally open from three to five, Cat."

"Could this woman come to my office on such short notice?" I asked.

"I think so. Let me text Gabby and see if that

will work. I don't have the other woman's direct number, otherwise, I'd call her myself."

Gilley and I cleaned up the dishes from our tea as Sunny texted Gabby. While we were setting the dishes in the dishwasher, Sunny's phone chimed. "Gabby says she can be at your office at three p.m. sharp."

"Perfect," I said.

"What name will the appointment be under?" Gilley asked, taking out his own smartphone.

"Scarlet," Sunny said.

"Ooh," Gilley cooed. "Great name."

"You think that's good, wait till I tell you that her last name is Rubi."

"Wow," I said. "For real?"

Sunny nodded. "*And* she's a ginger."

"She's a redhead?" Gilley asked.

"Yep. I've met her a few times. What a personality! Scarlet's as eccentric as they come and she's absolutely loaded, even by East Hampton's standards."

Gilley's brow rose. "Richer than the Entwistles?" he asked, referring to some dear friends of ours.

Sunny laughed. "Probably not quite that wealthy, but loaded all the same."

"How'd she come by her good fortune?" I asked.

"She's a romance writer," Sunny said.

My eyes widened. "She is?"

"Oh, yeah. Scarlet has been writing romance novels for fifty years, and her millions of fans adore her. She's made an absolute fortune from book sales, and at least twenty of her novels have been made into rom-coms."

Gilley's jaw hung open like a bat cave. He looooves a good rom-com. "*Where* can I find one of these treasures?"

"Oh, TNT airs them all the time! And a few of the spicier ones are on Netflix," Sunny added with a giggle. "Just do a search on Scarlet Rubi movies and they'll pop up."

Gilley began to furiously tap at his phone and his face lit up when he landed on what was likely a list of Scarlet's movies. "I've *seen* some of these!" he said. "And I loved them!"

I moved to peer over Gilley's shoulder. "Oh, yeah," I said. "I've seen some of these too. Scarlet can definitely spin a good yarn."

"And we get to sit down with her and have a little chat!" Gilley exclaimed. "Ooh, I just *love* getting to know famous people. Especially *rich* and famous people!"

"Whoa, whoa, there, Gil," I said. "There is no 'we' here. There is only me and Scarlet, sitting down for a *professional* discussion. And no matter what she says, you aren't allowed to repeat anything you hear, capiche?"

"Capiche," Gilley muttered. He'd learned his lesson since the last time he'd repeated something a client said and I'd very nearly fired him, which would've made our friendship and living arrangement awkward.

I eyed the clock and noticed that Sunny probably wanted to get on with her afternoon, so I said, "Thank you so much for spending some quality time with us, and for offering to watch Spooks."

"Of course," she said. "Finley adores that pooch. He'll be so excited when I tell him the news."

Gilley looked around. "Hey, where is that little guy, anyway?"

"He's with my cousin, Veronica, who's really more like an aunt to me. She offered to take Fin twice a week and give me a break, and she's been an absolute godsend. I love being a mom, but it can get pretty overwhelming if you're on duty twenty-four-seven."

I rubbed her shoulder as I moved past her into the hallway leading to the front door. "Sistah, preach!" I called out over my shoulder.

She laughed and followed behind me and Gilley to the door. "I can't imagine how you did it with twins, Cat."

"She had nannies," Gilley said. "Multiple."

I paused at the door to level a look at him. "He's not wrong," I conceded. "I did have some fantastic help."

"You should consider getting yourself one of those," Gilley said.

Sunny shook her head. "A nanny for one child? Not unless I decide to go back to work."

I eyed Sunny in surprise. "You're thinking about that?"

She nodded. "I got a nice settlement from the divorce, but it won't last forever. Marcus is encouraging me to study for the bar and take it to get my law license."

Gilley and I blinked rapidly at her. This was new information. "You went to law school, Sunny?" Gilley asked.

She nodded. "UC Berkeley. I married Darius shortly after graduating, and he convinced me not to pursue a law career because he knew it'd be a lot of hours away from him. Like an idiot I agreed."

"Hey," I said, reaching for her arm. "You're the exact opposite of an idiot, Sunny. And if there's anything we can do to support you in your pursuit of becoming a lawyer, please don't hesitate to tell us."

Sunny put a hand over mine. "Thanks, Cat. I appreciate that more than I can say. You guys have a great rest of your day, and remember, don't say anything about Marcus to Steve."

Gilley crossed his heart and mimicked locking his lips and throwing away the key. I smiled and took him by the hand. "Come along, Gilley. We have tickets to purchase and reservations to make."

Little did I know then that all our travel plans were in danger of being thrown out the window in the days to come.

Chapter 2

"How do I look?" Gilley asked me while keeping one eye on the door.

"How do *you* look?" I replied. "Fine. Why?"

"Because I want to make a good first impression with Scarlet, like duh," he said as if I was slow-witted.

"Gilley," I said sternly. "This isn't a social call and you are *not* to turn it into one. Understand?"

"Yeah, yeah," he said, literally waving me off as he moved to the door to peer out toward the street. He bounced with excitement and I was worried he'd be too much for Ms. Rubi and I'd lose a client because of it.

"Please, Gilley?"

He looked over his shoulder at me. "Please what?"

"Please don't overwhelm her, okay? If she's as

wealthy and famous as she appears, she'll be well-connected which means if she has a bad experience with us, she could damage our reputation."

Gilley pouted at me and rolled his eyes. "Fine," he said with a heavy sigh. "I'll treat her like I do every client."

"Thank—"

"Only I'll add in a little extra sizzle on account of her being so rich and famous."

I actually laughed when what I should've done was send Gilley out for refreshments or some other errand. Of course, he'd absolutely refuse to go, even if I ordered him, so I suppose finding the levity in the situation was bound to be the easier course.

I didn't have long to worry about it as just a moment later a woman with brilliant red hair, wearing a red satin suit, red stilettos, and adorned in rubies walked toward our door.

"I'm going to take a wild guess and say that's Scarlet," Gilley said, pointing toward her.

I put my hand on his arm and firmly lowered it because I didn't want Scarlet to see him pointing at her through the window. "Remember," I whispered as she came close. "Be cool."

"Got it," Gilley said, reaching for the door and pulling it open. "Ms. Rubi!" he exclaimed with a low bow like a knight before his queen. "What an honor to meet you!" he added, still frozen in that posture. "Won't you please come in? And whatever refreshments you require, consider me—Gilley Gillespie—at your beck and call."

I felt my face flush with embarrassment. Gilley was way over the top, but somewhat to my relief,

Scarlet didn't seem to mind. She eyed him with an amused smirk and tapped him on the shoulder. "You may rise, Sir Gilley."

Gilley popped back upright and added a hop. Scarlet had said the perfect thing to make Gilley's day. "What may I bring you?" he asked.

Scarlet smiled warmly at him. "I'd love a scotch. Got any?"

My eyes went wide with surprise, but Gilley didn't even flinch. "Glenfiddich? Macallan? Johnnie Walker Black?"

Scarlet's eyes held a twinkle and that amused smile never wavered. "Surprise me," she said with a wink.

Gilley practically danced in place, then he eyed me as if to ask if it was okay, and I merely inhaled deeply and waved my hand at him. "The store is right around the corner. Keep the receipt and I'll reimburse you," I told him.

Gilley was off like a shot and both Scarlet and I laughed at his antics. Extending my hand I said, "I'm sorry about him. He's a bit excitable."

"He's delightful," she replied, taking my palm for a gentle handshake.

I had the opportunity to study her features then, and I marveled at how beautiful she was. Her hair was a deep red, perfectly coifed in a French bun, and her skin was pale but mostly unlined, even though I'd put her in her seventies, especially if she'd been writing professionally for fifty years.

She had bright blue eyes that held what appeared to be a permanent twinkle, a straight thin nose, and lips adorned with bold red lipstick. She was quite tall, probably five-ten or five-eleven in heels and perhaps five-eight or so barefoot which still put her seven inches above me. The other curiosity was that her posture was straight as an arrow, which was surprising given that her profession required her to sit hunched over a computer keyboard for long hours.

"Catherine," she said warmly. "It's a pleasure to finally meet you. I've heard and read so much about you, it's wonderful to put a face with the name."

I warmed to this woman immediately. She was delightfully charming. "Lovely to meet you as well, Scarlet. Won't you come have a seat and we'll start our chat."

Scarlet followed me to my seating area, which was a comfortable, cozy little square in the center of my office space, set up with a wing chair for me and a love seat for my clients.

Once we were settled, I took up a pad and pen from the small side table next to my chair and said, "So! What brings you to my door?"

Scarlet sighed and her eyes held a faraway cast as she began to speak. "I'm afraid I've created a monster," she said. "Wait, correction, I'm afraid I've created a family of monsters."

"Sounds serious," I said.

"Oh, it is," she assured. "Catherine, from the articles I've read about you, it appears you're also a woman of means, is that correct?"

A flush hit my cheeks, but I nodded, wondering where this was going.

"And do you support your family?"

"I do," I said. "I support my sons, who're fifteen, and, frankly, I guess you could also say that I support my ex-husband and his new wife from the settlement of our divorce."

"And your extended family? Do you support them?"

"I have a sister, but she does fairly well for herself, and she's in one of the best marriages I've ever seen, so my financial support isn't something she wants or needs."

Scarlet nodded. "No one else?"

I grinned sideways. "Well, I might partially support Gilley. He's my permanent houseguest, living in my guesthouse, but it'd simply be an empty home without him and I enjoy his company, so it works for us."

"I see. So you don't support any parents, cousins, nieces, nephews, or aunts, uncles, etcetera, etcetera?"

I shook my head, thinking I knew where this was going, but I wanted to let her tell me.

"Smart," she said, as I shook my head. "Keep it that way."

"I'm assuming you support many members of your family?" I asked.

She laughed mirthlessly. "Many members indeed. I support the entire family tree, which isn't so much a tree anymore as it's a thick vine, wrapped around me now like a snake that is slowly choking the life out of me."

"Wow," I said, my eyes widening. "That's intense. And it must be hard to carry all that, Scarlet. A lot of weight on your shoulders."

"Definitely," she agreed.

At that moment, Gilley, flushed and sweaty, burst back into the office carrying a brown paper bag with the outline of a liquor bottle in it. Spotting us looking at him, he paused long enough to smooth out his hair and wipe a bead of sweat from his forehead. "How do you take your scotch, madam?" he asked formally.

"Neat," Scarlet said. "And I like a generous pour."

Gilley nodded enthusiastically and hurried over to our beverage counter to assemble Scarlet's cocktail.

We waited in silence while he got down a glass and opened the bottle of Johnnie Walker Black to pour out a "healthy" pour, then brought it over to Scarlet, holding the glass with both hands and serving it to her with another slight bow.

She flashed that gorgeous warm smile at him and said, "Thank you, Gilley. You can be my bartender any day."

Gilley's face, already flushed from exertion and excitement, turned absolutely crimson and he grinned so widely at her, I thought he'd split a lip.

"Gil," I said softly.

"Yeah?" he asked without turning his attention away from Scarlet.

"May I please have a bottle of sparkling water?"

"Sure, sure," he said, but didn't move. He seemed to be waiting for Scarlet to take a sip of her scotch.

And she in turn seemed to sense that because she lifted her glass and sang, "Cheers!"

Gilley bounced away to fetch my water with all the enthusiasm of Tigger on a new adventure with Pooh, and Scarlet winked at me as she took a healthy sip of her scotch. "Oh, that's the stuff," she whispered. "Now, where was I?"

"You were telling me that your family is currently imposing on your generosity," I said.

Beside me there was a gasp and I heard Gilley say, "How dare they!"

I startled and turned my head to stare at him with wide, furious eyes. He'd snuck up on me and he knew better than to listen in and/or comment on anything my clients said.

Sensing my displeasure, Gilley put a hand to his lips and muttered, "Excuse me. I think I have emails to answer."

When he was safely out of earshot, I leaned in toward Scarlet and said, "I promise you nothing you say here will be repeated."

She waved a hand in dismissal at me. "Of course," she said. "Like I said, I read up on you, and your reviews on Yelp are excellent with quite a few clients noting your discretion."

I have reviews on Yelp? I thought to myself. To Scarlet I merely nodded and sat back again in my chair. "How do you want me to help you, Scarlet?"

"Well," she said, taking a moment to consider my question. "I suppose I want your advice on how to cut off the worst of the customers at Bank of Rubi."

"Who might those be?"

"The question is more like, who wouldn't they be. There're my children, Masie and Grayson; my sister Siobhan; her son Luke; my nephew Carson; and my granddaughters, April and Lucy."

I sat up straighter in surprise. "Do any of them have jobs?"

Scarlet laughed like the question was hilarious. "Only Carson—he works for me. He's the son of my beloved brother who died in an automobile accident years ago. Carson was in the car and the crash left him a paraplegic."

"Oh, that's so sad. I'm sorry."

"Thank you," Scarlet said. "I loved David—Carson's father—so much. If he were alive today, he never would've allowed things to get this out of hand."

"I think you've done your best, Scarlet," I told her gently. She wore so much guilt, it was a miracle she didn't simply throw up her hands, retreat to her bedroom, and ignore the whole world.

"What about the others?" I asked, getting us back on track. "You said they don't work?"

"No. No, they do not."

"Why not?" I asked, genuinely curious about Scarlet's family dynamic.

"Well, to hear them tell it, they do work. My sister is an artist, although I've never actually seen her sell one of her paintings, but she claims that her art pieces are in hot demand. My daughter, Masie, does something with makeup or beauty or a thing on the internet where she influences other people to buy other people's products but as far as I can tell, she doesn't directly benefit from this because she's never been able to even earn enough to pay for her own groceries.

"Meanwhile, my son, Grayson, calls himself a promoter, whatever *that* means. Mostly what I've seen him promote are the glory days when he was in his twenties and handsome, smart, and quite the catch. These days I don't think that boy can buy a date."

From his desk, Gilley let out a loud giggle, but

quickly stifled it. I glared at him but Scarlet didn't pay him any attention. She simply sipped more of the scotch and continued.

"As for my nephew Luke, he claims to be a real estate developer. So far, I've had to bail him out of three bankruptcies and four foreclosures, and the only real estate he seems to actually be developing are ones with big giant holes in the ground in which to throw large sums of my money.

"And when we get down to the younger generations . . . well! Let me tell you, my two granddaughters, April and Lucy, make their parents and uncle look like success stories.

"Lucy and April are fraternal twins. Masie is their mother, but she never really was much of one when the girls were growing up. I tried to help raise them, but as I said, my work obligations kept getting in the way and all that dysfunction set both of the girls on a dark path.

"Lucy just got out of a rehab facility upstate. It was her fifth time at that center, which costs two thousand dollars a day. She'll be good for a few months and then she'll start hanging out with the wrong crowd again and I'll have to hire a private investigator to find her and bring her home, only to send her back upstate for another stint in rehab.

"And then comes April, and April makes Lucy look good. The girl is whip-smart, and such a talented writer in her own right; but she lacks discipline and focus, preferring to sleep her way through most of the Hamptons, hanging out with the wrong crowd, getting into mischief and trouble that always calls for expensive solutions. On her arrest record alone, I believe I've spent fifty thousand dollars to keep her out of jail for various petty crimes and misdemeanors."

I inhaled deeply when Scarlet finished, and said, "That's a lot."

Scarlet nodded. "It is. Much of it, I know, is my own fault, but to be honest, I've been so busy writing and touring the past forty years that I haven't had the energy to pay attention to the depths of their freeloading until very recently, when I had a health scare that made me take a long, hard look at myself and my family. I mean, I'm not going to live forever, Catherine. What will these people do without me?"

"Probably the same thing they're doing now," I said plainly. "Nothing of any substance, and they'll all pay a price in the end, but Scarlet," I said, leaning forward, "that's what life *is*! Our characters develop not in good times, but in difficult ones. It's how we respond to the hardships in front of us that makes us valuable, tested, and strong. If you keep removing all the obstacles for your family, then when the day comes that you're no longer there to provide for them, they'll fall flat on their faces and their struggles will really begin."

Scarlet chewed on the inside of her cheek. "That's what I don't want to have happen," she said.

"I know," I said. "And I know you love your children, your nephews, and your granddaughters, but Scarlet, they're going to fall on their faces either way. The difference is, if they start falling down now because you've stopped enabling them, then *you* at least will be able to get your life back instead of constantly trying to balance your work and their problems. If you continue to enable them, though, right up until you pass on, your family is still going to struggle, but you will have wasted all the precious time, money, and peace of mind you owe yourself between now and then."

Scarlet nodded and there was something in her eyes, something like a spark of courage, and I was thrilled to see it.

"So what do I do?" she asked. "How do I set them free of the bonds of my financial support? And before you answer that, Catherine, know that I'm not going to toss any of my family members out into the street. That would kill me because I bear some of this responsibility myself. I've enabled them all these years and they're not properly equipped to survive without any form of income."

"I understand," I said. And I did. "Maybe the place to start is by having an honest conversation with each of them to assess how difficult it'll be for them out in the big wide world without your safety net. Do they all live with you?"

"Oh, God no!" Scarlet said quickly. "That would truly drive me insane. No, they all have their own homes. Bought and paid for by yours truly."

"Wow," I said, somewhat surprised. This family really had milked Scarlet for all she was worth. "And they own these homes outright?"

I was thinking that, if all these family members owned their own homes, then they could probably sell them, move someplace far more practical and live off the proceeds until they got their act together—or didn't. The point was that they might have untapped assets that Scarlet could direct them to.

"No," she said, answering my question. "I own all the real estate, and pay for the upkeep and maintenance and utility bills, etcetera, etcetera, etcetera."

My eyes widened again. "Really?"

"Really."

"Are these homes especially valuable to you?" I asked next.

Scarlet shrugged. "All told, the real estate probably runs in the ten-to-fifteen-million-dollar range, so there is quite a lot of value there."

"And how much does it cost you to support your entire family for a year?"

Scarlet scoffed. "Oh, at least a million and a half if not more. These people always have their hand out. There's continually some crisis that requires large sums of cash, so maybe it's even more than that." Scarlet put a long, elegant finger to her lips and tapped them with it. "When I really think about it, and I remember that just last month the total tab to support them was in the hundred-and-seventy-thousand-dollar range, it's got to be at least two million each year."

"I see. So, in just five to seven years' time, if you let go of the real estate, you'd at least draw even, am I right?"

Scarlet cocked her head and squinted at me; I think she understood where I was heading. "Or less," she said. "You think I should sell their homes and give them the money from the proceeds, then tell them they're cut off?"

"No," I said. "I don't believe you should work quite that hard. I think, though, that if you're willing to part with the assets of their homes on your balance sheet, that you can assign the titles over to them and let *them* make their own decisions about how best to utilize that gift to support themselves. If you want to nudge them toward selling their homes and moving someplace less expensive to live off the proceeds of their house while they try to find jobs or simply get their act together, then I suppose that would be okay too."

Scarlet squinted at me. "I like this idea, Catherine. I like it a lot. If I assigned the title to their houses over to them, I wouldn't feel guilty about cutting them off. They'd be sitting on valuable real estate that they could sell in a heartbeat. They'd have the means to survive without my money, and anytime they came begging to me for more cash, I could simply point them back to the house I outright gave them."

"Exactly," I said, happily sitting back in my chair, proud that I'd found a solution.

And then I thought of something else, because I could see the potential for future trouble too. "Scarlet, I think you should consider drawing up a contract that they'd each have to sign before you'd assign the title to their house over to them. I think the contract should stipulate that in order for them to accept the transfer of title, they'd have to agree to never, ever, ever ask you for money again. Maybe if there was an agreement in writing, they'd be less apt to come begging to you for more coin."

Scarlet nodded enthusiastically. "Yes," she said.

"That's the perfect idea. I'll do it. But I'll want to do this right away. Tonight, if possible."

"Marvelous!" I said with a clap of my hands.

"I'll call my attorney—oh drat," Scarlet said.

"What?" I asked.

"My attorney just went on vacation yesterday. She's in Hawaii and won't be back for two weeks. If I wait even a day, Catherine, I know I'll scrub the entire idea. Who can I get to draw up these contracts on such short notice?"

"Who's your attorney?"

"Terry Gilman of Gilman, Dunlevy, and Bianchi."

I bounced in my seat. "Scarlet! We use the same firm! My attorney is Tony Bianchi."

"You don't say," she said.

"Yes! And I'm sure I can convince him to draft the contracts for you. Tony is a good man, and these would be fairly straightforward. A legal secretary could probably put one together in about a half hour if not less. Let me make a call."

I spent the next ten minutes explaining the situation to Tony, who agreed to draft the contracts and email them to Scarlet, but he cautioned me by saying, "I won't be available to oversee their signatures, Catherine. With Terry out of town I've got my hands full here covering her cases, and my wife and I are attending an event this evening so I'll need to leave the office by six."

"Do we need a lawyer present for the signing of the contracts?" I asked.

"No. But you will need a notary to verify signatures and the transfer of title."

My gaze traveled to Gilley, who for the past several months had been helping out our dear friend,

Channel Entwistle, as her real estate business grew and she struggled to find an adequate assistant. One of the things that Gilley had had to do to act as her helper was obtain his notary stamp. He'd even gotten it in the mail a few weeks ago.

"I know just the person for the job," I told Tony. "Thank you for doing this. I'll have Gilley send over all the relevant names and addresses of everyone involved right away."

"Perfect," Tony said. "Oh, and make sure to send over the value of each home. I'll need that to go into the contract as well."

"Got it. Thanks again, my friend. I owe you."

Once I'd hung up with Tony, I filled Scarlet and Gilley in on the plan. "Gilley, you'll need to attend the meeting tonight and bring your notary stamp."

"What about you?" Scarlet asked me. "Catherine, I'm not sure I can go through with this if you're not there to give me strength."

I blinked at her. I hadn't even thought about attending. "Um . . ." I said. "I guess, Scarlet, if you really feel it's necessary."

"I do. My family won't take this lightly. They're likely to be vicious, in fact. You *must* attend to buffer me from them."

"All right," I told her.

"I can pull up the values of the properties with a Zestimate," Gilley said.

"A Zestimate?" Scarlet asked.

"Yeah, you know, how Zillow gives an estimate of what a property is worth and all you have to do is plug in the address and voila! You know your house's current estimated value."

"Good," I told Gilley. "Pull up the values and make sure to include them in your email to Tony."

"On it," he said, clicking his heels and returning to his desk with the list of addresses that Scarlet had given him.

"While he's doing that, Catherine, I'll text everyone and let them know there's a family meeting tonight to discuss their monthly allowances and their attendance is mandatory."

"Will they all attend?"

"Oh, yes," she said. "When I put it like that, they'll definitely attend."

Two and a half hours later, Gilley and I pulled up to Scarlet's home. It was a grand affair that reminded me of the famous mansion in Kings Point, Long Island, that served as the inspiration for Baz Luhrmann's *The Great Gatsby* movie.

The chateau-inspired mansion was heavily invested in gray tones, giving it a hint of sinister character, and it had to be at least twelve thousand square feet with a fountain in the circular drive and a pathway that led to what appeared to be an enormous pool just off the left side of the main building.

The sound of surf echoed out from the darkening evening but there was no view of it in sight. Still, I suspected that Scarlet Rubi owned quite a bit of beachfront at the rear of the house.

In the driveway were half a dozen cars—all luxury vehicles and I concluded that they were owned or at least driven by Scarlet's family members who'd already gathered here for the family meeting.

We came to a stop in front of the central staircase leading up to a set of French doors, which were opened the moment I put the car in park. Out from the entrance and over to our car came a gentleman in a dark gray blazer and matching pants, wearing a cap to identify him as staff, and he paused in front of Gilley's door, opening it before Gilley even had the chance.

With a bow of his head to Gilley and then to me the gentleman said, "Mr. Gilley. Miss Catherine. I'm Carlos and I'm pleased to make your acquaintance. You're expected inside. May I park your car in a more advantageous spot for exiting the property after the meeting is over?"

I handed over my keys to him. "Thank you, Carlos," I said.

He bowed again and waited for me to get out of the way before hopping in the driver's seat to park the car in a better location.

Meanwhile, Gilley and I headed up the steps toward the French doors, one of which was still open. Gilley was dressed very professionally in a smart blue blazer, crisp white shirt, and a light-yellow-and-blue bow tie. "The bow tie sells it," I murmured to him as we climbed the steps.

"It's not too much?"

"No. It's perfect."

Gilley grinned bashfully at me, a rare look for him. "You look gorgeous too."

"Thank you," I said. I was wearing a cocoa-colored suede blazer and matching skirt with knee-high brown boots and lots of gold accents.

We made it to the top of the steps and heard the sound of boisterous conversation coming from just beyond the front foyer—which was divine, by the way, glistening with shiny blue-and-white tiles with an ornate fresco painted onto the cathedral ceiling.

Directly ahead of us was a grand staircase but to the right was a hallway and it was from this direction that the boisterous conversation was coming.

Gilley and I walked forward, led by the sound of a crowd of people talking excitedly. The hallway had a dining room off to the left and a library off to the right with the kitchen just behind the dining room, but then it opened up to an absolutely massive living room with multiple seating areas and floor-to-ceiling windows with a spectacular view of the ocean and plenty of beachfront to boot.

Gathered there were half a dozen people all talking over each other with what appeared to be a few arguments between individuals here and there. It was impossible to decipher.

Set apart from them all sat Scarlet. She was in a wing chair that resembled a throne in that it was the only one of its kind in the room and clearly drew attention to itself given both its size and deep red color.

Nearby was a man in a wheelchair who appeared to be in his late thirties, and who was eyeing the crowd very nervously.

I wondered why for all of about four seconds when something flew across the room and hit a tall, handsome man with silver hair and sharp features, wearing a large Rolex and a suit that matched his hair.

"Masie!" he yelled, bending down to pick up the missile. I realized it was a woman's shoe—a black pump with a red heel.

"I didn't mean to hit *you*!" the woman yelled in reply. "I was aiming for that troglodyte!" She pointed to another man—equally handsome with long brown wavy hair that draped a perfectly sculpted face inset with light brown eyes.

"You couldn't hit the side of a barn, you slag!" he sneered.

Masie immediately removed her other shoe and sent it flying. Gilley—having the reflexes of a cat—reached up and snagged the shoe right out of the air. It was a startlingly deft move, and it caused a momentary pause in all the yelling going on.

"Hello," Gilley said when he realized everyone was looking at him.

No one said anything in reply and the moment hung awkwardly in the air.

Scarlet rose to her feet with measured grace, like a queen from her throne. She then approached us with a steely, determined stare. It was good to see because I'd worried she'd cancel or abandon our plan.

"Catherine! Gilley!" she called as she made her way right past the cluster of people. "Thank you for coming on such short notice."

Scarlet reached us and stuck out her hand to me for a very businesslike handshake. She then did the same to Gilley, who took it and didn't seem to know what to do. For one brief moment it looked as if he was going to put his lips to the back of her hand and bow low, so I cleared my throat to warn him and he switched his posture to a rather clunky two-pump handshake.

Our host then turned to the crowd and said, "Here is my real estate agent and my attorney's representative."

My eyes went a little wide and I glanced at Gilley, who seemed a bit confused. He wasn't a licensed real estate agent, nor had he indicated to Scarlet that he was, and I certainly wasn't a legal representative, but Scarlet was clearly trying to strike a serious note here, so when Gilley caught my eye I mouthed, *Be cool.*

He nodded and straightened his shoulders a bit to present an air of confidence to the crowd.

I did the same.

Meanwhile, Scarlet pivoted back to us and said, "I'm assuming you've brought the contracts and the estimates for each address I gave you?"

"Yes," Gilley and I said together.

"Fabulous," Scarlet said, adding a wink that only Gil and I could see. "Come sit at the table near the window and we'll get started."

As we moved forward to follow Scarlet, the small, gathered crowd erupted in angry shouting and finger pointing all over again. It was hard to make out what any individual was saying, but I think I got the gist of it.

Scarlet had obviously already laid out the news that she was cutting them all off and would put their homes on the market if they didn't agree—in writing—to either take the house and never, ever bother her again about money, or face eviction when the house sold.

And it seemed *no one* was happy with the arrangement.

"Auntie!" the man with silver hair snapped. "This is untenable!"

"I agree, Luke. Which is why we're all here," Scarlet said, sinking back onto her throne with an air of supreme authority.

"You haven't given us any time to decide!" an older woman with hair that matched Scarlet's yelled.

"Siobhan . . ." Scarlet said, her voice dripping with impatience. "I've given you forty-five years to decide. You've simply chosen not to, and I've coddled you and all the rest of this family for far too long."

"Ohmigod, can I like trade my condo in for the money? Like, why do I have to put it up for sale? Can't you just give me the cash?"

"Lucy," Scarlet said, with a hint of worry in her tone, and I could see why. Her granddaughter was pale and limply postured with a slight slur to her speech. "Your condo will be assigned to you and your mother so that she may control the proceeds of any sale. I won't be funding any more trips to rehab, so I suggest you work to clean up your act."

Lucy blinked dully and she didn't seem to understand what Scarlet had told her. The young lady next to her, whom I assumed was April, said, "You're not getting any money, sis. But come to my place and we can hang out. You can play gopher for me until this ankle monitor comes off in two months." For effect, April lifted the hem of her pantleg to reveal a thick black strap with a small receiver attached which was blinking green. "I'm only allowed to be at my place or here," she grumbled. "It sucks. How am I supposed to find a new boyfriend when I'm held hostage at home?"

We'd reached the seating area by then and Scarlet waved for us to sit. We did but the yelling continued.

Scarlet folded her arms and shook her head at all the bluster, her expression both unimpressed and disappointed. I was so proud of her in that moment. She seemed to really be determined to rid herself of the burden of this crowd of grifters.

But they didn't seem to be backing down, either, and the rhetoric was getting abusive.

Now, I don't tolerate the bullying of women, especially women who've spent their whole adult lives doing nothing but sacrificing themselves on behalf of their families. So I stood, brought my fist down on the table hard enough to make a loud noise, and yelled, "Enough!"

That got their attention.

Scarlet looked over at me. And smiled.

Straightening my blazer I said crisply, "This meeting will either proceed with your cooperation, or without it, but I promise you all that it *will* proceed!"

The group gaped at me. It was glorious.

Scarlet turned her attention back to the small crowd, a smug expression on her face while she made a hand gesture to me that suggested I continue taking control of the meeting.

So, I turned to Gilley and said, "Which residence is up first, Mr. Gillespie?"

Taking a thick folder out of his satchel, Gil laid

it on the table and opened to the first page. "Four-seven-nine-five Ocean View." He then showed the printout of the house to Scarlet, who nodded first to him then to Siobhan, her sister.

"According to similar comparables in the area, I estimate the house to be worth in the two-million-dollar range."

Scarlet's brow shot up. On the way over, Gilley had told me that after doing extensive research on Zillow, he was surprised to discover that Scarlet had some *very* valuable real estate, well exceeding her initial estimate to us.

I wondered if it would change her mind about the arrangement, but then I doubted it would and it bothered me that, yet again, she was in a position to be taken advantage of, so I was glad that Gilley was making it clear to her exactly what she'd be giving up in exchange for the freedom from her family of freeloaders.

When I looked at Siobhan, however, I was somewhat surprised to find that she didn't seem at all surprised, and it made me wonder if she'd already done some research of her own.

"Ms. Forsythe," I said, lifting the contract Tony had sent me from the manila folder I'd carried into the house. "Please step forward and read over your contract. Once you sign it, Scarlet will sign over the deed to your house and you may do with it whatever you like."

Siobhan glared daggers at me before her attention shifted back to her sister. "How am I supposed to pay for maintenance and upkeep? You're cutting me off without any opportunity to earn enough money to keep my home!"

"Then sell it," Scarlet said dully, adding an inspection of her nails to drive the point of her disdain home.

You could've heard a pin drop in that room. Every single one of Scarlet's relatives stared at her with wide, disbelieving eyes. If their matriarch was unmoved by the plight of her own, elderly sister, then that did not bode well for any of the others, and they knew it.

Siobhan, however, seemed ready to test her sister's resolve. "You will *not* bully me into financial ruin!" she yelled, getting up from her seat ready to storm out of the room.

I cut my gaze to Scarlet, who very casually said, "Gilley, I'll be putting the Ocean View estate on the market immediately."

"Excellent!" Gilley said, his eyes sparkling as if he really was going to earn a commission on the sale. Reaching into his satchel he pulled out another thick folder, and I wondered what was inside until he opened it to reveal a stack of real estate papers and I realized Gilley had come well prepared for just such a scenario. "I have a listing agreement for that property right here," he said, handing a stapled group of legal-sized paper to Scarlet.

She eyed the paper, which I could see actually was a listing agreement, but most of the home-specific details had been left blank. Still, Scarlet pretended to skim the paperwork and then hovered her pen over the bottom of the last page, ready to sign on the dotted line.

Siobhan had paused long enough to watch this act play out, and the second Scarlet seemed ready to sign, her sister stomped forward and paused in front of our table.

With an absolutely vicious glare at Gilley and me, she snarled, "Where's the damn contract?"

I lifted the contract and attempted to hand it to her. She angrily ripped it from my hand, then skimmed it, her eyes darting back and forth across the two pages of terms and conditions.

The contract itself was very straightforward. This was a simple transaction, really; title to the house, free and clear of any liens or mortgages, would transfer to the named party along with two months' living expenses in exchange for the solemn vow never, ever to request either by word, deed, or written contract any money, compensation, or anything of value from Scarlet Rubi ever again.

The penalty for defaulting on the agreement would be an immediate transfer of title back to Scarlet, or, the equivalent worth of said property at the time of transfer.

Siobhan got to the end of page two and she looked up to curl her lip and snarl at her sister. "I'll want my attorney to look this over before I sign it."

Scarlet smiled at her like the white queen before a petty black pawn. "*Your* attorney, Siobhan? Do you mean Terry Gilman? Who is actually *my* attorney and very dear friend?"

Siobhan's face turned crimson, but she simply settled for glaring even harder at her sister.

"Terry is on vacation in Hawaii for the next two weeks. Good luck getting her to take your calls. Her partner at the firm oversaw the drawing up of these contracts and every loophole was thought through. If you don't sign on the dotted line here and now, the house you reside in, the house that *I* own, *will* be put on the market—and I'll likely accept an offer on it well before Terry returns your call."

Siobhan was literally trembling with rage. She had no card to play and we all knew it. Still, I suspected that the people who hadn't yet been called upon to sign their own contracts were willing her to find a loophole that they could also exploit.

We sat there waiting for her to make her decision for a solid minute. Maybe two. At last, Siobhan snatched up the silver pen on the table, scrawled her name across the signature line of the agreement, and threw the pages at her sister. They fluttered in the air and dropped to the floor, and it was the only sound in the room.

Gilley shook himself a little and reached for another piece of paper. Handing it to Scarlet, he said, "Here is the title to that property, Ms. Rubi. Sign on the bottom to transfer title over to Ms. Forsythe and I'll notarize it, making it official."

Scarlet accepted the paper, signed the bottom with a flourish, handed it back to Gilley, who signed it as well, then used his notary stamp to emboss the signature line with an official seal. Once that was done, he handed it to Siobhan, who snatched it, eyed it for a moment, then turned on her heel and walked out of the room without another word.

When she was out of view, I let go of the breath I'd been holding and exchanged looks with Gilley. Sweat had broken out across his brow and he appeared a bit shaken by the encounter. But Scarlet simply continued to sit in her seat and stare out at the rest of her family with that same smug smile.

And then she turned her attention to us again and said, "Who's next, Mr. Gillespie?"

For all the turmoil of that evening, we ended fairly quickly, all things considered. There were theatrics and hysterics and much raving, ranting, and moaning, but eventually, by seven thirty p.m. we had all six contracts signed and notarized and only one remaining title transfer agreement, which Scarlet had personally instructed us about prior to our coming here.

After Scarlet gave Gilley a nod, he took it out of his folder and laid it on the table. Scarlet pulled it close and fiddled with her glasses to read it through, nodding when she got to the end. She then signed it, handed it back to Gilley, who notarized it, then gave it over to Scarlet once again.

Holding the document, she looked at the man in the wheelchair and said softly, "Carson."

Carson seemed a bit startled to be called on, but he dutifully rolled his chair closer to his aunt. "Yes, Auntie?"

"This is for you," she said, handing him the title for the house she'd provided for him.

His brow shot up, and he seemed almost alarmed as he took the paper and stared at it with wide eyes.

"I should've assigned that house over to you years ago," she said. "I'm correcting that error tonight. Your home is now yours, free and clear.

You'll never have to worry about having a place to live."

Carson's hand shook a little as he stared at the title page and it touched my heart that tears sprang up in his eyes. "Auntie, I . . ."

She laid a hand on his shoulder. "It's the least I can do for your many years of loyalty and service, Carson. You'll continue under my employment, of course, and I've also decided to give you a raise. I'm upping your salary another ten thousand dollars a year."

Carson lifted his chin and stared at her, so moved a tear leaked down his cheek. I blinked hard to try to hold in my own emotion, and reached out to lay my hand on Gilley's arm because I was so moved by the scene.

He patted my hand and when I looked at him, his eyes were moist as well.

"Thank you," Carson said. "I don't know what else to say other than that."

"I'm the one who's grateful," she told him. "Now, who wants champagne? The night calls for a celebration!"

As if on cue a plump woman with graying hair wearing a dark blue uniform entered the room carrying a silver tray laden with champagne glasses. Behind her came Carlos, carrying two silver buckets of ice and two bottles of Cristal champagne.

"Ah, Mariana, your timing is perfection!" Scarlet sang.

As Carlos popped the cork on the first bottle and began to pour us each a glass, Mariana rushed away to retrieve some snacks to go with the champagne. Meanwhile, Scarlet reached over and picked up the stack of contracts to flip through them with a broad smile. "I am so thrilled that we actually pulled this off!"

"They all signed," I said, shaking my head in wonder. "I thought for sure Luke wasn't going to. Especially after you told him you weren't going to invest in his big development deal."

Scarlet rolled her eyes. "He'll find other funding," she said. "Or he won't, but it's no longer my concern. He has his house to use as an asset to raise funds if he chooses, but the bank of Scarlet is *closed*!"

Gilley clapped gleefully. "Good for you, Scarlet!"

I nodded happily too, but my mind reflected on one person in particular, namely, Grayson, Scarlet's son. He'd been the only one who hadn't protested or attempted to talk Scarlet out of the deal she was offering him. He'd merely gotten up from his chair, come to the table, and signed on the dotted line. But as Gilley was notarizing his deed, Grayson had leaned in close to his mother and whispered, "This isn't over." And then he'd snatched the deed from Gilley and walked out.

When I looked at Scarlet to see her reaction, it surprised me that he alone out of all of her other relatives had seemed to rattle her with just that simple phrase. I wondered why, and her unease had caused a similar chill to travel down my own spine.

Still, I put it out of my mind because, after all, he *had* signed the agreement and that was completely binding, so claiming that the argument wasn't over was moot—legally speaking—and there wasn't a thing he could do about it.

"What a rush!" Gilley said, pulling me out of my thoughts. He then lifted his glass of bubbly in a toast. "To you, Scarlet! You did it. And now you're free!"

We all lifted our respective glasses and clinked them together before taking a long, delicious sip of champagne. "Oh, that is so delightful," I whispered, holding my glass at eye level to inspect the bubbles. I love champagne. I'd once taken a bath in it, in fact.

"Just think, Cat," said Gilley. "This time next week we could be sipping this stuff *in* Paris!"

Scarlet eyed him keenly. "Oh? You two are heading to Paris?"

"Paris, Brussels, Cologne, and Amsterdam," I said.

"How marvelous!" she said. "Paris is one of my favorite cities in all the world."

"Do you travel much?" I asked.

Scarlet nodded. "I take a week's vacation every time I finish a novel."

"Which is four times a year," Carson said. Then he added, "And I'll remind you that you finished your last novel two weeks ago and you still haven't booked an adventure."

Scarlet smiled, but there was something off about it. Something sad. "I will soon," she told him.

Gilley bounced in his seat as an idea seemed to strike his mind. "You should come with us!" he announced.

My eyes widened. I couldn't believe he'd just invited a relative stranger along to crash our party. But then I remembered that this trip wasn't about me. It was about distracting Gilley long enough to get through what would've otherwise been a very difficult time for him. If he found joy in the company of someone like Scarlet, who was I to protest?

"Oh, I couldn't impose," our host said.

"It'd be no imposition, Scarlet," I said. "Gilley's right. You should come."

Scarlet's smile looked forced, and there was something in her eyes, something I couldn't place, but it was a hint of something sad again. "Really," she insisted. "I couldn't possibly. Next time, perhaps." Then she lifted her own glass and said, "To adventures abroad!"

We all clinked glasses and I felt joy in my heart for this marvelous woman.

Little did I know how short-lived that joy would be.

Chapter 3

Gilley and I were just sitting down to a breakfast of croissants and fruit when we got the news. My phone rang and I eyed it crossly. "Who's calling me at seven thirty in the morning?" I grumbled.

Gilley pointed to my phone, which was face-down on the table. "It's never good news when it comes that early. Do you want me to answer it?"

I lifted the phone off the table to eye the caller ID, immediately smiling when I read the name. "It's Shepherd," I said. "We haven't seen each other in a few days—he's been so busy with work and the remodeling of his kitchen." Ever frugal, Shepherd had decided to do most of the home improvement work himself.

"Answer it and see if he wants to come over for breakfast," Gilley said. "There're plenty of croissants and there's no way you and I can eat all this fruit."

"Hello, lover," I whispered when I answered the call. "Miss me?"

"Cat," Shepherd said, and his voice was anything but flirtatious. "I need to speak with you."

My brow furrowed. "Aren't you right now?"

"In person," he said, and I swear I detected a hint of irritation in his voice.

"Care to tell me what this is about?"

"Not on the phone. Take down this address and get here as soon as you can."

"What's happening?" Gilley asked.

I shook my head and held up my finger to let him know he needed to wait a moment. "Okay," I said, getting up from the table to head over to the kitchen counter where I kept a pad and pen. "What's the address?"

Shepherd rattled it off to me and my heart skipped a beat.

"What?" Gilley whispered. He'd been watching me closely and could tell something was very, very wrong.

Ignoring him I said to Shepherd, "What's happened to Scarlet Rubi?"

Gilley gasped and put a hand to his heart. "Something's happened to Scarlet?" he whispered again.

I held up my index finger again. He was distracting me.

"She," Shepherd began, but quickly changed course. "Just . . . come over here as soon as you can."

"Okay," I said meekly, then clicked off the call.

Gilley sat riveted in his seat, staring at me intently. I gave him props for not peppering me with questions I didn't have any answers to. "Come on," I said softly. "We have to go."

"To Scarlet's?"

"Yes. I'll drive."

The ride over to the house was a blur. I don't think Gilley or I said more than five words to each other. I think we both knew that something terrible had happened, and more than once I found myself welling up when I imagined the worst.

Shepherd was waiting for us outside in the driveway, which was lined with police cars and an ambulance. When I saw the ambulance, I felt a tiny ray of hope. Maybe Scarlet was only hurt. Maybe she'd had a bad fall? Maybe I was just jumping to conclusions when I imagined the worst.

But as we got out of the car the front door opened and two men pushing a stretcher appeared. On the stretcher was the outline of a body, wrapped tightly in a bright white sheet.

"Oh, no," Gilley whispered as we watched the stretcher being eased down the stairs. "Oh, no, no, no, no, *no*!"

"Hey," Shepherd called, as much to get Gilley's attention before he had a full-scale meltdown as it was a greeting.

I felt several tears drip down my cheeks. I've seen more dead bodies than any layperson should, but nothing ever prepares you for the sight of someone taken before their time. Especially when you'd been sipping champagne with them only the night before.

Shepherd stopped in front of us and his expression was so sympathetic. He pulled me into his arms and hugged me tightly. "Gil," I heard him say. "Come here."

Gilley's body pressed against my side and I could feel Shepherd hug him too. I embraced Shep in the tightest hug I could manage. I loved that he'd brought Gilley in on it too.

I squeezed my eyes closed while he held on to us. I didn't want to see them load Scarlet into the ambulance. I wanted to remember her the way she was, vibrant and full of life.

"What happened?" I finally managed to say.

Gilley backed out of the hug but Shepherd continued to hold on to me. "She was murdered," he said simply.

I gasped, and Gilley repeated himself by saying, "No. No, no, no, no, *no*!"

Letting go of and stepping away from Shepherd, I tried to gather myself. Swallowing hard, I said, "Who did it?"

My beautiful man, with his light brown hair and eyes the color of topaz, sighed tiredly. "Right now? We don't know, but you two aren't off the suspect list."

My jaw fell open. "You're joking!"

Gilley glared hard at Shepherd. It was a well-earned glare. My significant other had a habit of arresting first and asking questions later. "This again, Shepherd?" Gilley growled. "My God, you treat threatening to arrest Cat like it's foreplay!"

"Gilley!" I said as heat seared my cheeks.

But Shepherd chuckled. "No one's threatening to arrest either of you. But I do need a statement from the both of you. Separately. According to the victim's nephew, you two were the last two people to see her alive."

"No," I said, feeling a bit indignant that Shepherd would even suggest that we'd been party to anything so criminal. "We weren't. The person who killed her was."

Shepherd nodded. "Agreed. But Cat, I have to do this by the book, okay?"

I sighed heavily and Gilley put his hands on his hips to show the good detective just how he felt about this conversation.

"Do you want us to come downtown, or something?" I asked when the atmosphere started to feel hostile.

Shepherd also sighed and stared down at his shoes when he said, "No. We can use the library inside. It's already been dusted for prints and cleared." Turning to Gilley he added, "Could you wait in the car while I take Cat's statement?"

Gilley made a face at him. "Whatever," he said, and stalked off toward the car.

"What's with him?" Shep asked me.

"Don't know. Maybe he's not especially thrilled to be labeled a suspect in a murder investigation before nine a.m."

"He knows I don't really consider him a suspect," Shepherd snapped. "I mean, come on, Cat."

I slid a glance at him as we walked toward the front door. "Your record doesn't exactly support the most open mind."

"My *record*? What's that supposed to mean?"

"Well, just rattling off the names of people in

our circle that you've arrested for murder, how about we start with me, your sister, Maks Grinkov—"

"You can't hold that guy against me," Shepherd interrupted. "I mean, come on, Cat. *That* guy? You know he's trouble."

Maks Grinkov was a former lover of mine. He was all rolled up with the Russian Mafia; however, as far as I could tell, he actually played for the good guys. When I'd known him, he'd been acting as an informant for the CIA and the FBI. Maks's job was insanely dangerous, and one of the reasons we'd never worked out. Well, that and the fact that Shepherd had finally shown an interest in me.

"No, I don't know that, Shep," I said, responding to the accusation. "I only know that Maks isn't the bad egg you've convinced yourself he is."

We'd reached the front door by now and Shepherd held back to allow me to enter first. As I passed him, I swear I saw a flash of jealousy in his eyes. This was perhaps proven when he said, "Have you been in touch with good old Maks recently? Set up any clandestine meetings? Have him over for drinks? Just the two of you?"

I let out a short, mirthless laugh. "You can't be serious."

"Yes," he said, stopping in the doorway to stare hard at me. "I am, actually."

"Wow," I said. "Wow."

Shepherd shook his head, and I could see the internal battle he was having, knowing he'd just made an ass of himself but unable to fully deal with that green-eyed monster pouring out of him right now. "Forget it," he said stiffly.

"I don't think I will," I said crisply. Being accused of being unfaithful was a low blow; jealous or not, it was over the line. "But let's table your insane and insulting assumptions for after we talk about Scarlet, shall we?"

It was Shepherd's turn to blush. "Yeah. Let's." He moved past me then to lead me to the library.

On our way we passed the staircase and I put a hand to my mouth when I realized that around the back of the stairs where there was a small nook was a large pool of blood. "Oh, my God!" I whispered, covering my mouth with my hand in horror.

Shepherd stopped and looked back at me, and I think he realized his mistake in leading me past the scene of the crime. "Damn," he muttered. Backtracking quickly to my side, he wrapped an arm around me, pulled me into him, and quickly led me down the hallway. "I'm sorry, babe. I wasn't thinking."

I shuddered as I moved along with him. "Don't let Gilley see that. He's in a fragile state."

"Why is he in a fragile state?"

"Remember? He signed his divorce papers two days ago."

"Oh, yeah. I did forget. Sorry."

We had reached the library by then and Shepherd moved to the desk at the far corner, and pointed to a chair in front of the desk while he moved around to the back to have a seat. Already placed neatly on the blotter was a laptop opened and ready to take notes.

"Okay," Shepherd said once he'd gotten settled. "Tell me how you and Gilley came to be here last night and all of the events that took place between the time that you arrived and the time you left."

I took a deep breath and began. I talked for probably a good thirty minutes before Shepherd paused his typing to ask, "What time did you leave, exactly?"

I bit my lip, trying to remember. "It was late. We'd had a few glasses of champagne and they hit me a little harder than I was comfortable driving with, so I believe I waited to sober up a bit and we left here around ten thirty."

"And you were the only two people present besides Ms. Rubi?"

I nodded. "Yes. Carson had gone home around nine, and I believe that Scarlet's housemaid—Mariana—had also gone home."

"What about Carlos DeLeon?"

I blinked and then it came to me. "The driver?"

Shepherd nodded.

I shrugged. "He poured us all a glass of champagne to celebrate then he headed out and I didn't see him again, so I assume he went home."

"So, to your knowledge, Ms. Rubi was all alone here in the house when you two left?"

"Unless there was another staff member here that we weren't aware of, yes."

Shepherd sat back in the chair and steepled his fingers. "Carlos and Mariana say that the alarm was set when they arrived this morning at seven a.m. Scarlet likely set the alarm after you two left. Whoever murdered Scarlet was either in the house at the time she set the alarm and then waited for one of the staff to arrive to deactivate it and sneak out one of the exits, or, someone knew the alarm code and got in, murdered her, then reset it on their way out."

I shuddered. Both of those scenarios were awful to contemplate. "Who knew the alarm code?" I asked.

"That's what we're trying to find out. Carlos said Scarlet would often change the code—she was a little paranoid after an incident a few years ago when a mentally unstable fan began to stalk her—and as far as Carlos and Mariana know, Scarlet never gave out her alarm code to any members of her family."

"Well, *someone* had access," I said. "Someone got in and killed her."

Shepherd nodded but he looked quite troubled. "The ME says that Ms. Rubi's liver temp suggests she died within a three-hour window, sometime between ten p.m. and one a.m."

My heart started hammering in my chest. I suddenly had a very bad feeling about all this. "Shepherd," I said firmly. "She was *alive* when Gilley and I left!"

"I believe you," he said. "Still, Cat, this doesn't look good."

I glared at him. "How was she murdered?"

"She was shot."

"Whoa," I said, taken aback.

"At point-blank range," he added. "Execution style. She was on her knees when the gun was fired. We think she was pleading for her life."

I put a hand to my mouth and felt my breakfast threaten to come up from my stomach. "My God," I said when I could speak again. "That is awful!"

Shepherd looked at me intently. "My gut says that someone else was here besides the three of you. Someone who was here lying in wait, and I have a feeling that if they'd have had to wait much longer, it wouldn't have been just one body on the floor out there. It would've been three."

I felt a cold shudder travel up my spine. "Who could it have been?" I asked softly.

"Anyone that was here last night. Carlos parked all the cars and laid the keys out on the table in the foyer, labeled so that every family member had the right key after they got their individual deed and left. He spent most of the rest of his shift in the garage where he also has a small office to eat his dinner and wait for his wife—Mariana—to finish waiting on you. She says that Scarlet sent her home around nine."

"That's true," I said, remembering Scarlet dismissing her housekeeper about an hour and a half before Gilley and I left. "And Carson left about a half hour before that."

Shepherd nodded. "I've spoken to him by phone. He's headed here now and I'll get his statement too."

"Do you really think someone from her family could've murdered her?"

"Given what went down here last night before the champagne broke out, I'd say it's far more likely to have been a family member, angry about having been cut off. Plus, we can't find a single thing that's out of place or missing, so it doesn't appear to have been a robbery gone bad. This has the feeling of vengeance to it."

"What about the contracts?" I asked as the thought suddenly occurred to me. "Are they missing?"

Shepherd lifted up his laptop to expose the manila folder I'd brought along to the family meeting last evening. "All here and accounted for."

My brow furrowed. "But how does that make sense?"

"Well, Cat, I'm no Sherlock Holmes, but if there was a contract missing that'd pretty much tell us who dunnit."

I scowled at him. "No, you dolt. My question wasn't referring to any single contract, it was referring to all six of them. Every single family member is still bound by the terms of the contracts they signed unless that contract—or all the contracts—go missing. There were no duplicates made and I doubt Scarlet would've had a chance to scan them and send them to her attorney, who I might add is currently on vacation."

"The contracts are beside the point, Cat. If a family member pulled the trigger, then they were probably hoping that Scarlet's will would provide them some extra dough."

"I wonder what's in the will," I said. "If they stood to inherit a lot of money and/or assets, that would be a firmer case for you, wouldn't it?"

Shepherd shrugged. "Maybe. What we really need is some hard evidence, and right now I'm not seeing a lot that can point to any one individual. The crime scene, as you saw, was messy, but beyond that there're no bloody footprints, no discarded cartridges, no security camera footage, no deactivated alarm, no forced entry, and no smoking gun."

"Yikes," I said. "This sounds like a tough case to crack."

"It will be."

"I wish I could say that I'll be around to support you through it, but Gilley and I are leaving next week for Europe."

Shepherd's eyes widened. I'd told him about the trip, of course, but I could see that he'd forgotten about it. "Cat, you two can't leave town."

I blinked. "What? Why?"

"Because the D.A. would have my ass if I let the two last people to see Scarlet Rubi alive jet off to Europe, possibly never to be seen again."

"I thought you didn't suspect us!"

"I don't. But the D.A. isn't going to let you slide outta town just cuz you're my girlfriend."

"How could he keep us here?"

"He could force the EHPD to issue a warrant to hold you for forty-eight hours on the day your flight leaves. And, trust me, this new D.A.—Don Symanski—he'd do it. He'd do it in a heartbeat, only he wouldn't make *me* do it. He'd get some rookie to pull you two in and there wouldn't be a damn thing I could do about it."

"But what about Gilley? He *needs* this vacation, Shep!"

He shook his head sadly. "I wish I had a solution, babe, but, unless I solve this case in the next week, I'm going to have to convince you to stay on U.S. soil until I do."

I stared angrily at him. Deep down I knew it wasn't his fault, but still. "Fine," I said curtly. "May I go?"

Shepherd nodded. "Yeah. Of course you can. But if you think of anything else that might help me out on this case, let me know, okay?"

I simply stared coldly at him.

Shepherd cleared his throat. "Okay, well, I can see you're mad, so would you just do me the favor of sending Gilley in here so I can take his statement?"

I got up without a word and walked out of the library. Marching past the awful scene behind the stairs, I continued on until I got to the car and rapped on the window. Gilley was inside keeping warm and he had his AirPods in and appeared to have been listening to music the way he'd been rocking back and forth before I knocked on his window, after which he screamed and threw his phone into the passenger seat. He then put a hand over his heart and stared at me with wide eyes. "You could've killed me!" he shouted from inside the car.

I opened the door. "How exactly?"

"You could've given me a heart attack!" Poor Gilley. He looked truly rattled and I didn't blame him. The last several days had been hard enough without this newest twist, and I could only imagine what his mood would be like when I told him we were going to have to cancel our vacation.

"Shepherd wants to see you in the library," I said, pointing to the house.

Gilley got out of the car. "You look like it was a rough interrogation. Did he grill you? Did he play bad cop the whole time?"

I shook my head. "No. It was fine. But listen . . ."

"Yeah?"

I was trying to work up the courage to tell him about our canceled plans when out of my mouth came the words, "Tell him everything you can remember and then come straight back here. We gotta get home to brainstorm."

"Brainstorm?"

"Yeah. We've got to form a plan."

"For our trip?"

"No. A plan to help Shepherd solve this case before we leave for Europe."

Gilley pulled his chin back. "We do?"

"We do."

"Cat, I know our track record for amateur sleuthing is pretty darn good, but don't you think we should focus on packing and getting ready to leave instead of helping Shepherd figure out who killed Scarlet?"

I scooted by Gilley to get into the car. "No, Gil. No, I do not. Trust me on this. We've got to help solve this case. Quick."

"Okay, I trust you."

"And don't mention any of this conversation to him, okay?"

"Do I *look* stupid?"

I managed a tiny grin. "Nope, so scoot! Give your statement, then hurry back. We've got a list of suspects and a lot of work to do."

Gilley saluted smartly and set off. I watched him go and wondered if I'd be able to keep my promise to take him away to Europe before Michel came to town and broke his heart all over again.

Chapter 4

For a long while after we got home, Gilley and I simply sat at my kitchen counter, sipping tea and staring off into space. As gung-ho as I'd been when I left Shepherd in the library, by the time we got home I felt more shell-shocked than enthused.

Much of that, I'm sure, was the fact that Scarlet had made a brief but memorable entrance into our lives. I felt very much that we all could've been good friends, and maybe Gilley was feeling the exact same way. To think about such a vibrant, lively, and fabulous soul dying the way that she did . . . well, it was more than unsettling. It was chilling and horrible. I kept imagining her crouched there, behind the stairs, knowing she wasn't going to survive the encounter with whoever had pulled the trigger, and it haunted me. That her last moments were spent in terror sent a cold shiver right up my spine.

"What an awful way to die," Gilley muttered, and I realized he'd been thinking the same thing.

"Isn't it?" I agreed. "And isn't it infuriating that someone in her family is likely the person who did the deed. I mean, she took care of those people! For almost half a century she looked after them, provided for them, housed them and what do they do? They murder her."

Gilley turned to me. "They?"

I waved a hand and said, "Yeah, they. Her family. Her own flesh and blood."

"No, I meant they as in plural."

I squinted at him. "She has more than one family member, Gilley."

He sighed. "No, Cat, I mean what if it was more than one person? What if two or more family members conspired to murder her?"

"Huh," I said. "You're right. We don't know that she was murdered by only one person. It definitely could've been more than one family member."

"I think we're just very lucky we weren't there when it happened."

"Agreed," I said, shuddering at the thought.

Gilley sighed sadly. "Poor Scarlet. She was such a cool old bird. I was really looking forward to getting to know her."

"Me too, Gilley. Me too."

Gilley got up from his chair and headed toward the hallway leading to other rooms on the first floor. He was back in a jiff with the easel and whiteboard I kept in my home office.

I smiled when he appeared with it. It was a sign that he was ready to get to work, and it helped me mentally shake off the shocked stupor I'd fallen into.

"Right," Gilley said when he'd set up the whiteboard and uncapped the marker that went with it. "I think we should start with all the usual suspects."

"We need to identify our Keyser Söze."

"Exactly," Gilley said, pointing at me. "Which means we should start looking at each family member that Scarlet cut off financially last night."

"That eliminates Carson," I said.

"Agreed. Plus, Scarlet looked like she could've outrun a guy in a wheelchair. No way would he have been able to corner her and shoot her at point-blank range. I mean, how do you hold a gun while you're using both hands to roll yourself after the person you're trying to murder?"

"Another great point," I said. "Carson is definitely on the non-suspect list. Plus, the man is just sweet, am I right?"

"Yep," Gil said. "And he loved her. You could tell."

"You could."

Gilley turned to the whiteboard and hovered the marker over the surface. "That leaves us with the other six members of the family."

"Siobhan's objection to the contract was probably the most vocal and dramatic," I said. "She was absolutely livid with her sister."

"She was," Gilley replied, beginning to write Siobhan's name on the whiteboard. "Wait, how do you spell her name again? I always want to write it phonetically. S-h-i-v-o-n."

"It's spelled the Irish way, Gil. S-i-o-b-h-a-n."

Gilley wrote her name out and stared at it. "That's just weird," he said. "It looks like her name is pronounced See-oh-bhan."

"I get it, but it's pronounced 'Shivon.' "

"If you say so," he said. "Who's our next most likely suspect?"

"Well, I'd have to go with Grayson, I mean, did you catch how he leaned in toward his mother and whispered, 'This isn't over,' to her?" I shuddered at the memory.

"I didn't catch that," Gilley said. "You were sitting closer to them, though."

"Well, he said it, and Scarlet had this look in her eyes like she was actually afraid of him."

Gilley wrote out Grayson's name on the whiteboard. "I can't imagine being afraid of my own son," he said. "Poor Scarlet."

"Yeah," I said. "I know. And did you catch Masie's reaction? She flat-out threatened her mother, remember?"

"You mean when she vowed to air the family's dirty laundry? Yeah, I got that. I wonder what she had on Scarlet that she thought she could use as leverage?"

I shrugged. "All families come with secrets. I doubt there was anything Masie could've told the press that would've been juicy enough to harm Scarlet's reputation. At most it probably only would've caused some embarrassment."

Gilley wrote Masie's name under Grayson's.

"She and Grayson are siblings," he said. "Maybe they conspired together to murder their mother."

"I hope that's not the case," I said. "I'd hate to think that Scarlet gave birth to, raised, and supported the two people who actually murdered her."

"We have to consider every possibility," Gilley said.

"I know, but I don't have to *like* considering that particular possibility."

He smiled at me over his shoulder. "You've got a soft heart, Cat." Turning again to the whiteboard, he said, "What about Masie's daughters, Lucy and April."

"Were they a trip or what?" I said.

"They were," he said, writing down their names underneath Masie's, but then he seemed to think better of it and erased them before turning around to me and saying, "In fact, they were such a hot mess that I wonder if they'd even be capable of an act like this."

"Lucy was definitely stoned last night, did you notice?"

"Stoned out of her mind," Gil said. "I thought it was a miracle she could walk out of the room under her own power."

"And April couldn't have done it because, with that ankle monitor, she was being monitored by the police, and I'll bet dollars to doughnuts that Shepherd already checked to see if she was at her condo during the time of Scarlet's murder."

"For sure he checked her out," Gil agreed. "Do either of the twins strike you as capable of murder anyway?"

"No," I said quickly. "Lucy was too stoned to do much beyond stay upright and April didn't have the opportunity given the ankle monitor."

"Yep, yep," Gil said with a vigorous nod. Then he turned back to the board and began a second column marked *Non-suspect,* writing down Carson's, Lucy's, and April's names.

"That just leaves Luke, right?"

"It does," Gilley said. "He was probably the calmest and most levelheaded of them all, don't you think?"

"Maybe," I said. "But did you catch the look on his face when he asked Scarlet if she was still going to help fund his latest real estate project and she said no?"

"I did, but he looked more stunned than mad."

"True," I agreed. "But that doesn't mean that, after he got over the initial shock, that he didn't get mad enough to come back to the house and murder her. Plus, Scarlet cut both him *and* his mother off. Maybe the double whammy was enough to send him over the edge."

"He and Siobhan could've conspired together to murder Scarlet," Gilley mused. "If we have to consider that Grayson and Masie may have colluded in her murder then we also have to consider Team Siobhan and Luke."

I nodded. "Sounds fair."

Gilley wrote Luke's name in the suspect column then stood back from the whiteboard, tapping his lip with the capped marker. "If you had to pick, which one of them feels most likely to have murdered Scarlet?"

I squinted at the board. "Honestly? Siobhan. I

mean, she was apoplectic when Scarlet forced her hand."

"'*She was raging! She was raging! And a storm blew up in her eyes* . . .'" Gilley sang, taking liberties with a lyric from his favorite band, U2. He'd had their Best Of album playing nonstop for the past several weeks, and that song, "Running to Stand Still," seemed to really speak to him as it was often on repeat alongside "With or Without You," cuz, like, duh.

"Yes. She was raging," I laughed, but then quickly sobered because Scarlet's murder was no laughing matter. "There was a determination to Scarlet that I hadn't thought she'd exhibit, frankly."

"Me either. I think that's what really threw all of her relatives. She had a backbone of steel last night," Gilley said.

I shook my head sadly. "It was likely the thing that led to her murder."

"What do you mean?"

"Well, we believe that was a change in her behavior, right?"

"From when she talked to you earlier in the day yesterday, it was."

"Exactly. And if her family noticed, then at least one of them accepted that she wasn't about to change her mind to cut them all off, which is why at least one of those people . . ."—I paused to wave at the whiteboard—"killed her."

"Oh, and remember that Scarlet mentioned to Siobhan in front of everybody that her attorney was on vacation for the next couple of weeks. The killer or killers probably thought that they had to act before Scarlet had a chance to change her will."

"Oh, my God, Gilley!" I gasped. "I bet that's exactly right. And we're the ones who pushed her to have her family sign those contracts even though her attorney was out of town. We did this!"

Gilley came around the counter to put his hands on my shoulders and stare intently into my eyes. "Catherine Cooper, we did *not* do this. We're not responsible for her murder. The killer is. You can't know if we had anything to do with the timing. We don't know that. It could've been a convenient cover for what was already planned."

I took a deep, shuddering breath. "You're right. Of course. You're right." I then sat back in my chair and sighed. "I like that," I said, waving at the whiteboard. "It feels like it's not too big of a suspect pool to tackle."

"I wonder who Shepherd has as a primary suspect?"

"We can't ask," I warned. "He'll know we're meddling, and you know how he feels about our meddling."

"Super chill?" Gilley said with a giggle.

"Volcanic," I said. "I'm not risking a breakup right before we leave for Europe. I want things to be nice between us until you and I skip across the pond."

"I can wheel it back to your office and turn it around so that he won't see it when he comes over."

I sighed again. "*If* he comes over."

"Yeah, I've noticed that too," Gilley said. "He's been boyfriend in absentia lately. What gives?"

I shook my head. I realized that I was more frustrated with Shepherd's absence from my mornings, evenings, and weekends then I'd thought. "He's working that damn kitchen remodel and he's been telling me he's insane at work."

"Working on what?" Gilley said. "Cases?"

I shrugged. "I guess."

"Have we had a murder spree around these parts that I don't know about?"

"Only the one," I said glumly.

Gilley made a face. "Sorry," he said. "What other cases does he work on?"

"B and Es, shoplifting, property damage, hit-and-runs, all of that and probably more."

"I didn't realize crime was up," Gil said. "Sorry, sugar."

I love the way Gilley says "sugar." He's from the South (Georgia), and when he calls me that it's so soothing, like a whispered hug. I smiled at him. "It's okay," I said. "It's just that I almost never see him these days. We had one night out together eight days ago and it's only been a few text messages and quick phone calls since. I miss him."

"Why do you look worried?"

I consciously un-furrowed my brow. "I didn't realize I did."

"You do. Even now while you're trying not to."

"Is he pulling away?" I asked, feeling a tightening fear wrap itself around my chest.

Gilley eyed me with concern. "Is he?"

"I don't know. I'm asking you."

Gilley sat down on the counter chair next to me. "Let me ask you a delicate question; has there been a little less hanky in the panky?"

I thought about that for a minute. "It's been *eight* days, Gil."

"Okay, but how *was* it eight days ago? Did he phone it in? Or did he shiver your timbers."

I felt the vice around my chest loosen when I couldn't help but laugh. "Your metaphors are ridiculous."

"Your cheeks are bright red," he said.

I put my palms up to my cheeks. They were indeed hot. "This is private stuff we're getting into."

"I realize that, Cat, but if you're worried that he's pulling away, maybe you should look at the most obvious sign, which would be a disinterest in . . . you know. Bow-chicka-bow-wow."

"Ohmigod, *Gilley*!" I squealed.

"What? I'm trying to be delicate!"

I shook my head and shoulders to rid myself of the embarrassing shivers traveling up and down my torso. "He was as *enthused* as he's always been."

Gilley grinned at me. "You lucky, lucky b—"

"Do not say it!"

"—rat. I was saying *brat,* Cat."

I leveled a look at him. "I'll bet. But yes, to your point, I am lucky. Shepherd has always made me feel desirable. That hasn't waned. Still, I can't ignore the fact that he's been finding excuses not to come around regularly. He says he's either working late on a case, or up early to work on his kitchen."

"Well, maybe it *is* that," Gilley said, "Maybe there's nothing to read into here and we're making mountains out of molehills."

"You think?"

"How long before he's done with the kitchen remodel?"

"It's been three weeks already."

"Have you seen it?"

"No. I asked to, but he said the place is a disaster and he'd be too self-conscious to have me over."

"Okay, so three weeks to do the work himself doesn't feel overly long to me. I'd give it another three weeks before I panic."

"Which will be about the time we return from Europe."

"Exactly. If he's still making up excuses not to come over by then . . . that's when I'd worry."

"Okay," I said, but the truth is, I was already worried, and I doubted waiting another three weeks before being totally concerned was going to work.

Turning back to the whiteboard, Gilley asked, "Where do we start?"

I inhaled a deep, cleansing breath and said, "Well, I think the best place to start is with the family itself. Carson seems to be the only loyal person in the family. He might be willing to give us some insight into the other family members. I'm sure he'll have a theory about who might've pulled the trigger too."

"I wouldn't start with him," Gilley said, eyeing the whiteboard keenly.

"Why not?"

"Well, for two reasons; first, he's bound to have biases that might favor one suspect over another, and that could send us in the wrong direction; and second, he's probably shellshocked and deeply upset about his aunt and questioning him now the day after her murder just feels cruel."

"True," I said. "The poor man. Do you think we should at least check in on him?"

"Definitely."

"Good. I think we should too. But back to your point, if not Carson, then who do you think we should start with?"

"The best gossip always comes from the staff, Cat," Gilley said. "They're privy to everything because most people treat them like they're invisible."

I pointed at him. "Mariana and Carlos," I said.

"Yep. They're probably also upset, but maybe slightly less than Carson, plus they have each other to lean on. We really might be able to get some good information about the family dynamics from them."

"How do we find them to talk to them?" I asked next.

"We go back to the scene of the crime. Just because Scarlet is dead doesn't mean those two will abandon their posts just yet. They'll want to clean up after the CSI crew gets done with their forensics."

"Good plan," I said, getting up off the barstool to walk over to where my purse was sitting on the far countertop. Grabbing it and without looking back at Gilley, I made a swirling motion with my index finger and said, "Saddle up, Gil, and let's ride."

Gilley and I found a spot down the street near Scarlet's house to sit under the shade of a tree and wait for the CSI team to leave. Luckily, we didn't have that long to wait as, only fifteen minutes after we parked, several people in uniform emerged from the front door and began shoving equipment into a big white van. Within a few more minutes, they were gone.

"Let's give it another five," I said when their van was just a speck on the horizon down the road. "I want to make sure they didn't forget something and come back."

"Good thinking," Gilley said.

We sat in silence, alternately watching the digital time on the dash and the road leading to Scarlet's house, but no one appeared and after the requisite five minutes, I put the car into drive and crept toward her home.

"I wonder if they're even here," Gilley said, as I turned into the drive.

"I think they'd be here, if only to clean up and lock up, right?"

"Mmm," Gilley grunted. "Probably."

I parked near the front door and we got out, climbed the steps, and rang the doorbell. I'll admit that my heart was pounding in my chest.

The door was opened by Mariana, who seemed very surprised to see us and her watery eyes suggested that she'd also been crying. "Oh! Miss Catherine, Mr. Gilley. What are you doing here? Did you not hear the news?"

"We heard, Mariana, and I'm so, so sorry for your loss."

Mariana immediately welled up. She wiped her cheeks and it was then that I noticed she was wearing latex gloves. "I'm trying to clean up," she said hoarsely. "The police left everything a mess."

"There are services that can do that for you, you know," I said gently. My stomach lurched at the thought that she might have to clean up the bloodstain behind the stairs.

"I know, but Miss Scarlet wouldn't want strangers in her house. Carlos has been doing most of it, thank God. There are certain things I couldn't . . ." Her voice broke off and she put a hand to her mouth to try to stifle a sob, but couldn't quite manage it.

Gilley—God bless him—stepped forward and wrapped her in his arms. "There, there, love," he said, patting her back and rocking her slightly back and forth.

Mariana clung to him and sobbed into his shoulder, and I found tears streaking down my cheeks as well.

After a bit, she let go and stepped away from Gilley to wipe at her cheeks, clearly embarrassed. "I'm so sorry," she said.

"Mariana, we totally understand," I said, fishing around in my purse. I found the travel pack of tissues I always had on me and handed her one. "Please don't concern yourself over a little display of emotion." I paused to take a tissue out for myself. "It's clear to us that you genuinely cared about Scarlet."

The housekeeper nodded. "She was the best boss. Carlos and I always felt so lucky to be employed by her."

"How long did you work for her?" Gilley asked.

Mariana sniffled. "Twenty-seven years."

My eyes widened in surprise, as did Gilley's. "Wow," I said. "That's a long time."

She nodded. "We thought of her like family. We took care of her and she took care of us. She paid us well and gave us a car, and she even helped us buy our house. Carlos and I don't have any children, and our parents are long gone, so we only had her, really. We loved her like a favorite aunt."

I glanced at Gilley and found he was looking intently at me. It was now time to ask her about the suspect list, so I took a big breath and dived in. "Mariana, do you know who might've wanted to hurt Scarlet?"

She welled up again. "No. Not really."

There'd been the slightest hesitation in that statement, and I knew that Gilley had also picked up on it because he said, "You sure, sugar?"

Mariana sighed heavily. "Well, you saw her family, right? They've been taking advantage of her for years and years. When she told us she'd finally had enough and was going to make sure they were cut off, Carlos and I worried about her."

"Worried about her . . . safety?" I asked.

Mariana nodded and then spoke in a whisper, as if the walls had ears. "Yes."

"Who worried you the most?" Gilley asked.

Mariana glanced to either side of her. Clearly, she felt uncomfortable speaking about Scarlet's family. "Miss Siobhan."

My brow arched. "Really? Grayson didn't worry you as much as Scarlet's sister?" There was something cruel in Grayson's eyes when he looked at his mother with that veiled threat. I wouldn't forget it.

"Mr. Grayson isn't a kind man," she admitted. "But he never beat up his mama."

I blinked and glanced at Gilley, who seemed equally surprised.

"Siobhan *beat up* Scarlet?" I asked.

Mariana nodded. "Oh, yes."

"Recently?" Gilley asked, like he couldn't believe it.

Mariana nodded again. "About two years ago Miss Siobhan got mad about something and went after Miss Scarlet. Carlos had to pull her off her sister and poor Miss Scarlet was pretty banged up."

"*Why* would Scarlet ever allow that woman back into her home?" I asked, completely aghast at Siobhan's violence against her sister.

Mariana shrugged and shook her head. "Miss Siobhan used to drink. She had a real problem. Miss Scarlet didn't talk to her for a year, but she continued to support her, of course. Then, Miss Siobhan got sober and we haven't seen her take a drink since. Miss Scarlet let her back into her life when she started going to AA, and since then, she's been better, but I've never trusted her since she beat up Miss Scarlet."

I crossed my arms and shook my head back and forth. "Drinking is no excuse for violence," I said.

"Oh, I know. We wanted Miss Scarlet to call the police on her sister, but she wouldn't. So we patched her up like we used to and took care of her until she was better."

I cocked my head. "What do you mean when you say you patched her up *like you used to*?"

The housekeeper put a hand to her mouth as if she hadn't meant for that to leak out.

"It's okay," I said. "You can tell us. Scarlet was my client and I'm bound not to mention anything I learn about her private life to anyone. It's the life coach oath."

Of course, there was no such oath, but I wanted Mariana to trust me, and besides, I would never gossip about a client to anyone I knew. Well, except to Gilley.

"Her ex-husband used to abuse her," Mariana whispered.

I bit my lip. I hated the idea that Scarlet had endured such physical violence from both her sister and her ex-husband. The thought infuriated me. "Tell us about him," I said, trying to keep the anger out of my voice.

Mariana pressed her lips together for a moment and her eyes held a faraway stare. "Mr. William . . . he liked to drink too. And like Miss Scarlet, he was also a writer, but he'd only had two books published and they didn't do so well. I think it made him really angry that Miss Scarlet was so successful. He was always telling her that what she wrote was 'junk food for simple minds,' and sometimes, when he'd had a lot to drink, he'd slap her, or he'd throw something at her.

"We begged her to call the police on him, but she never would," Mariana continued. "She was afraid of the scandal, and I think there was a part of her that believed him when he said she had no real talent. But over the years her books just got more and more popular, and his abuse got worse, until one day she'd had enough and she kicked him out and filed for divorce.

"He hired a really good lawyer, though, and he took her to the cleaners. We offered to testify that he'd been abusing her all those years, but again, she was too afraid of the scandal. She said she wrote about strong women and that's who her fans expected her to be. She couldn't let them see her in any other light, so she ended up forking over a lot of money to him, and then there were the alimony payments, which finally ended a few months ago."

I could personally empathize with Scarlet. My ex had taken me for half my net worth, but at least I'd avoided paying him alimony.

"Since the alimony checks stopped going to Scarlet's ex-husband, has he tried to contact her?" I asked.

"I think so," Mariana said. "Two weeks ago, Carlos and I got here and Miss Scarlet was shaken up. She said she needed to run an errand but she wouldn't let Carlos take her. She wanted to drive herself, and Miss Scarlet almost never drove. When she got back home, she went straight to her room and stayed there, telling me she didn't feel well so she was going to bed for the rest of the day."

"Why do you think it was her ex who contacted her?" I asked.

"Carlos looked at the car's GPS when Miss Scarlet came back. He recognized the address. He said it was Mr. William's address."

Gilley looked at me knowingly. We'd just added another suspect to the list.

Chapter 5

We left Mariana and once back in the car I looked at Gilley and asked, "Should we go have a talk with William?"

"I think we have to," he said.

"Agreed. What's our cover?"

Gilley shrugged. "Well, he's probably already heard the news—"

"Especially if he did the crime."

"Right, especially if he's our trigger man, but I think we should say that we were close friends of Scarlet's and we're putting together a retrospective of her life and since he was married to her for so many years, perhaps he has some fun anecdotes to share, or some photos of happier times."

"Ooh," I said. "I like that. Yeah, let's go with that."

"The only problem is, Cat, if he did murder

Scarlet, then we'll have to be very careful about the questions we ask him. If he's a violent murderer, no way do we want to set him off."

I pointed at Gilley. "Too true, my friend. So, how about this: you ring his doorbell and I'll pretend to be on the phone with someone, and when he opens the door, I'll say, 'I have to go, we're at William's house now,' and that way he'll assume that we've already told someone our whereabouts and he'll think twice about making us disappear."

"I like it!" Gilley said. "And maybe you could subtly hit the RECORD button on your video camera app, just so we have a record of what he says."

"Yes. That's brilliant, Gilley." And then I took a moment to really look at him and I added, "We're getting so good at this undercover amateur sleuth thing, right?"

He grinned. "We are, sugar. We are."

"Okay, do your supercomputer sleuth thing and give me William's address."

Gilley got out his phone and hovered his finger over the screen. "His last name again . . . is it Rubi?"

I thought about it for a moment and said, "No, that's Scarlet's maiden name. Remember? Her nephew Carson's last name is Rubi and his father was Scarlet's brother, so after the divorce she must've reverted back to her maiden name, which means that her son Grayson's last name should be the same as William's."

"Which is?"

I closed my eyes to try and remember the name on the contract I'd handed him and it suddenly bloomed in my mind. "McMillen. Grayson McMillen."

"So I'm looking for William McMillen," Gilley said, already tapping away at the screen. "Got the address," he announced a moment later, which was much sooner than I'd expected.

"Fabulous. Let's roll."

We arrived at William's place about fifteen minutes later. He lived in the southern part of town with a condo on the golf course.

As homes went, his lacked character, personality, and taste. Two stories of drab, beige siding and deep red brick, without a hint of landscaping, a black door, and matching shutters. It looked about as inviting as a stone-cold hearth on a windy frigid day.

"Charming," Gilley said drolly as we headed up the walkway.

"Maybe it's better inside?" I told him.

"Want to bet on it?"

"No. No, I do not."

We reached the front door and I pretended to be on a call while Gilley pressed the doorbell. The door was opened by a disheveled man with white chin stubble, bloodshot eyes, and an outer rim of white hair around his mostly bald head.

His clothing was rumpled and he wore only one shoe.

If I was a bettin' woman, and, on occasion, I am, I would've said he slept in those clothes, if he slept at all.

"Yeah?" he asked when he saw us on his doorstep.

Before Gilley could answer I spoke to my imaginary caller. "Yes, I'll remember. Listen, I have to go. We're at William's house. You know, Scarlet's ex-husband? I'll update you later." Pretending to click off the call, I actually activated the video function on my phone and held it in such a way that I hoped the lens captured McMillen and anything he might say.

"Hello!" Gilley said jovially.

"What time is it?" McMillen grumbled, holding up his wrist to look at the time. It was a moment before he realized he wasn't wearing a watch.

"It's well after noon, sir," I said to him. When he eyed me crossly, I offered a friendly smile.

"What do you want?" he demanded.

"We're here about Scarlet," I said.

His brow furrowed. "Why?"

Gilley cleared his throat. "We're putting together a retrospective for her, and as her ex-husband, we were hoping you might share some touching or funny anecdotes about your time with her."

McMillen blinked. Then blinked again. "What the hell are you talking about?!" he shouted.

Both Gilley and I took a step back, but I decided not to abandon ship just yet. "Scarlet," I said slowly, like cooing to a hungry lion. He shook his head at me and I placed a hand to my chest and said, "Surely you've heard the news?"

"What news?"

"Oh, I'm so sorry to tell you this, but your ex-wife passed away last night."

McMillen's brow shot up. "What time last night?" he asked, and there was an eagerness in his voice that really set the hairs on the back of my neck on end.

"We're not sure, sir," I said. He frowned, like he was disappointed I didn't know what time his ex-wife died. "She was murdered, Mr. McMillen," I added, hoping that might get a proper emotional response.

Instead, he merely grunted and then, using air quotes, said, "One of her 'fans' finally got to her, huh?"

Gilley and I stared at him without speaking. I think we were both a bit too stunned by his reaction. He took the moment of silence from us to say, "Thanks for letting me know. I got a call to make." And with that he slammed the door in our faces.

"Wow," I whispered.

"I hope Michel doesn't react to the news of my death like that," Gilley said.

I squeezed his arm. "Let's go, Gil."

We turned as one and headed back down the walkway, neither of us saying a word. Once inside the car again, however, we'd regained our senses and our tongues.

"Why would he want to know what time Scarlet died?" Gilley asked.

"Absolutely no clue, Gil. But that was creepy."

"We still think he's a definite suspect for Scarlet's murder, though, right?"

"One hundred percent. Did you see how rumpled he was? He looked like he didn't get any sleep last night, and probably was only able to fall asleep sometime before we showed up. Which leads me to think that, if you murder your ex-wife, you might come home amped up on adrenaline, and it may take you a while to catch some z's."

"For sure," Gil said.

We were quiet in the car as I steered us toward

home. I hadn't routed us in that direction on purpose; I'd done it on reflex. Still, it'd be good to get back to the whiteboard and discuss McMillen's reaction to the news of Scarlet's death and perhaps posit some theories about why he'd needed to know the time.

"Maybe he needed to make sure his alibi will hold up," I said.

"You lost me," Gil said, and I realized I'd been having most of that conversation in my head.

"Maybe the reason McMillen needed to know what time Scarlet died was to make sure whatever alibi he offers will hold up."

"But, Cat," Gil said, "he needed to know what time she died *before* we told him she'd been murdered."

I sucked in a breath. "You're right! And that's a question you ask when you already *know* she's been murdered!" Fishing around for my cell I pulled it out of my pocket. It was still recording. I wiggled it at Gilley. "And I got it on video!"

"Great!" Gil said. "If Shepherd starts looking into McMillen as a suspect, we can show him that we think Scarlet's ex knew she'd been murdered. But that also means that McMillen probably didn't pull the trigger."

"Right," I said. "If he was working to establish an alibi, he would've made sure he had one at the time of Scarlet's death, which means, someone *else* murdered her, which means the two might've conspired together."

"True that," Gilley said.

"We need to dig into McMillen a little more. Find out who he's been hanging out with. He could've arranged for a professional to murder Scarlet, you know. It didn't have to be another family member."

"But why?" Gil said. "What's his incentive?"

I shrugged. "Revenge?"

"For what?"

"Well," I said, tapping my finger against the steering wheel. "Didn't Mariana say that the alimony checks to William ran out a few months ago?"

"She did."

"Maybe he called Scarlet up, got her to come over to his condo where he demanded she continue to pay him, and when she didn't, he murdered her."

"But why would Scarlet ever agree to that?" Gilley said. "I mean, we know she drove over to his house, but did they actually meet?"

I sighed, frustrated that I couldn't connect the dots. "Gil, we need to dig a little into McMillen's financials and see if he's in debt and by how much. Can you pull a credit report on him?"

"Not without his Social Security number."

"Can you get that?"

"I can try," he said, as we pulled into my driveway where we were both surprised to find Shepherd's car already parked near the door.

"Uh-oh," Gilley said. "Think we've been caught?"

My face felt flushed as I put the car into park. "Why would you say that?"

"Because Shepherd's usually suspicious of our antics whenever there's a dead body connected to us. And I just realized that there've been far more dead bodies connected to us than I care to admit."

"You're not wrong about that," I said. I got out of the car and Shepherd's door opened. He stepped out looking tired and irritable. "Hi!" I said, perhaps a bit more jovially than I'd intended. "What brings you by?"

Shepherd rubbed his eyes. "I haven't had a chance to hang out with my girlfriend in a while. Thought I'd fix that."

I reached him and stood on tiptoe to kiss him. "You look tired."

He wrapped me in his arms and kissed me again. "And you look amazing."

"Have you had any sustenance today besides coffee?"

"There's sustenance that's not coffee?" he asked with a grin.

"Ha, ha," I mocked. "Come on in, I'll make you something to eat."

Shepherd looked over my shoulder. "Is Gilley coming?"

"No. He's . . . um . . . still trying to decide what to pack for Europe, right, Gil?"

"Right," he said, giving me a subtle wink. "You two have fun. I'll catch up with you later." He then trotted away over to Chez Kitty.

When I turned my attention back to Shepherd, I was surprised to find him looking cross.

"What?" I asked innocently.

"Cat," he said. "Come on. Cut me some slack. You can't expect me to solve this case in time for your trip."

"Why couldn't you? You're an amazing detective. I believe in you."

"It's pressure," he said softly. "And I'm gettin' it from all sides right now."

"What sides?" I asked.

"Scarlet was dating the mayor."

"She was *what*?"

"It was new. Only a few months old. But he's really broken up about her murder."

"Are you sure he didn't have anything to do with it?"

Shepherd rolled his eyes. "Come on, woman. Not *everyone*'s a suspect."

I took him by the hand and led him inside. "But you checked to see if he had an alibi all the same, right?"

He squeezed my hand as we entered the front door. "I did," he said softly.

"Lady Catherine," Sebastian said. "And Detective Shepherd. So good of you to join us."

Shepherd eyed the small speaker to the side of the door. "How does he know I'm with you?"

I pointed toward the ceiling. There was a small camera mounted there. "He's got very good facial recognition."

"It's creepy."

I laughed. "Sebastian is not creepy."

Shepherd made a face and from the creases in his forehead and dark circles under his eyes, I could tell the lack of sleep from all that he had going on was really taking its toll. "Come sit," I coaxed, leading him into the family room just off the kitchen.

Shepherd plopped down on the couch and took up my hand when I sat down next to him. "I've missed you," he said, lifting my hand to kiss my knuckles.

"Ditto," I said. "What can I do for you?"

"Do for me?"

"Yeah. You look exhausted and spent. Like you've got too many balls in the air and your arms are tired from juggling."

"That is an apt description of how I feel."

"Maybe it's time to set one or two things down."

Shepherd rubbed his face and scratched at the stubble on his chin. "Like what?"

"Like the remodel on your kitchen."

Shepherd shook his head. "There's not a whole lot left to do. It's nearly done."

"Then hire someone to help you finish it."

"No way," he said. "I'm not paying some contractor to charge me an arm and a leg to finish something I can do myself."

"Then let me pay them," I said.

"What?"

"Let me pay someone to finish your kitchen."

Shepherd rolled his eyes. "That's definitely not happening."

"Why not?"

"Because I'm not going to have my girlfriend throw money at my problems." He was acting like I'd insulted him.

"Shep," I said softly. "If the situation were reversed, and I were struggling to keep up with all my obligations, and *you* had the means to help me, would you?"

"That's different," he said, still irritated.

"Oh, you mean because I'm the woman and you're the man?"

"No! Listen, I'm the kind of guy that wants to make his own way in life. I'm not interested in your money, Cat. I'm interested in *you.*"

Shepherd yawned and he tried to stifle it.

I got up and physically picked up his legs to stretch him out on the sofa. "What's happening here?" he asked.

"You're taking a nap," I said. "When you wake up, I'll have something delicious prepared and we can have an early dinner together."

Shepherd sighed. "That sounds great. But I can't stay long. I gotta get back to my place. My cabinets were delivered two days ago and I haven't had a chance to install them yet, and I got the countertop guys coming tomorrow morning so I have to get those cabinets installed tonight."

"You're not staying?" I asked.

Shepherd yawned again and closed his eyes. "Can't, babe. Too much to do."

I stared down at him with irritation, but even as I watched him his breathing slowed down and became more rhythmic. The beast had fallen asleep.

I placed an afghan over him and headed out of the family room to my home office. There I sorted through the contacts on my phone and made a call. "Hi, Trevor! It's Cat Cooper calling. Listen, I have a project for one of your guys and I'm willing to pay triple his hourly rate if he'll come over right now, pick up a key, and go install some kitchen cabinets for me. . . ."

Shepherd woke up from his nap around five, which was perfect timing because I had just taken the lid off some beef stew I'd been slow cooking. "That smells delicious," he said.

I smiled when I saw his sleepy face, staring over the back of the couch at me. "It is," I said. "I'll serve you up a plate in just a sec. I've got to run this over to Gilley's."

I took up the tray with two bowls of stew and Shepherd asked, "Gilley's getting a double helping?"

"No," I sang as I walked toward the front door. "One of these is for Spooks."

After dropping off the bowls of stew for Spooks and Gilley—who was still working on finding out anything he could about William McMillen—I checked my phone because a text had come in right as Shepherd had peeked over the couch at me.

The text was from the worker Trevor had sent to install Shep's cabinets. It read, **All set, Ms. Cooper**.

I smiled and Venmoed the young man the money I'd promised him, then headed back across the courtyard to Chez Cat.

Shepherd and I ate dinner by candlelight and enjoyed each other's company. After helping me with the dishes, he said, "I gotta go."

"You're sure?" I asked him, batting my eyes and cuddling up to him.

He groaned. "Man, babe, I would like nothing more than to stay here with you tonight, but like I said, I gotta get those cabinets in so that the countertop can be installed, and it's too late to reschedule."

I thought about telling Shepherd that his cabinet installation was all taken care of, but didn't want to ruin the surprise, so I merely said, "Well, if you get done with your project early and want to come back this way, please do."

He chuckled. "I wouldn't count on it. Installing cabinets properly takes time. I'll be up past midnight for sure."

"All right," I said dramatically. "Off you go, then."

Shepherd left and I puttered around the house, all the while sporting a smug grin. I looked at my watch after twenty minutes, knowing he would get home at any moment and see the work completed. I imagined him turning right back around and coming here personally to thank me and that made me head to the bedroom for something sexy to put on.

My phone rang right on time. "Hi, lovey!" I said happily. "Are you surprised?"

Shepherd was silent for a long moment but then he said, "I told you I didn't want you to do that."

I was taken aback by his tone. I'd been expecting gratitude and instead he sounded seriously mad. "Shep," I said. "You needed the help and it was nothing for me to call my contractor and—"

"Dammit, Cat!" he swore. I pulled the phone away and stared at it. As mad as Shepherd had ever been at me, I didn't think he'd ever sworn at me. "I told you I wanted to install the cabinets myself!"

My eyes welled with tears. I was so hurt; I didn't even know what to say. "I was only trying to help you," I said wetly.

"You're always trying to *help* me!" he roared. "Stop it, okay? Just stop it!"

With that he hung up and I will admit to crumpling into a chair and having myself a good cry.

* * *

I slept fitfully that night and by the time the sun was rising I decided to call Shepherd and apologize. I didn't really understand why he was so mad, but I felt like an apology was the right thing to do. I called his phone and muttered, "Pick up, pick up, pick up!"

But he didn't. The call went to voice mail.

I sighed heavily as I listened to his outgoing message, and when the prompt beeped I said, "I overstepped. I'm sorry. And I mean that. I would never, ever do anything to intentionally upset you, Shep. My heart was in the right place, and I just wanted to help. I'm sorry you got upset. I love you, and I hope you'll call me soon so we can put this behind us."

After hanging up the phone I stared at it for at least a half an hour, willing Shepherd to call me, but he didn't.

With a sigh I finally got out of bed and dressed in a pale raspberry crossover cardigan that cinched at the side, black skinny jeans, and a pair of open-toed black suede booties. I thought about sharing what'd gone on between Shepherd and me with Gilley, but I decided against it for the moment. The truth is that I was too embarrassed to admit that I'd upset Shepherd so much. I needed a little time to process it before I confessed it all to my bestie.

Once I was dressed, I texted Gilley and headed downstairs.

Just as I reached the front hall, the door opened and my best friend stood there looking quite fetching in a soft yellow V-neck cashmere sweater and dark blue jeans. "Hey," I said, giving him the up-down once-over with an eyebrow bounce of approval.

"Hey," he said, matching the optical gymnastics. "Nice," he added, wagging a finger at me.

"You too. Breakfast?"

"Yes."

"Dine in? Eat out?"

Gilley sighed dramatically. "Let's have someone else cook and clean up for once."

I offered Gilley my arm and we headed out together.

We ended up at the Carissa's Bakery on Pantigo Road. The bakery is the stuff of rom-coms—imagine a pristine all-white bakery with gleaming marble countertops, dreamy baked confections piled high under polished glass, staff in crisp white attire, and a smell that I'm convinced is pumped into the shop directly from heaven.

I could exist on the smell of Carissa's baked goods alone.

"Ohmigod," Gilley said, inhaling deeply. "Nothing inedible could ever smell this good."

"What're you having?" I asked as we stepped up to get in line.

"A macchiato and the snail," Gilley said, pointing to a glass dome containing a half dozen of the light croissant pastry filled with almond frangipane and golden raisins, then topped with an apricot glaze. Trust me on this: as off-putting as the name was, the snail was every bit as delicious as its combination of ingredients sounded.

"Me too," I said.

"Are we committed to having only one each?" he asked with a bounce to his eyebrows.

"Yes," I said, already wavering. "But if you want to have one and then split another one with me, I wouldn't say no."

"Deal," he said.

We put in our order and headed to a nearby table by the window to wait for a staff member to deliver our food. As we settled in, I saw Gilley glance to my left before his eyes widened.

"What?" I asked, turning to look where he was staring. He didn't need to reply. I saw for myself what had caused him to look so startled. In the far corner of the bakery sat Siobhan and William McMillen. They were huddled close together speaking softly but earnestly. And there was something intimate about the way they were leaning in toward each other. Something that suggested more than a platonic relationship. "What're Scarlet's sister and ex-husband up to?" I said quietly.

"Don't know," Gilley whispered. "But boy would I love to know why they look so chummy."

A server stopped in front of us and offered us the three snails we'd ordered plus our beverages and it was all I could do not to shoo him away so that we could get back to ogling Siobhan and William.

Once the young man had left us, Gilley and I focused our attention at the pair and it was right around that time that William got out of his chair and got stiffly down on bended knee.

Gilley and I both gasped.

William then reached into his pocket and pulled out a black ring box, opening it for Siobhan as she nodded at him and snatched the ring box from his hands.

His grin was ear to ear while she pulled the ring from the box and shoved it onto her finger. Then she threw her arms around William, and several customers who'd seen the display began to clap.

Gilley and I looked at each other and refrained from joining in.

Siobhan and William laughed and turned to the patrons still clapping for them, and the couple waved in gratitude, and right around then is when the pair noticed us. Sitting there. Ogling them with judgmental expressions.

All happiness faded from their faces, and a flood of red blush overtook their complexions. "Hey there," I said loudly. "Congratulations. Scarlet would've been *so* happy for you both."

It was mean, I know, but the gall it took to propose to your ex-wife's sister—the day after she'd been murdered—was too much to stomach.

They disgusted me.

Siobhan leaned in and whispered into William's ear, pointing at us. He seemed surprised, then he turned and spoke to her in soft tones, also pointing at us. And then the pair turned as one to glare in our general direction.

Gilley waved. "Lovely ring," he said. "Best get it appraised, though. Lots of cubic zirconia floating around these days, being passed off as the real thing."

Siobhan got to her feet and motioned for William to follow her. Without a word she stalked past us, her nose in the air. William followed her path, but he stopped momentarily to snarl, "Spying on us?"

Gilley and I shook our heads. "Why would we do that?" I asked him, oh so casually. "Are you two lovebirds trying to hide something worth spying on you both for?"

McMillen's face turned a deeper shade of red, the fury in his eyes so intense he was scary. "I could call the police," he growled.

Gilley rolled his eyes. "Go for it. Ask for Detective Shepherd. I'm sure he'd *love* to hear how you just proposed to a murder victim's sister. And make sure you identify yourself as Scarlet's ex-husband. That's a detail I'm sure he'd simply *adore* to hear."

McMillen's complexion went one shade darker. "I could sue you, you know. This is stalking and harassment!"

I smiled gamely at him and wiggled my phone. "Bring it on. My attorney is on speed dial."

Scarlet's ex gave a frustrated, angry huff, and stormed out of the bakery, chasing after his new fiancée.

I turned to Gilley after he'd gone and gestured toward the table the couple had vacated. "What *was* that?"

Gil tore off a chunk of pastry, popped it into his mouth, and said, "Murder, Cat. That was about murder."

Gilley and I made swift work of breakfast—even forgoing the splitting of the third snail—and headed home. We had much to discuss and we both felt a whiteboard was in order.

"What we need to do is start drawing some lines of connection," I said just a bit later, as I stood back and studied the whiteboard, colored with our lists of suspects and other family members.

"Agreed," Gilley said. "And we can start by drawing a direct line from Siobhan to McMillen."

I uncapped a marker and drew a line between the two. "We both agree that they probably conspired to kill Scarlet, right?"

"I think anything is possible, but I also think that *that* is starting to look more and more attractive as a theory," Gilley said.

"Okay, so what's the motive?" I asked.

Gilley tapped his chin. "Money," he said succinctly.

"Obviously—but how would they benefit?"

Gilley frowned. "That I don't know. Especially once the alimony ran out and Siobhan was cut off."

"Her home is worth two million dollars, though," I reminded him.

"Right. And as of the day before yesterday, she owns it outright. There's no reason to kill Scarlet if that's the motive. She's already got the house," Gilley said.

I tapped my lip with the end of the marker. "Then what else could be their motive?" And then something bubbled up in my mind and I gasped when I thought of it.

"What?" Gil said, knowing I'd just connected two dots.

"When I was divorcing Tommy, within my divorce decree our lawyers put in a mandate that he and I both carry fairly sizeable life insurance policies until the twins turn twenty-three."

"Okay . . ." he said, staring at me quizzically.

"We're also mandated to make the recipient of that life insurance policy each other."

Gil's eyes widened. "You think Siobhan and McMillen could've killed Scarlet for some sort of insurance policy?"

"It's the only way I can think of that they'd benefit from Scarlet's death."

Gilley nodded and reached over toward his messenger bag where I knew he kept his laptop. After pulling it from his bag he opened it up and began to type. I simply stood by and waited, because I'd learned that once Gilley employed his supersleuthing hacking skills, it was best to allow him to concentrate.

"McMillen's net worth is about five hundred thousand," he said.

I whistled. "That low?"

Gilley nodded. "Yeah, and that includes his condo, which, as far as I can tell, doesn't have a mortgage on it."

"That condo is worth at least that amount," I said.

"Yep. Which means he's broke."

I waved impatiently at him. "Okay, now do Siobhan."

Gilley once again focused on his computer screen, his eyes darting back and forth while his fingers flew. "She's estimated to be worth one fifth what he has," he said. "But that doesn't include the house that Scarlet signed over to her."

My eyes widened again. "So, if she wants to hang on to her house, she's *also* essentially broke."

"By East Hampton standards—definitely."

"How can we find out if they're going to benefit from an insurance claim?"

Gilley stretched and cracked his knuckles. "Leave it to me," he said.

For the next hour Gilley typed and searched and worked the dark corners of the internet while I did a load of laundry, watered the houseplants, then made lunch for Spooks and brought him over to Chez Cat to eat it and keep us company.

Finally, I saw Gilley's bent-over posture straighten and he said, "Found it!"

"You found the insurance policy?" I asked hopefully.

"No. I found the divorce decree."

"Between Scarlet and William," I said, wanting to make sure.

"Yes. And listen to this, Cat," Gilley said excitedly, never taking his eyes off the screen. "According to the divorce papers, Scarlet was required to carry a five-million-dollar life insurance policy naming McMillen as benefactor if she should die before the age of seventy-five years and six months old."

I blinked. "That's specific."

"It was probably based on an actuary table."

"How old was Scarlet, again?"

Gilley smiled but it contained no humor. "At the time of her murder, she was seventy-five years, five months, and twenty-nine days old."

My jaw dropped. "You're telling me that, at midnight on the night she died, the policy would've reverted back to her estate?"

"That's *exactly* what I'm telling you," Gilley said.

"No *wonder* McMillen wanted to know what time she died!"

"Right? And the ME probably won't help with that because the time of death is usually given within a three-hour window. Once the family gets wind that there's an insurance policy where they could benefit, I think they'll line up to sue him for it."

I paced back and forth along the counter opposite from Gilley while I thought that through. "The timing of her murder *can't* be a coincidence, can it?"

"If she'd died of natural causes, I'd say it could be, but the fact that we know she was murdered sort of removes any skepticism I may have harbored."

"But wouldn't McMillen know that, being the recipient of that claim, he'd immediately become a suspect?"

"He would, which is where I think Siobhan came in."

"She killed her sister for her lover?"

"Yep. And to also cash in on the money, of course."

"We need to do some more snooping around, maybe find out what's in Scarlet's will."

"Agreed."

"Can you do some more of your hacking thing?"

"I could, but I'd need access to Scarlet's computer. Which is at her house."

"Darn," I said. "So that's a no go."

"Not necessarily," Gil said.

"What does that mean? I'm not breaking into her house, Gilley, if that's what you're thinking."

"I'm not," he said. "What I'm thinking is probably perfectly legal."

"Probably? It's *probably* legal? Gilley, if there's even a question then the answer is a hard pass."

But Gilley held up a finger to me and said, "Hold on, Cat, before you shoot my idea down I have just one question for you."

Smelling a trap, I narrowed suspicious eyes at him. "Which is?"

"Have you ever been at a party, excused yourself to the restroom, and snooped through the host's medicine cabinet?"

I scowled at him. "There's a big difference between taking a cursory glance through someone's medicine cabinet and breaking into her home to snoop around."

"I'm not talking about breaking and entering, Cat. I'm talking about going over there to check on Carlos and Mariana, something we should do anyway, right?"

I continued to glare at him without offering an answer.

"I'm right," Gilley said rather smugly. "And while we're there *checking* on them, making sure they're doing okay, one of us . . . let's say, me, could excuse himself for some emergency or other, and use that time to snoop through Scarlet's desk and hack into her computer."

"Snooping around in Scarlet's personal files feels wrong to me," I said. "I don't like it."

"Cat," Gilley said, adopting his most patient tone. "If Scarlet were still alive, yes, snooping through her personal effects would be very, very wrong. But she's not alive, and what's more she was *mur-*

dered likely by the person or persons who stood the best chance of collecting once she was dead."

"But it makes no sense if Siobhan was also about to benefit from her sister's death by marrying the man who would collect that five million dollars from her insurance policy, Gilley. Siobhan would be looked at as a suspect too."

"Oh, I think just about everyone in that family is suspect, my dear, *but* if McMillen convinced her to murder her sister in exchange for a proposal of marriage where they could live on the proceeds of the life insurance policy, then that makes them our primary suspects, right?"

"It all sounds so convoluted," I said, rubbing my temples.

"Murder ain't neat, sugar."

I sighed. "Fine."

Gilley arched his brows. "Really? You'll go along with the plan?"

I threw up my hands. "We need inside information, and how else are we going to get it if we don't sink to a new moral low and snoop around a little."

"That's the spirit," Gilley said, his smile a mile wide.

Chapter 6

Gilley and I called Mariana and told her that we wanted to stop by to see how she and Carlos were doing. The sweet woman got a little choked up at the idea of Gilley and me caring about how she and her husband were coping.

When I hung up and motioned to Gilley to follow me to the car, I felt an elephant-sized level of guilt. "We need to be nicer," I said as I backed us out of the garage.

"We're plenty nice," he said.

I eyed him skeptically. "Are we though?"

"Where is this coming from?"

"Would we have offered to check in on Mariana and Carlos if we didn't have the secret agenda of snooping around, looking for clues?"

"You mean, would we check in with them if we

weren't otherwise trying to solve the murder of their former employer?"

I nodded.

"Of course we would've," he said earnestly. "Cat, you're a good, kind, thoughtful person. If you weren't so distracted by Scarlet's murder, you definitely would've made a point to circle back to Mariana and Carlos."

I considered that for a moment and decided that Gilley was probably right. I hate to see people in pain, and I would've been concerned about the lovely couple—especially since it was so obvious how much they cared about Scarlet.

"While you're snooping, I'll try to find out what their plans are now that Scarlet's gone. They must be worried about finding new jobs—especially as I'm sure they'll want to stick together."

"That'd be a tall order," Gilley said. "To find employment someplace in need of both a driver and a housekeeper?"

"Oh! I know who we could reach out to!" I said, suddenly brightening. "We could ask Julia Entwistle if she knows anyone who could hire them as a team."

Julia was one of the Hamptons' wealthiest residents. She was practically royalty around these parts, and we were good friends with her, her grandson, and her granddaughter-in-law.

"That's a great idea!" Gilley said. "See?" he added. "You're a good person, Cat. Of course you would've checked in on them without an agenda if we weren't trying to solve this murder."

"I think you're right," I said, feeling better about the whole thing.

We arrived at Scarlet's a bit later and Mariana answered the bell, greeting us warmly, but there was still a good measure of sadness in her eyes. "Come in, come in," she urged. "I've got tea and some treats in the kitchen."

We followed her to the kitchen. We had to hope that Carson wasn't here, of course, because as Scarlet's personal assistant, he might be occupying the very place Gilley needed to snoop.

As we walked behind Mariana I casually asked, "Is Carson here? We'd like to check in with him as well. He must be so devastated."

"He's not here right now," Mariana said. "He called earlier and said he'd been having panic attacks since they told him about Miss Scarlet. He's really struggling."

"Oh, that's so hard," I said, feeling sympathetic toward Carson while guilty about the fact that I was also relieved he wasn't here.

We reached the kitchen which was mostly white and soft grays and Mariana nodded to the left where a lovely silver velvet couch and two white velvet, shelter arm swivel chairs created a cozy seating area.

We took our seats as Mariana gathered a tray full of delicious-looking confections and a quirky-looking teapot with art deco details. "The house has been so quiet the past two days," she said softly while setting down the tray on the ottoman in front of us.

I could see the pain etched in Mariana's expression but she seemed to be fighting it, trying her level best to be cheerful. I reached over and took her hand in both of mine. "I'm so, so sorry, Mariana. I know you cared for Scarlet very much. She would be very grateful that you and Carlos are still here, tending to the property."

Mariana's lower lip trembled and her eyes filled with tears, but again she fought to hold herself together. Swallowing hard and taking a deep breath she said, "Mr. Carson told us we can stay on either until we find a new employer or the house sells."

"Oh?" Gilley said. "Carson is already moving ahead with selling the property?"

"Not yet," Mariana said, "but we all assume that's what it will come down to. Miss Scarlet's lawyer called him yesterday. She's been in Hawaii and she said she just heard the news. She took the red-eye last night and she'll be over tonight to deliver the reading of the will."

Gilley's brow shot up, and so did mine. "So soon?" I asked. Scarlet wasn't even buried yet.

Mariana poured out the tea, then sat back on one of the swivel chairs. "The lawyer said that Miss Scarlet's will was to be read within three days of her passing. Miss Scarlet didn't want anyone to worry about what they'd get after she'd gone."

"I hope you'll let us know when the funeral will be held," I said, thinking that as long as the funeral were taking place before we left for Europe, we'd definitely want to be there. "Gilley and I would very much like to attend."

Mariana nodded, and looked unable to speak, so she distracted herself by reaching for the plate of confections and offering it to each of us.

After bingeing on the snail earlier in the morning, I shook my head gently and declined her offer, but Gilley thought nothing of reaching for the two most enticing treats on the plate, popping one into his mouth immediately. He moaned with pleasure and offered Mariana a soft smile. "These came from Louis on Seventh, am I right?" he asked.

Mariana looked quite surprised. "Yes. Miss Scarlet would have us bring her a box of his mixed pastries from Southampton once a week. She liked to have them on hand should any company come over. How did you know?"

"I took several classes from Chef Louis. He's a master pastry chef, and a brilliant artist."

Mariana brightened for the first time since we walked through the door. "I've always wanted to take his class!" she said. "I love to bake."

"You should!" Gilley replied, matching her enthusiasm.

The two chatted for a few moments longer about Louis and his pastry shop and I took the opportunity to discreetly call Gilley's phone. He jumped as his back pocket vibrated, then met my eyes as he took out the phone. Looking at the display he made a show of sighing heavily and frowning. "That's my attorney," he said glumly. "Mariana, is there someplace private where I can take this call?"

Mariana immediately pointed to the hallway. "You can use Miss Scarlet's office. Down the hall, it's the third room on the left."

Gilley got to his feet, nodded his thanks, and hurried out of the room, pretending to answer the call by saying, "Hello, counselor. So what does my soon-to-be ex-husband want now?"

Alone again with Mariana I smiled sheepishly. "Poor Gilley. He gets one of those phone calls at least once a day."

"He's getting a divorce?"

I nodded.

"That's so sad," she said. And then her gaze traveled to the ring finger of my left hand where I wore a large gemstone. "You're married?"

"No," I said with a sigh. "Also divorced."

Mariana nodded. "So many people getting divorced lately."

"Well, sometimes you need more than love to hold a marriage together, and when marriages go bad, they can get really, really bad."

"Oh, I know," she said. "When Miss Scarlet got divorced, it was terrible. Her ex-husband put her through a lot."

"What're your thoughts on William McMillen?" I asked.

"I don't like to speak ill of anyone," she said almost in a whisper. "But he is *not* a good man. He was so mean to Miss Scarlet. To all of us, too."

"Gilley and I saw him this morning when we were getting breakfast," I said, hoping she'd take the bait.

"You did?"

I nodded. "He and Scarlet's sister, Siobhan, were getting engaged."

Mariana actually gasped. "*Engaged?*"

"Yep," I said, taking a sip of tea.

"You must be mistaken!"

"I'm not, Mariana."

"You're sure it was them?"

"Positive. William even spoke to us on the way out."

Mariana made the sign of the cross and said, "Such disrespect for poor Miss Scarlet! She would be so upset if she knew!"

"Are you sure she didn't?" I asked, taking another casual sip of my tea.

Mariana began to blink some more, and I could see her mind racing to pinpoint a time when her boss might've discovered the truth.

To nudge her in the right direction, I said, "Remember the phone call she received and how she drove herself over to William's home? Maybe she went there to confront him, or even threaten him."

Mariana gasped again. "I never even suspected," she said. "Miss Siobhan was over here all the time, usually to ask Miss Scarlet for more money. I never heard her even mention Mr. William once the divorce was final."

"Well, maybe she did hate him and dismiss him a few years ago," I said, pretending to give Siobhan the benefit of the doubt. "But this morning, she'd definitely gotten over any ill will she wished him. They were clearly in love."

"I'll have to tell Carlos. He'll be so mad for Miss Scarlet! Sisters should never betray each other like that!"

"Siobhan must figure that, now that her sister is dead, she's free to marry William."

"But to get engaged so soon after Miss Scarlet was murdered?" Mariana said, her voice going up an octave or two. I could tell she was starting to connect the dots, just like Gilley and I had.

I allowed her mind to spin without speaking, hoping it might prompt something that would lead us to another clue, but she merely sat there, shaking her head, making tsking sounds.

She looked up after a few moments and said, "I hope Mr. Gilley isn't getting bad news. He's been gone for a while."

"Oh, his attorney is a talker. You know, the better to run up the bill. I'm sure he's fine. They're probably just talking strategy."

To distract her from Gilley, I focused our conversation back on family. I told her about my sons and her mood seemed to brighten as I spoke about their antics. I even had her laughing at one point, which was such a welcome sight as she'd been so sad since Scarlet's death.

Gilley finally came back into the room then and the way he looked at me, I knew he'd found something interesting. "Sorry," he said to Mariana while he took his seat. "My soon-to-be ex-husband is pulling some shenanigans again."

"Oh, no," Mariana said. "I'm so sorry."

Gilley waved nonchalantly at her. "It's nothing. My attorney is going to handle it just fine. Oh, but Cat, I do have to get back to the house to find some paperwork my attorney wanted me to email him."

"Of course," I said, getting to my feet. "Mariana, thank you so much for seeing us. The tea and the treats were lovely."

Mariana walked us to the front door, but seemed

reluctant to see us leave. "Thank you for coming," she said sadly, and I suspected it must be quite lonely in that grand estate all by herself. And then I had another thought.

"Mariana," I said, "would you like for us to wait until Carlos gets back just to make sure you're safe?"

Mariana's face turned slightly pale, and I suspected she'd just had the same thought as me: a killer had entered the house undetected and had murdered her employer. Who was to say that the killer couldn't come back?

"No," she said after a momentary pause. "Thank you, Miss Catherine. I'll be okay. Carlos should be here very soon."

"You're sure?" Gilley asked, and I could see he was feeling almost guilty for getting us to leave so abruptly.

"Yes," she assured us. "I'll be fine."

We took her at her word, but I'll admit that I was more than a little reluctant to leave her unprotected. Not that I could do much to protect her. Or Gilley, for that matter.

When we got into the car I said, "Okay, spill it. What did you find?"

"Scarlet was dying," he said. Just like that. Just blurted out a shocking statement without any preamble or buildup.

"She was . . . dying?"

"Pancreatic cancer," he said. "She probably only had weeks to live."

"Shut the front door!" I said to him.

"Oh, I shut it, gurl, I shut it."

"How did you find this out?"

Gilley reached into his pocket and pulled out a prescription bottle. "I found this in her desk. I didn't know what it was prescribed for, so I looked it up online, and it's primarily used for patients with pancreatic cancer, and taking that as a clue, I dug a little deeper into her desk and found a file labeled MEDICAL. In there was her diagnosis."

"But she seemed so healthy!"

"Pancreatic cancer is deceptive, sugar. You can have high functionality until you suddenly don't. Her cancer was only recently discovered, and it'd spread to her liver, intestines, gallbladder, and lymph nodes."

"It'd turned metastatic," I said.

"Yep. At the time of her murder, she was not long for this world."

"No wonder she looked so sad when we asked her to come with us to Europe. She knew she wouldn't make it in her condition."

"That's my guess," Gilley said.

"Did anyone else know?"

"I doubt it," Gilley said. "The way her family reacted to the news of being cut off makes me think that they didn't know, otherwise, at least one of them would've mentioned it."

"But why come to see me if she was dying?" I asked. "In a few weeks' time it wouldn't have mattered if her family was still sponging off her, right?"

Gilley sighed sadly. "I think, but don't know for certain, that it may have been Scarlet's one last attempt at gaining back her own power. She'd been so abused over the years, both emotionally and physically, that to have that one final grasp at asserting her self-governance over her finances and her family was something worth doing."

I stared at Gilley for a long time. "I love that," I said at last. "It makes me feel like we contributed to Scarlet's last wishes in a way."

"Yeah," he said. "And isn't that a great feeling?"

"It is."

A bit later we arrived home and both Spooks and Sebastian greeted us at the door. Spooks crashed his big head into us and Sebastian said, "Hello, Lady Catherine, and Sir Gilley. Might I order you some lunch?"

I looked at the time on my watch. It was already quarter to noon.

"Yes, please, Sebastian," Gilley sang. "I could go for some French onion soup and a Roquefort-walnut salad from Rowdy's. How about you, Cat?"

"Ooh, Rowdy's. We haven't had lunch from there in a long time. Sebastian, I'll take an order of Rowdy's chopped salad."

"Excellent choices, you two. Placing that order now."

Gilley and I ventured into the kitchen and sat once again at the island. "I feel like all we do lately is eat," I said.

Gilley grinned wickedly. "Think of it like we're in training for Europe. Gotta stretch the stomachs for all of that glorious dining we'll be doing."

"If we're not careful, we'll be stretching our waistlines more than our stomachs." My eye fell on the whiteboard across from us. "We need another angle to work this case. I'm convinced that Siobhan and McMillen killed Scarlet for the insurance money, but how do we prove that?"

"We need access to them," Gil said. "But no way would they allow us within fifty feet of them from now on. They know we're onto them."

"Then we need to find them out in public and follow them. Maybe they'll lead us to the gun used in the shooting."

"Shepherd didn't recover it?"

"Not to my knowledge," I said.

"Well, there *is* the reading of the will tonight," Gil said. "That's going to come with its own drama."

"Drama we should be in on," I said.

"Agreed. Okay, new plan. We've got to figure out how to listen in on the will being read."

And that's when an idea hit me. "What if we told Mariana that we left something behind and needed to come back for it?"

"Like what?"

"Well, like . . ." I looked down at myself, trying to think, and that's when I remembered I was wearing one of my favorite rings. Set in platinum, the large, five-carat, square-cut sapphire glinted in the light from the kitchen. "My ring," I said, holding it up for Gilley to see. "Mariana already commented on it this morning. I could call her—sounding panicked of course . . ."

"Of course."

". . . and declare that I've lost my precious sapphire and that we need to come back to the house to search for it."

Gilley snapped his fingers. "I like it! But what do we do in the meantime?"

The doorbell rang and Sebastian announced, "Your lunch is here, Lady Catherine!"

I got up and grabbed my purse from the counter. Fishing through it for a cash tip, I excused myself to fetch our lunch. When I came back to the kitchen, I set the food on the counter and answered Gilley's question. "What we're doing in the meantime is eating lunch and then we'll do a little shopping for our European trip."

Gilley frowned, which wasn't an expression I'd seen him wear any time I'd mentioned the word *shopping*.

"What?" I asked.

"Are we really going to be able to make our trip, Cat?"

My eyes widened in surprise. "Of course!" I might've put a bit too much enthusiasm into that statement.

Gilley leveled his eyes at me. "Shepherd would really allow us to skip town?"

"Why wouldn't he?"

"Come on, Cat," he said. "I know him almost as well as you do, and that man wouldn't let us leave town in the middle of an investigation where we're on the suspect list."

I bit my lip. "Why do you think we're on the suspect list?"

"How could we not be? We were the last two people to see Scarlet alive."

"Three people," I corrected.

"Who's the third?"

"The murderer."

"Ah," he said. "Still . . ."

I sighed. "Shepherd doesn't suspect us."

"Of course he doesn't. But he has a sergeant or lieutenant to answer to, doesn't he? And above them there's the D.A., right?"

"Gilley," I said, trying to put some earnestness into the lie. "We can leave town whenever we want. Legally, Shepherd can't stop us."

"Yeah, I know, but if we did that, and he got heat from above, wouldn't that put more strain on your relationship?"

I gulped. "Why do you think our relationship is strained?"

"Because you guys haven't been spending much time together, and this morning when you met me at the door, not only wasn't he here, but you looked like you'd had yourself a good cry, so sugar, *something*'s going on."

I turned away from him to hide what I knew was a worried expression, and covered the move by grabbing two plates from the cupboard. "Nothing's going on. He's been very busy. That's all. We'll spend more time together once he's finished remodeling his kitchen."

Gilley said nothing as I got the plates, and the silverware. But as I sat down and pulled our bagged lunch toward us, he said, "That's how it started to fall apart with me and Michel. He was busy. Always busy. Always putting something else in front of our time together."

I bit my lip again and turned in my chair to take up his hand and look him earnestly in the eye. "That's how it fell apart with me and Tom, too, Gilley. Only I was the one always putting something in front of our time together. But that's not going to be me and Shep. I'm determined to insist on time together should this go on much longer."

"And yet . . ." he said without finishing the thought.

"And yet, what?"

"And yet, we're taking off for three weeks during a murder investigation where we know he'll get heat from upstairs if they find out that the two people last to see Scarlet alive have ventured off, out of the country."

I sighed. "We're going, Gil. End of story. Shepherd and I are fine."

He looked doubtful, and I couldn't tell if he was doubting that we'd actually head to Europe or if Shepherd and I were okay, and, admittedly, that bothered me the whole rest of the day.

Chapter 7

Gilley and I arrived back at Scarlet's house about ten minutes before the will was scheduled to be read. Mariana had told us to come right up to the garage and when we got there, the door lifted, revealing Carlos, who waved us forward. When we got out to greet him, he put a finger to his lips and whispered, "Please speak softly, Miss Catherine and Mr. Gilley. If the family knows you're here, they'll throw a fit!"

"We'll be quiet as mice!" Gilley promised in a hissy whisper. Then he crossed himself and pretended to lock his lips and throw away the key.

Carlos smiled.

I rolled my eyes. He was laying it on a little thick, if you asked me.

We followed behind Carlos up the ramp and entered the kitchen where Mariana was busy loading silver trays with small triangular-shaped sandwiches, cheese, crackers, and bite-sized quiches.

"You're feeding them?" Gilley asked, his tone surprised.

Mariana hustled from one tray to the other, barely pausing to glance up at us as we entered. "If they eat something they might not be so angry," she said quietly and then she allowed herself one quick nervous glance toward the door leading to the hallway. Just beyond that door came the muddled sound of conversations. No raised voices, though, as far as I could tell.

"Is Mr. Carson here yet?" Mariana asked her husband.

He shook his head. "He called from the funeral home. He's making the final decisions on her casket and services and he'll be here very soon."

"And the attorney isn't here either, yet, right?" Mariana asked.

"No, *mi vida*," Carlos said.

Mariana frowned, then paused long enough to take another worried look at the shut door leading to the central hallway which led to the living room where I suspected everyone was gathered.

"I'm worried they'll start taking things if there's no one in there to watch them," she said.

Carlos glanced over his shoulder in the direction of the garage. "I have to get back outside to wait for Mr. Carson and the attorney and any stragglers that might arrive late."

Mariana donned an oven mitt, then ran to the oven door and pulled it open a crack to peer inside. "These quiches need another two minutes or so. I can't leave them yet."

"We'll keep an eye on the family for you," I said, thinking quickly.

Mariana and Carlos both shook their heads. "I don't think that's a good idea, Miss Catherine," Carlos said. "Remember how angry they were the other night?"

"You mean, at least as angry as the person who murdered Scarlet was?" Gilley said drolly.

"Yes," Mariana said. "It's too risky."

"Well, someone should be in there to watch out for Scarlet's things," I insisted.

Just then the door from the garage opened and in stepped my sweetheart, who took one look at me and Gilley and instantly became less sweet. "What the hell are you two doing here?" he demanded.

Gilley and I exchanged panicked looks and we were saved by Mariana. "Hello, Detective Shepherd. We weren't expecting you. Miss Catherine and Mr. Gilley are here because Miss Catherine lost her ring and she thinks it might've dropped off her finger somewhere in the house. I've been so busy, I haven't had time to look for it."

Shepherd barely acknowledged Mariana. "What ring?" he demanded, staring at me.

I gulped. "My . . . saph-sapphire," I stammered. For good measure I held up my empty ring finger.

Shepherd squinted at me suspiciously. "When did you lose it?"

"Earlier."

The squint narrowed even more. "Earlier when?"

"It's a good thing you're here, Detective!" Gilley said, stepping in front of me like a human shield. "The family is all in there and Mariana and Carlos were just saying they were worried that one or two of Scarlet's relatives might decide to get sticky fingers before the attorney arrives to read the will."

In that moment it was as if Shepherd became aware of the din of conversation happening in a nearby room. He pivoted his gaze from us to the door and back again. "How long have they been here?"

Mariana answered him. "At least a half hour, Detective. I've been preparing some snacks for the family, and Carlos has to watch out for Mr. Carson and the attorney. It would make us all feel better if you could be in there just until Mr. Carson arrives."

Shepherd considered Mariana for a long moment, but he finally allowed himself one curt nod and began to move toward the door leading to the hallway and the living room beyond. As he passed me, however, he took up my hand and whispered, "Come with me." And even though he'd said that softly, there was no mistaking the commanding implication.

I thought about resisting, I mean, his appearance had made all thoughts of spying on the reading of the will vanish. Had Shepherd not had ahold of my hand, I would've grabbed Gilley and bolted the second Shep's frame was through the doorway. But my choice now was either to pull away and make a scene or allow him to quietly berate me on the way to the living room. I figured if I walked quickly the berating wouldn't be so intense.

So I allowed him to tug me along and when we got to the other side of the doorway, I tried to keep walking but Shepherd surprised me again by pulling me in close to him and pressing me up against the wall of the hallway. "What. Are. You. Doing. Here. Cat?" he said, enunciating each word to let me know how royally ticked off he was, because he damn well knew what I was doing there. And it wasn't looking for a lost bauble.

"We were curious," I admitted, hoping the truth—or the partial truth—would set me free.

"About?"

"The will."

"Why?"

"What do you mean why?"

Shepherd shook his head and swore under his breath. "Stop it, Cat," he said. "I know you're here, sticking your nose in where it doesn't belong, and I'm still so pissed off at you for hiring that contractor to invade my personal space and now this . . . this nosing into other people's business is just so typical of you and yet also so disappointing."

I stared at him with watery eyes as a long, tense silence spindled out between us.

At last, he stepped back from me and let go of my hand. And then he turned his back on me and headed down the hallway alone.

I stood against the wall and felt a few tears slide down my cheeks. Somehow, hearing Shepherd say he was disappointed in me was worse than if he'd actually yelled at me. So I took a moment to dab at my eyes and was prepared to go back into the kitchen when the door opened on its own, and out from the entry came Carson in his wheelchair and a slight woman with curly brown hair and an air of intelligent confidence strolling along behind him.

"Catherine," Carson said, coming up short when he saw me, his tone warmer than Shepherd's by about a zillion degrees. "What brings you here?"

"Hi, Carson," I said. "So sorry to intrude. I lost a ring earlier today and I thought it might've slipped off when I came by to check on Carlos and Mariana. And you, actually. I've been so distraught over your family's tragedy. It's just so upsetting." I was babbling, I knew, but Shepherd had thrown me for a loop.

Carson's brow wrinkled. "Oh, I'm sorry. Did you find it?"

"Find what?" I asked.

"Your ring."

"Oh!" I said, feeling my cheeks heat. For the record, I'm a terrible liar. "Um . . ."

"Found it!" Gilley announced as he too stepped through the door, offering up my sapphire ring like a conquering hero holding aloft his sword.

I assumed he'd been listening on the other side of the door, and I was so relieved he'd come to my rescue, and announced the discovery of my lost bauble just like we'd planned.

"Oh, thank goodness!" I said, scooting around Carson and the woman to clutch Gilley's hand and take my ring from him. "I'm so relieved!"

Carson offered a bit of a forced smile, then he indicated the woman next to him and said, "Terry, these are two of Scarlet's friends, Catherine Cooper and Gilley Gillespie. Catherine is a client of one of your partners, but I don't think you've actually met in person yet, right?"

Terry sized the two of us up in about three nanoseconds and I couldn't be sure, but I suspected she was onto us. Those intelligent blue eyes glinted with a twinkle of knowing. "Only over Zoom," she said, extending her hand to me.

I pushed a big old smile to my lips, shook her hand, and said, "Hi, Terry. Great to meet you."

Gilley shook her hand next, and he added a curtsey . . . because . . . of course he would. After that a slightly awkward silence ensued until I gestured to the hallway and said, "Please don't let us keep you from the task at hand. I know the family is probably very anxious to hear the details of the will."

Carson scoffed. "That's putting it lightly. My voice mail is completely full of messages from them. I don't think they realize that even I don't know what's in the will until Terry tells us."

There was a look that crossed Terry's face, an expression that I couldn't quite place, but I got a bad feeling from it.

"Let's proceed, shall we?" she said, and waited for Carson to take the lead.

I think he'd noted her expression too, though, because he hesitated ever so slightly before he wheeled himself forward. As the pair were about to turn the corner toward the family room, the door behind us opened again, and out stepped Mariana and Carlos, both carrying a silver platter loaded with goodies.

Mariana was biting her lip nervously. "Why do you think she wants us there, Carlos?" she was saying.

"I don't know, *mi vida*. Maybe Miss Scarlet left us a piece of art or something."

Mariana focused on me as she began to pass by

and said, "The attorney wants us in the room when she reads the will."

"Oh?" I said.

She nodded and bit her lip again.

"That's a good thing, Mariana," I tried to reassure her.

"I don't know," she said. She looked scared and that worried me. What did she know that we didn't?

"Why wouldn't it be?" I tried.

Mariana looked back at her husband, and Carlos seemed to understand. "If she left me and Mariana anything of value, the family will fight us for it. We don't have money for fancy lawyers. We can't fight back."

Gilley and I exchanged a silent look, and he nodded as if he could see where the couple was coming from.

And the fact that I also could see where they were coming from pissed me off. I glanced in the direction of the family room and said, "Mariana. Carlos. If you'll allow Gilley and me to escort you into the family room and stand with you during the reading of the will, I'd be willing to also stand up for you against the family if they protest anything that was left to you from Scarlet's will. I'm not an attorney, but I have a few on retainer, and one or two others who actually owe me a favor. I'm sure I could convince one of them to waive their retainer and represent you should it come to that."

Mariana's expression bloomed in relief. "Oh, Miss Catherine!" she said. "That would be so good if you could do that!" Nodding toward where the family was gathered, she added, "Those people scare me!"

"Understood," I said.

Gilley stepped up to her and lifted the silver platter from her hands. "Let me help," he said. "You walk next to Cat. Show them you've got allies, okay?"

Mariana smiled at Gilley. "Thank you," she said shyly.

We walked down the hallway together, the din of conversation growing louder as we went. When we turned the corner into the family room it was like déjà vu. Everyone was seated in the exact spot they'd been seated in two days before with one exception, and that was the appearance of William, who was sitting beside Siobhan. Even though they weren't touching, it was obvious that they were now a couple, and I could tell that this had sent a ripple of discord through the rest of the family.

Carson rolled forward to park his chair in the same spot next to Scarlet's throne, and he looked at her empty chair with a pained expression.

Terry was already seated at the table on the other side of the throne, where Gilley and I had sat, and her posture was every bit as commanding as Scarlet's had been.

The family all looked up as we entered, and most of the conversations amongst them stopped abruptly. I leveled my gaze at them—double-dog-daring them to challenge whatever Scarlet had left to her two loyal employees, and I thought I did a pretty good job of looking intimidating until my eye caught Shepherd's. He was standing across the room, near the French doors leading to the beach, and *his* look took my tough-girl expression to *school.*

I barely resisted the urge to shudder and managed to accompany Mariana all the way over to a set of chairs near where Terry sat. I waved for Mariana to take a seat, and gave a nod to Carlos, who set down his tray of hors d'oeuvres and came to take the chair next to Mariana.

I stood behind Mariana, and Gilley trotted to the coffee table to set down the second tray, then followed Carlos to his chair and took up sentinel behind him as well.

All of this was firmly noted by the family . . . and by Shepherd, whose glower became even darker.

I set my gaze on Terry to avoid a chance glance his way, knowing he was furious with me. At this point, I was in for a penny and a pound, so I didn't think it mattered how much I pushed my presence at Scarlet's will reading.

Once we were all seated and the room had settled into a tense silence, Terry extracted an iPad from the briefcase she'd carried in, and opened the flap covering the screen before addressing the gathering. "Thank you for being punctual. Normally, I would simply email you each a copy of the will and notify anyone who was about to receive an inheritance, but Scarlet insisted that her last will and testament be read aloud in front of the whole family.

"To that end," she continued, her voice reverberating around the room, "I should tell you that if any of you are anticipating a specific inheritance due to the fact that Scarlet told you she would leave something for you—please brace yourselves. Scarlet changed her will considerably approximately ten days ago, shortly before I went on vacation."

There were some nervous shifts in chairs and a look or two exchanged among family members. I thought it intriguing that Scarlet had so recently changed her will. I wondered what'd prompted it.

"The total of Scarlet's estate has recently been assessed," Terry continued. "She had holdings of cash, stocks, bonds, real estate, and material possessions in excess of eighty million dollars."

An audible gasp escaped several witnesses, including Gilley and myself.

"She also had substantial monthly income of about four million generated by the royalties from her seventy-seven books in print, and an advance of three million on a manuscript recently completed and sent to her publisher just four days ago."

"Two days before she died," I whispered to Gilley.

"Pending approval of said manuscript, her assets would increase by that amount less her agent's commission, of course. The total estimated value of Scarlet's entire estate if everything were liquidated today would be in the neighborhood of ninety to one hundred million dollars."

A new series of gasps echoed around the room. I noticed that several family members had either gone pale or red-faced, likely depending on which way they felt they'd come out in the will.

"To that end," Terry said once the attendees had had a chance to absorb the news, "Scarlet's estate will be divided up as follows."

Scarlet's son and daughter, Grayson and Masie, leaned forward eagerly, while her sister, Siobhan, her nephew Luke, and her two granddaughters, Lucy and April, all grimaced, likely because they knew what was coming. Or, more to the point—what wasn't.

"To Scarlet's ex-husband, William McMillen, Scarlet leaves the sum total of twenty-five million dollars in cash, stocks, bonds, and other liquid assets."

The family's reaction was one of absolute stunned silence. A few gasps escaped, but mostly everyone's jaw dropped—including mine. Then, almost as one, we all turned to stare at William McMillen . . . who seemed the most stunned of all.

Still, Terry wasn't finished. She continued with, "In return, William McMillen will agree to never marry Siobhan Rubi, and that he will end all contact with her immediately upon signing receipt of said funds and assets set forth in this last will and testament."

Siobhan's complexion drained of all color. She'd been gripping William's hand tightly as the first lines in the will were read, but now that the stipulation for William's inheritance was laid bare, her eyes watered as William forcefully pulled his hand from hers, pressing his palm against his knee and staring at Terry as if he expected her to yell out, "Gotcha!"

But she didn't. Instead, she turned to Carson and said, "Carson, Scarlet wanted to make sure you were taken care of, so she left you four million dollars in a secure trust to be administered by me or my successor when I retire. With careful management, you should be able to live off the interest for many years to come." She turned to Mariana and Carlos. "This next paragraph Scarlet wrote directly to you."

The pair looked at each other nervously, but they also nodded to Terry to continue. Terry cleared her throat and read, " 'To my faithful employees, Mariana and Carlos DeLeon, I leave all the rest of my assets, material possessions, rights to royalties, and real estate. It is my fondest wish that the two people who never betrayed me, took care of me in my darkest hours, and were more my family than my own family—be safe and secure in the knowledge that this house is theirs, along with everything in it, and that all future income from any royalties, advances, and subsidiary rights on the sale of my books become their income to spend or distribute as they please for as long as they both shall live.' "

If the attending family members had been stunned before when they heard about William's inheritance, it was nothing compared to how they looked now. All of them swiveled their gazes from Terry to the DeLeons and back again, as if the very notion that these two *servants* could *possibly* be the inheritors of the rest of Scarlet's vast fortune was too far beyond belief to even contemplate.

And for their part, Mariana and Carlos both seemed ready to faint. "No," Carlos said weakly. "No, that can't be right. Can it?" he asked Terry.

Terry eyed him over her half-rimmed glasses. "It's right, Carlos. Scarlet wanted to take care of you. She was very specific about it."

"This is outrageous!" Siobhan snapped, standing tall and glaring first at Terry and then at Carlos and Mariana. "My sister was out of her mind! She would've taken care of family over any money-grubbing moochers!"

"She did," I said boldly, and for emphasis I placed my hands on Mariana's shoulders. "She did take care of the only family that ever took care of her. And if you contest the will, I promise you that you'll lose and be out attorney fees. I have some very powerful friends in the legal community, Siobhan, and I'll make sure Mariana and Carlos are *quite* well represented."

A tense standoff followed as Siobhan shot daggers with her eyes at me while everyone else looked on. I had a feeling she was close to violence and truth be told, the look on her face frightened me but I wasn't about to back down.

Right about then someone cleared his throat and I allowed myself a quick glance in that direction. Shepherd was pushing himself away from the wall he was leaning against and came across the room to stand next to me, adding his protective presence—and his badge—to the situation. Siobhan backed down. Barely. Turning to William she snapped, "Come on. Let's get out of here."

William stood tall and regarded her in a way that suggested he wasn't about to tell her something she'd approve of. "I'm going to stay, Siobhan, and talk with the attorney. You and I can chat later."

Siobhan's face became as red as her maiden name. She snarled at him, turned on her heel, and walked out. One by one the others also got to their feet and filed out of the room. I couldn't help noticing that several of them glanced a bit too long at some of the artwork on the walls—and I had no doubt that the art Scarlet had in her grand home was the type of art bid on at auctions.

Shepherd must've noticed that too, because he tagged along after the crowd, no doubt making sure they got to the front door without being weighed down by any souvenirs.

Meanwhile, Gilley and I came around to face Carlos and Mariana. They were holding hands and still looking quite stunned. "How do you feel?" Gilley asked them.

Carlos shook his head and then he raised his chin and looked around the ornate room. Just in this one room was probably more material value than he or Mariana had ever had in their whole lifetime.

"I don't even know what to say," he said. "It's too generous. It's too much."

Terry tucked her iPad back into her satchel. "It'll take six months or so to wind its way through probate court," she said, "but at the end of it, all this will be yours."

"But why?" Carlos pressed.

Terry smiled kindly. "Scarlet always spoke highly of you two, Carlos. She's revised her will at least a dozen times over the past two decades, and in each revision, she would give more and more to the two of you. You took very good care of her, and she even told me once that you saved her life. . . ."

Terry paused to look meaningfully at William, who stood in front of his chair, blinking as if trying to comprehend this turn of events. Given his history with Scarlet, I couldn't understand why she would leave him so much of her fortune.

As if he also needed an answer to that question, William said to Terry, "Why? We were divorced. She had stopped paying me alimony. Why would she leave me so much money?"

Terry's lip curled. "Would you have left her sister for anything less?"

William stared at Terry with wide eyes. And then they narrowed angrily. "Scarlet always had to have the last word, didn't she? She was always dictating the course of my life, and finally, *finally* when I find the one true love, she has to go and wreck it!"

Now, I'm not one for violence, but in that moment, I wanted to punch William, I truly did. He had the *nerve* to complain about being left twenty-five million dollars by a woman he'd routinely mentally and physically abused?

"You're despicable," I hissed at him.

His attention turned to me. "*What* did you say?"

"I said, You. Are. Despicable! How *dare* you disparage the woman cut down before her time, murdered in cold blood, and who left *you* twenty-five *million* dollars! Have you no shame? No sense of decency? No sense of gratitude?!"

"Cat," Gilley whispered, placing a gentle hand on my shoulder. I knew I was shouting and I knew that my display of anger was perhaps a bit over the top, but this man had struck a real nerve with me. My ex-husband had taken exactly half of *my* hard-earned money when he left me for a country club bartender. He'd waited until after the very profitable sale of my marketing firm to announce that he was leaving me. In other words, he'd waited for the cash to come in, knowing he'd get half when he filed.

So I was yelling at William as much as I was yelling at Tom—my ex. And I knew all of that, yet I couldn't seem to contain my anger. It was like a genie let out of the bottle. "You're nothing more than a bitter loser, William!" I snapped. "Scarlet was the one with the talent. The drive. And the imagination to not only make a name for herself, but to become one of the best in her craft! Meanwhile, what did you do other than complain and abuse her? Huh? Did you use your time to turn out a bestseller, William? No. No, *you* just sat around and felt sorry for yourself. No *wonder* she ordered you away from her sister! If you abused Scarlet—the woman keeping you housed, clothed, and fed—I can only imagine what you would've done to her sister had you two moved forward with your plans for marriage!"

In a sudden moment, moving quicker than I could've imagined he would, William flew at me and grabbed me around the neck, choking me with his bare hands. I rocked backward, gripping his wrists and trying to pry his hands from around my throat. All around me there was commotion and clatter. Chairs were overturned as I backed up to try to get away from William, desperate to free myself from his grasp. I could hear Gilley screaming, and as the darkness started to creep into my vision, I saw his hands grabbing at William, trying to pull him away.

And all this time I couldn't breathe. My heart hammered painfully in my chest, and I could feel my face grow hot with the effort to get some oxygen, but William's grip was too tight. And then, like a miracle, his hands released me and I stumbled backward, kept from falling to the ground by Carlos, who caught me and helped stand me up.

I coughed several times, trying to inhale as much oxygen as my lungs would allow, but my breath was ragged and my throat burned. The skin at the base of my neck felt scratched and raw, and I doubled over to cough some more and try to get my breathing under control.

"I'll get her some water!" Mariana cried and from my bent-over position, I saw her feet go running off. And then there were strong hands on my hips, and the presence of someone trying to comfort me.

"Breathe in slow," Shepherd said. "Come on, Cat, slow that diaphragm down. You can do it, just inhale and hold it for a second or two before exhaling."

I closed my eyes, which had filled with tears, and tried to follow Shepherd's direction. After a minute or two I felt better, opened my eyes, and stood tall again. "I'm okay," I said to the gathering of worried faces. And then my eye caught William, sitting on the ground with his hands behind his back, a swollen eye and a fat, bleeding lip. He looked dazed and my mind was having trouble putting the sequence of events together. "What happened?" I asked.

Mariana appeared with the water and I took it meekly.

"Shepherd punched McMillen," Gilley said, practically giddy over having witnessed it. "He came flying into the room, took one look at McMillen trying to kill you, and punched him so hard he flew five feet, landing over there!"

Shepherd scowled at Gilley. "The use of force was justified."

"Oh, was it ever!" Gilley agreed. Pointing to McMillen he said, "That man is a menace and a danger to society! You should arrest him."

"Relax," Shepherd said. "He's cuffed and he'll be formally charged in a minute, okay? What I want to know is what set him off?"

Gilley explained everything—a bit too well, but Shepherd seemed nonplussed when Gil got to the part where I'd yelled at William.

Turning to me after Gilley was through, Shepherd said, "You'll file a complaint, right?"

"I will," I promised. And then, because I couldn't help myself, I added, "I hope you're considering him for Scarlet's murder. Especially since Mariana told us that Scarlet visited William two weeks before she died and appeared visibly upset when she returned from that visit. I bet he threatened her. There's a history of abuse, you know. He used to physically and mentally abuse her when they were married, right Mariana?"

"It's true," she said meekly.

I pointed an accusing finger at McMillen. "I think he threatened her and she changed her will leaving him a sizeable chunk of her fortune, possibly under duress. The timing fits for both her visit with him and the changing of her will, Shepherd."

"You don't know what the hell you're talking about!" William yelled at me. "I didn't kill her and I didn't force her to change her will!"

Shepherd stepped away from me to walk to William and stand menacingly over him. "That's enough out of you," he said softly, but there was no mistaking the implied physical threat of his stance or his words.

William shrank away from him, and I shook my head, thinking how typical of an abuser like William to cower in front of someone like Shepherd, a true protector and defender of women. In that moment, he was very much my hero.

Turning back to us, Shepherd pointed at Gilley and said, "Get her to urgent care and make sure she's okay. Bring a report back to me of anything they find, and make sure they take photos—tell 'em it's for a police report. I'm going to take McMillen to the station and get him booked. Cat, I'll need a witness statement from you as soon as you can come to the station after urgent care."

I nodded and waited until Shepherd had hauled McMillen out the door before I turned to Gilley and said, "No."

Gilley sighed heavily. He knew exactly what I meant. "Sugar," he began. "You know I always take your side over Shepherd, but in this one case he's right. We do need to get you to a doctor and get you checked out—"

"I'm fine," I insisted. "Truly."

"There are scratches, Miss Catherine," Mariana said. She placed cool fingers on the side of my neck and it helped to take a little of the sting out.

"Mariana," I said, taking her hand in mine and squeezing it affectionately. "Do you and Carlos live nearby?"

She pointed to the south wall of the room. "We

live in Southampton. We have a small house there."

"Does it have a security system?"

Carlos and Mariana both shook their heads. "Why would anyone bother with us?" Mariana asked.

"You stand to inherit a huge fortune that several family members might think you stole away from them. Why *wouldn't* someone bother with you?" Gilley said.

Mariana wrung her hands and looked to her husband for reassurance, but he looked just as disturbed. "Maybe we should get an alarm, *mi vida.*"

"Carlos, those are expensive," she said. "And we don't have a paycheck coming in anymore. You heard Miss Terry; it'll take months to sort all this out. If we lock all our doors and windows, we'll be okay."

I shook my head. "That settles it," I said firmly. "You two are coming home with me until this murderer is identified and brought to justice."

"Oh, we couldn't impose," Carlos said, taking his wife's hand.

"You're not imposing, and I'm insisting. You two head home and gather enough clothing and essentials to last you at least a month. Gilley and I will be in Europe late next week, and you'll be doing me a favor by house-sitting until we get back."

Mariana bit her lip and Carlos looked unsure, so I wagged my finger at them and said, "No arguments. You're coming home with me. We can keep you safe at Chez Cat."

"And while they're gathering their things, I can take you to urgent care," Gilley said.

"We'll take some pictures," I told him, waving him off.

"Cat," he said, ready to argue.

"I'm fine!" I insisted. "It's much more important to get Mariana and Carlos someplace safe, just in case the killer has it out for Scarlet's heirs."

The color drained from both Carlos's and Mariana's faces as they thought about it.

Terry helped our cause when she stepped forward with some wisdom. "As I said, it'll take about six months to get everything settled. Moving somewhere with a security system is probably the safer move for you two right now."

Because the DeLeons still appeared unsure, and just to drive the point home, I asked Terry, "Was there a stipulation in Scarlet's will, should Mariana and Carlos not be able to inherit her wealth, about who the money would go to?"

Terry grimaced. "Yes. There is a clause that states that, if the DeLeons are unable to take physical possession before the estate is settled in probate, it would then be equally divided among the remaining members of Scarlet's family. I know she planned to amend that clause, but she wanted time to think on it. Time she never got.

"I'll file all the motions necessary for moving the estate through probate," she continued while gathering up her things. "For now, you two be safe." Terry waggled her finger between Carlos and Mariana and then she left the room.

After she'd gone, Carson wheeled himself forward into our small circle. He'd been so quiet I'd almost forgotten he was still present. "I think it's a good idea, Carlos. I think you should take Mariana away until Detective Shepherd identifies who killed Aunt Scarlet."

"But what about the house?" Mariana asked.

Carson smiled kindly at her. "The dusting, vacuuming, and cleaning can wait. It's more important that you two are someplace safe."

"But what about you, Mr. Carson?" Carlos asked. "Who will look after you?"

Carson rolled his eyes. "I'm handicapable, remember?" he said with a heavy dose of sarcasm as his expression turned sour when he spoke the ableist word. Then he seemed to soften. "I'll be fine," he assured the couple. "No one's interested in my little trust, anyway. If the person who murdered Aunt Scarlet comes back here, he or she will be hunting bigger game. Like the two of you."

Mariana became pale again. She stared at Carson as if he'd just read out her death sentence. And perhaps he had.

"Okay, Mr. Carson," Carlos said, clasping his hands in front of him in a show of gratitude. "When everything gets settled, I'm sure I can speak for Mariana and myself when I say that we would like it very much if you would stay on as this fine house's manager."

Carson beamed. "I'd love that, Carlos. But you'll need to drop the 'Mr.' when you speak to me. From now on, I'm just Carson, okay?"

Carlos let out a sigh of relief. "You got it, Mr. . . . I mean . . . Carson."

The pair chuckled but I couldn't get the thought of a certain impatient detective wondering what might be taking me so long, and risk having him come back to find out.

"I think we should go," I said to them. "Let's lock up the house, send you two to your house to gather enough of your things for an extended stay, and get you settled at Chez Cat—my place. There're plenty of bedrooms to choose from. You'll feel right at home. And I have a killer security system. His name is Sebastian and no one gets past him."

Chapter 8

On the way to Chez Cat, we stopped at an urgent care facility with an empty parking lot and no waiting. Gilley insisted I do as Shepherd asked and get myself checked out, especially since it would take Mariana and Carlos some time to get to their house, gather their things, and head back toward us.

Reluctantly (and mostly because Gilley was driving and refused to hand over the keys once we entered and parked in the lot) I sat patiently while the doctor assessed my "injuries," which were, as I had said, nothing more than bruising and a little burning feeling when I took a deep breath.

Still, the doctor was thorough and told me he'd email me a copy of the report to use when I filed my complaint with the EHPD.

By the time we got home again, we'd already

heard from Mariana that she and Carlos were on their way.

And, as expected, the second we got in the door, my phone rang. "Hello, Shep," I said, noting the caller ID.

"Cat," he said almost casually. "Where the hell are you?"

"Gilley and I just got home from urgent care. There was a long wait," I lied, "but I've been thoroughly inspected head to toe and I'm fine."

"That's good," he said. "But why aren't you *here*?"

"I've invited Mariana and Carlos to come stay at Chez Cat. As soon as they get here, I'll come see you to file that police report."

There was a significant pause on Shepherd's end, then, "Why exactly are the DeLeons staying with you?"

"Because, as the inheritors of the bulk of Scarlet's estate, I don't think it's wise for them to be in a place where they could be *murdered*."

"So dramatic," Gilley whispered, clearly listening in on the conversation.

I glared at him and he held his hands up in surrender, then busied himself by moseying over to the fridge to peer inside.

"I might have Scarlet's murderer in lockup, you know," Shepherd told me.

"You might have *one* of Scarlet's murderers in lockup. If McMillen did the deed, I don't think he did it alone."

"Why do you say that?"

"Because Scarlet happened to die the night her life insurance policy—the one naming McMillen as beneficiary—expired."

There was another pregnant pause. "*How* do you know *that*?"

I squared my shoulders, even knowing Shepherd couldn't see me. "Gilley and I have been looking into the case."

I held the phone away from my ear while Shepherd expressed his deep, deeeep displeasure at my admission. When he paused long enough to inhale a ragged breath, I continued with, "I know you told us not to, but it's imperative that Gilley and I take our European vacation, and I don't want anything to get in the way of that."

Shepherd was practically spitting with anger, and I was actually relieved to be having this conversation by phone rather than in person. "Why is it *imperative*?" he demanded.

"Because," I said.

"Because . . . ?" Shepherd repeated.

I eyed Gilley at the sink, filling a big pot of water. He glanced over his shoulder at me, obviously still listening in, and he nodded in a way that suggested he was okay with my telling Shepherd the whole story.

"Michel is coming back here to pack up the rest of his things next week."

"So?" Shepherd said.

It irritated me that he wasn't fully grasping why that might be painful to Gilley, so I turned it back on him. "Let me ask you something," I said. "When you and your ex-wife split up, do you think it wasn't painful for her the day you packed up all your belongings from the house you shared with her during your marriage?"

He made a growling sound. "She wasn't even in

town when that happened," he snapped. But then he seemed to catch himself as I'm sure the meaning of what he'd just admitted to hit him.

"Exactly my point," I told him.

"Come on, Cat," Shepherd insisted, still not conceding the battle. "You can take Gilley to the City for the day. You don't have to pack up and leave the country."

I watched as Gilley moved the pot of water over to the stove and lit the burner. The set to his slumped shoulders told me that even hearing me discuss the day Michel would be here to take back his things was so obviously painful to him, that there was no way I *couldn't* take him. "Yes," I told Shepherd. "Yes, we do need to leave the country, Shep. We need to be on the other side of the ocean when Michel comes here, and I know you may not understand that, but it's what Gilley needs and as one of his best friends, it's also what I'm bound and determined to give to him."

Shepherd sighed. I could tell he was still very angry with me, and didn't want to concede the point. "You're drifting very close to the line of obstructing my case, you know."

"How is helping you considered obstruction? Didn't I just provide you with information you might not've had?"

"I would've discovered that on my own probably very soon," he said. "Can't you see that while I'm trying to investigate this case, worrying about you meddling in the middle of it would be distracting for me?"

"We can help, Shep," I said plainly. "In fact, I can even suggest that, because William McMillen would obviously find himself at the center of suspicion—given the life insurance policy angle—he probably had Siobhan do the deed, promising to split the insurance settlement with her."

Shepherd didn't say anything for a long moment, so I continued. "Gilley and I think that Siobhan was willing to be the trigger-woman if McMillen promised to marry her. Heck, they got engaged *yesterday*! And I know that because they did it in front of us, but did you know that?"

"It was obvious they were a couple at the reading of the will," he said.

"Did you also know that Scarlet changed her will right around the time she went to a secret meeting with William? Mariana said that Scarlet drove herself over to McMillen's condo, and came back looking very upset, much like she used to look when William was still her husband and abusing her."

"What did William and Scarlet talk about?" he said, momentarily sidestepping the abuse angle.

"I don't know and neither do the DeLeons. But I believe Scarlet found out about Siobhan and William and she went there to demand William stop seeing her sister."

And then my eye drifted to the prescription bottle that Gilley had taken from Scarlet's desk drawer. He'd set it on the kitchen counter before our lunch had arrived.

"Annnnd," I added, feeling like I could make an even more solid case to Shepherd about what good amateur sleuths Gilley and I were. "Did you know Scarlet had cancer?"

"No," he said quietly. "The ME's report isn't finished yet."

"It's not?"

"No. He's been covering most of the autopsies in the Hamptons, since the pandemic left him so shorthanded. He's backlogged. But he said he'd get it to me by tomorrow."

"Good. I hope he notes that Scarlet's cancer was metastatic. She had only weeks to live."

"How do you know *that*?" he asked, his voice becoming irritated again.

"We did a little more snooping."

Shepherd growled again and muttered under his breath a few words that aren't worth repeating in polite company.

His reaction irritated me. Couldn't he see how helpful Gilley and I were to his cause? I'd just provided him with a plethora of new information that he wasn't aware of. Why wasn't he happy?

"I gotta go," he said.

I blinked. "You do?"

"Yeah."

"Oh. Okay. Well, as soon as the DeLeons get here and get settled in, I'll be down to give my statement about McMillen."

"Fine."

My brow furrowed. He wasn't letting go of his anger or softening. "Did you want me to bring you some dinner?"

"Nope."

"Um . . . okay. I'll see you in about an hour."

"I'll tell the boot on duty."

"The . . . boot on duty?"

"Yeah. We've got a rookie at the intake station. He can take your statement."

I blinked a few more times, feeling a little stung. "Where will you be?"

"I'm headed home, Cat."

He said nothing more. Just that. "Oh. Okay. Did you want me to come over later?"

"No."

"Did you get my voice mail from this morning?" He'd never responded to my heartfelt apology.

"Yep," he said without further comment.

My eye caught Gilley's. He was looking at me with a curious expression. But I shook my head, trying to keep the waver out of my voice as I said, "Okay, Shep. Have a good night."

"Mmhmm," he said, and hung up.

I set the phone down and stared at it for a solid thirty seconds. "Want to talk about it?" Gilley asked.

"He's upset."

"Duh," Gil said.

"I think . . . I think he's upset about more than just our sticking our noses into his investigation. I mean, he didn't seem to want to yell at me, and whenever we poke our noses in, you know how he gets—"

"Apoplectic?"

"Yeah," I said, pointing at him. "That."

"What did he say this time?"

"Nothing. I mean, he said he was leaving the station, heading home, and he didn't want me to come over."

Gilley dropped some pasta into the boiling water

and then he eyed me over his shoulder. "Not surprised," he said.

"What does that mean?" I asked sharply.

Gil came over to stare at me across the kitchen island. Looking me deep in the eyes he said, "A few years ago, I read a survey that'd polled a very large group of men and women from all across the country, and that survey asked only one question."

"Which was?"

"The question they asked was: 'Would you rather be loved or respected?' "

I squinted at him. The answer seemed too obvious. "Loved," I said. "Naturally."

Gilley pointed a finger gun at me and clicked his tongue. "The overwhelming majority of women responded that way, Cat. But equally overwhelmingly, the men responded that they'd rather be respected."

"You're kidding me."

"Nope," he said, moving back to the stove to stir the pasta. "The article spoke about how men are pretty much hardwired to see themselves as heroic. Noble. Good guys. In some psychological circles, it's referred to as the hero instinct, but basically, the theory goes that men connect to purpose. Women connect to emotion. Women love and want to be loved, but men don't *need* to be loved as much as they need to have a driving purpose in their lives. Something to strive for. A goal to achieve, and on that journey, they want their women to respect their ambitions as much as they want them to love them for who they are."

"What does this have to do with Shepherd and

me?" I asked, although I already knew what Gilley was getting at.

"You're emasculating your boyfriend," he said bluntly. "Shepherd's a good guy, but lately, you haven't been allowing him to show you how good he is, either at domestic projects or at his job. He's struggling to finish his kitchen but still making headway, and what do you do? Swoop in to speed up the process by sending in a contractor." I'd told Gilley about what I'd done while we were shopping.

"Then," Gilley continued, "he's working his butt off to solve this crime and what do you do? Swoop in again to solve it for him. If you don't back off your head-on approach, you'll lose him, Cat. And trust me on this—losing someone you truly love whom you've pushed away, even without meaning to, is just the worst. The *worst*, because you can't ever get it back. You can't say, 'Sorry! My bad!' and think that your relationship will magically go back to being super strong. Some things are beyond repair. Don't go that route with him."

"Ohmigod," I whispered, seeing it clearly for the first time. "Gilley, you're so right!"

"I know," he said with a hint of sadness.

Just then the doorbell rang and Sebastian's muffled voice through the door said, "Welcome to Chez Cat. May I inquire as to who you are and the nature of your visit?"

"The DeLeons are here," I said, jumping off my barstool to head to the hallway.

"Lady Catherine," Sebastian said as I rounded the corner. "A Mr. and Mrs. DeLeon are here. Would you like me to open the door for them?"

"Yes, please, Sebastian. The DeLeons are my guests. They'll be staying on the premises for the next month or so."

"Excellent," Sebastian said. I heard the lock on the front door click and Sebastian said, "Please do come in, and make yourselves at home, Mr. and Mrs. DeLeon."

The door opened and Mariana and Carlos were staring all around, as if they thought they could place the disembodied voice. "Hello!" I said, waving to them. "Come in, come in!"

The couple stepped over the threshold a bit cautiously and looked about my foyer with wide eyes.

"Miss Catherine," Mariana said with a shy smile while pulling a suitcase on wheels into the hallway. "Where should I put this?"

Gilley came up behind me and waved to Carlos and Mariana. "Hey, you two! I've got some chicken zucchini and cashew pesto pasta brewing in the kitchen. It's delicious. You'll love it."

"It smells wonderful," Mariana said while her husband nodded eagerly.

Turning to Gilley I said, "Gil, I was thinking . . ."

"Always a time to worry," he muttered.

I poked him with my elbow. "I think it might be a good idea to give Mariana and Carlos Chez Kitty. Sebastian is wired over there and they'd be just as safe at the guesthouse as they would here."

Gilley's posture stiffened and I regretted asking him in front of the DeLeons. Still, he pushed a smile to his face and said, "Can I take the bedroom off your office?"

I grinned. That bedroom was the only one on

the ground floor. "You just want to be closer to the kitchen for those midnight snacks."

"Duh," he said.

"Of course, lovey. Take any room you'd like!"

Gilley nodded and turned back to the DeLeons. "Chez Kitty is the perfect solution for you two. You'll have privacy and security and feel much more at home than being here with our prying eyes."

I smiled gratefully at him. "Thank you, Gil."

"Of course," he said, waving his hand like it was nothing. Then he pointed to the couple and said, "Let me just bounce over real quick to grab a few things for myself here, and of course grab my pooch—you'll love him, his name is Spooks—and then you two can get settled. I'll have dinner ready in twenty minutes, okay?"

As Gilley was gathering some things at the guesthouse, I escorted the DeLeons into the kitchen and set them up at the island counter with a glass of iced tea for each and some assorted nuts to snack on before dinner.

The second Gilley was back, however, I said, "Could you keep a plate warm for me? I've got to head to the station and give that police report."

Gilley eyed me slyly. He knew my mission would involve more than that. "Of course, sugar," he said. "I'll make sure Mariana and Carlos have everything they need, so you take your time, okay?"

I hugged him, waved to the DeLeons, and left.

Shepherd answered my knock dressed in jeans and a torn T-shirt that was covered in dirt and sawdust. "Hey," I said when he stood there, looking annoyed by my sudden appearance on his doorstep.

"I thought I said I wanted to be alone tonight," he said curtly.

"You did. And I heard you, but Gilley pointed something very important out to me after we ended our conversation, and I didn't want to go another night without telling you about it."

Shepherd worked his jaw and offered me a slow blink. "What?" he asked without even a hint of warmth.

I cleared my throat and said, "I haven't told you this lately, but I think you're one of the very best people I've ever known."

That won me a skeptically arched brow.

I pressed on. "The reason I think that is because, over these past few years, I've watched you put everyone else first. You take care of everyone in this town, Shep, the citizens, the tourists, your family . . . me. And never once do you ask for anything in return. Not even a thank-you. You just get up every morning with one sole purpose, and that is to protect and serve.

"And you do that with such determination and selflessness, completely unconcerned for your own safety. Especially when I'm in the mix."

Shepherd had released the skeptical eyebrow and was looking at me intently. I made the point just then to reach up and touch the spot near his shoulder where a large circular scar was still tender to the touch. "You've even stepped in front of a bullet for me. You've literally saved my life,

Steven Shepherd. That's a debt I don't think I can ever repay, but I think I've been trying in the years since that moment to somehow give to you as much as you've given to me and the citizens of this town. I've wanted to help you. I've wanted to help you do the thing that you are most adept at, and I can see in this moment how incredibly pompous I must seem to you. How snide and arrogant I must've sounded on the phone earlier."

Shepherd continued to stare at me intently, but I could see that my words were having an effect. I was reaching him. The wall that'd gone up between us was showing some cracks in the mortar.

"I want you to know that I'm ashamed of myself for being so insensitive," I said next. "I want you to know that I don't just love you, Shep, I admire you. I'm in awe of you. I'm so, so proud of the man you are. The good man. The noble man. The kind and thoughtful man. The earnest, sincere, hardworking man. And, the man who has come to my rescue over and over again, caring little for his own safety in the process. You amaze me every day, and to think that I've done anything to suggest that I'm less than in absolute awe of you breaks my heart because I never, not for one moment, have ever lost that feeling of admiration and marvel at the things you do to keep me and this entire town whole and safe. I more than love you, my sweet man." I paused to reach up to stroke his cheek. "You're my hero, Shep. My knight. My world."

A long, long silence played out between us and I had to swallow hard because my voice had started trembling at that last part and I didn't want to get too emotional and take away from the earnestness of my words, but damn if Shepherd's own eyes weren't a bit misty by then too.

At last, he took a deep breath, stepped to one side, and waved to the kitchen area behind me. "Coffee?" he asked.

"Love some," I said, stepping forward.

As I moved into the kitchen, I felt Shepherd's hand slide into mine, and he squeezed my palm and I let go of the tense set to my shoulders. We could fix what hadn't been working between us. I had renewed hope, thanks to Gilley's wise, wise words.

"I don't have any real cream," Shep said. "Just some nondairy stuff in the pantry."

"That works," I assured him. Then I waved my hand in a circular motion. "Amazing," I said, taking in the dramatic change to his kitchen.

Shepherd's old kitchen had been dated but functional. The peach-and-black granite countertop and camel-colored cabinets hadn't been a *bad* combination—just not very interesting.

But this new look . . .

"Kerpow!" I said, smiling at him and making a motion like my mind was blown.

"You like?" he asked, and I could see how proud he was of his own choices.

Shepherd had done away with everything dated and replaced the bland factory-made cabinets for some that were obviously handcrafted real oak with knots and swirls and small cracks. In the center of the kitchen was the island, which had a dark ebony base and a beautiful piece of panda marble—white with black swirls—for the countertop.

Contrasting that were the cabinets and countertop along the base of the U-shaped kitchen, with cabinets painted bright white and an absolutely gorgeous countertop of black marble with varying streaks of white throughout in a chaotic pattern that reminded me of an intense thunderstorm, with bolts of lightning shooting across a night's sky. I moved to the nearest countertop and ran my hand over the marble. "This is incredible," I said.

"Isn't it?" he said, fishing around for a mug in one of the boxes where all of his dishware was stored until he was able to unpack it. "It took three of us over three hours to install it this morning, but we got it done."

"I *love* it, Shep!" I said. "Where'd you get it?"

"A friend of mine from high school imports exotic stone from all over the world to supply most of the luxury hotels on Long Island. He had some of that left over from a big project and he cut me a deal."

Shepherd stepped close to me and stroked the countertop as well. "This type of marble is called Vulcano Black, and even with the deal it cost me a fortune but it's a showstopper, right?"

"It truly is," I said. "If this place were on the market, this kitchen would sell it all on its own. No doubt about it."

Shepherd grinned, and he even added a chuckle as he headed to the coffeemaker to pour me a cup. "Thanks for that insight. It's actually helpful."

"Oh?" I asked curiously.

"Here," he said, handing me a steaming mug of black coffee and a spoon. Nodding to the pantry door next to me, he added, "The creamer is on the third shelf in there, and once you get your fill of creamer, follow me into the living room. There's something there I think you might like."

Even more curious I rushed through putting a few spoonfuls of the powder into the coffee, then took his hand when he offered it and followed him into the living room where I came up short.

"Oh, my God!" I gasped. "Shep! That is spectacular!"

At the far end of the room was the most incredibly gorgeous marble fireplace I'd ever seen. Cut from the same Vulcano Black stone as in Shep's kitchen, the massive traditional Canterbury-styled mantel was embossed with vines and flowers and engraved blocks along the top part of the mantel. It both dominated and set the tone of the room, taking what had been a fairly plain living space and transforming it into something much more elegant and inviting.

I also noted that Shepherd had acquired two new distressed Brazilian leather chairs which were set right in front of the fireplace making the space even more enticing.

"Isn't it great?" he asked, and I could hear the pride in his voice.

"It so, so is," I gushed. Moving forward I went to touch the mantelpiece, which was just as smooth to the touch as his countertop. "This must've also cost a fortune," I whispered. And knowing Shepherd as the practical and otherwise almost always frugal man that he was, I was really surprised that he'd splurged at least a couple of months' salary on a fireplace of all things.

Shepherd came forward to stand next to me

and wrap an arm around my shoulders. "I saved a bundle buying everything wholesale and doing most of the renovation myself, so when I went to the showroom to pick out the marble for the kitchen, my buddy—Sean—showed me this in the back of his warehouse. One of his guys put a big chip in it with a forklift . . ." He paused to show me the bottom right section of the base where it buttressed up against the wall. I didn't know what I was looking at until he pointed to a fist-sized notch in the stone. "Because of that, Sean had to carve out another fireplace for his client because they refused to take something that wasn't perfect, even with a huge discount, so he sold this puppy to me for a song."

"You can't even see the chip unless you go looking for it!"

"I know, right?" Shep said, clearly pleased by the acquisition.

"I'm so proud of you," I said, hugging him. "You've done an amazing job. And I'm so sorry that I ever sent someone here to do your job for you. I promise to be more patient with your home projects from now on."

Shepherd enveloped me into a big bear hug, nuzzled my neck, and whispered, "Thank you."

That was all he needed to say, really. I could feel our love for each other strengthen rather than weaken for the first time in months and it did my heart a lot of good.

I stayed over that night, while we sat in the two new chairs for hours and simply talked about things that didn't involve murder, or impending trips. Instead we spoke about a whole range of other topics and I felt like we not only reconnected, but connected on a much deeper level than we ever had.

He told me things I'd never known about him before, how he'd played guitar in a garage band all through high school, how he'd been a state champion freestyle swimmer and had won a partial scholarship as a result; how his first job out of college was as a process server—a job that routinely had him ducking punches from soon-to-be ex-husbands—and wives—and some of the stories he told about hiding out in the bushes, waiting to jump out and yell, "You've been served," had me howling with laughter.

The next morning, much of that magically recharged energy was still sparking because as we were sipping more coffee together, Shepherd said, "Thanks, Cat."

"For what?"

"For helping me out on the Rubi murder. McMillen is going to try to get bail today, and I want to talk to the A.D.A. before the bond hearing so that I can make a case to her to push for bond denial. I don't have enough to charge McMillen with Scarlet Rubi's murder, but with some of the things you and Gilley discovered, I think I can gather enough evidence in the next day or two to bring that charge, and keeping this guy off the street is in the public's best interest."

I took his hand and kissed it. "I'm so glad we could help, Shep. From this point on, Gilley and I will focus solely on packing and finalizing our travel arrangements. We'll leave the detecting to the expert." I added a wink, just to let him know I meant him.

"I hope you guys have a great time in Europe, babe," he said, pulling me close for a kiss. "I'm gonna miss you like crazy, but by the time you get back the kitchen should be done and McMillen could be in jail for Scarlet's murder, meaning we can focus on us again."

"I'd love that," I said. And meant it more than I could say.

Chapter 9

The next evening, I was gathered with Gilley and the DeLeons in the kitchen, having just finished washing up from dinner and talking about playing either a game of Trivial Pursuit or Pictionary, when Shepherd's name appeared on my caller ID. I'd heard from him earlier when he called to tell me that, despite his best efforts, McMillen had gotten out on bond. Still, his passport had been confiscated so at least he wasn't a flight risk. I wasn't thinking Shepherd was calling with anything serious when I picked up his call with a playful, "Hello, lover. Whatcha wearing?"

"Cat," he said, his tone all business and I immediately knew something was wrong.

"What's happened?" I asked, my heart racing.

"It's McMillen," he replied. My eyes roved to the kitchen window, subconsciously bracing for some sort of sighting of the man, thinking that Shepherd had called to warn me that William was out for revenge.

"Should I lock all my doors and have everyone get upstairs?" I whispered.

"What?" he said.

"Are you calling to tell me that you've discovered McMillen is thinking about harming me? Or that he's made some sort of public threat to me?"

"No," Shepherd said. "It's worse."

My breath caught. What could be worse? "Tell me," I said.

"McMillen is dead."

My jaw dropped and immediately after registering what Shepherd had just said, I told myself I must've misheard. "He's what?"

"Dead. William McMillen is dead."

I put a hand to my mouth. "Suicide?" I asked meekly. Perhaps the guilt of killing his ex-wife was too much and he'd taken his own life.

"Nope," Shepherd said. "He's been murdered. I'm on my way to the scene."

"*He's what and you're what?*" I exclaimed. None of that made sense!

"McMillen's been shot. Execution style. Just like Scarlet."

"What's happening?" Gilley said, and I jumped when I realized he'd come up next to me.

Ignoring Gilley, I focused on Shepherd. "Who murdered him?"

"It sounds like Siobhan did," Shep told me.

I gasped again.

"Who's been murdered?" Gilley whined. "Cat, tell me!"

I waved at him and kept my focus on my conversation with Shepherd. "Well, that makes sense, doesn't it? Scarlet made sure that McMillen wasn't going to get a penny unless he gave up Siobhan, and that woman doesn't strike me as the type to take that news well. I bet she killed both her sister and McMillen."

"That's my theory too," he said. "Anyway, I wanted to tell you the news first before you heard it from another source, and also to let you know that I won't be able to come over tonight like I'd planned to. I'll be working this case all night."

"I completely understand," I said. "Don't worry about tonight. We'll find time to be together soon."

"You know it," he said. "Love you, babe."

I grinned. Shepherd didn't often tell me he loved me—he usually tried to show me and settled for implying that he did. "Love you back, Detective. Get some sleep when you can and we'll talk later."

After hanging up with Shepherd I filled Gilley and the DeLeons in on the news.

"No," Mariana said when I explained that Siobhan had likely killed both her sister and McMillen. "Miss Siobhan wouldn't kill Miss Scarlet!"

But Carlos didn't seem to share that opinion. "Remember how violent she got with Miss Scarlet, *mi vida*. I think she could've done it."

"Oh, she definitely did it," Gilley said, nodding his head vigorously. "That woman is *scary*!"

"If it was her, Shepherd's going to get to the bottom of it," I said confidently and then scowled at Gilley when he eyed me skeptically. Wanting to change the subject I pointed to the closet where I kept all the games for game nights and said, "I'm feeling more like Pictionary than Trivial Pursuit. Who's with me?"

We played Pictionary until bedtime and as Mariana and Carlos were headed back to Chez Kitty, Carlos said, "Since the danger seems to be over, Mariana and I can return home in the morning."

"Oh, Carlos," I said, squeezing his arm. "Please don't feel the need to leave in a hurry. Stay as long as you like, okay?"

He smiled gratefully at me. "Thank you, Miss Catherine, but we don't want to be a burden, and I'm sure Mr. Gilley would like to have his home back."

Gilley stood next to me and simply smiled sweetly. I wanted to elbow him, because it was clear he had no intention of protesting the couple's abrupt departure in the morning.

And as much as I wanted Gilley to have his own space again, I still worried about the DeLeons. Scarlet's relatives were cutthroat, and I didn't put it past them to try to talk Carlos and Mariana into agreeing to give them part of the estate. I wanted to protect them from that, and if they were here under my watchful eye, I could do that at least until Gilley and I left on our trip.

But I was the only one who wanted that, apparently, so I settled for extending the invitation and allowing them to make their own choices.

I was out like a light as soon as my head hit the pillow that night, and don't think I was asleep longer than six hours when my cell phone rang and woke me up.

When you're a parent, middle-of-the-night

phone calls immediately set your heart racing and your mind to mild panic.

When I looked at the caller ID, that reaction ratcheted up a notch. "Marcus?" I said, my voice croaking like a frog. "What's going on?"

"Catherine," he said softly. "I'm sorry to wake you, but my client insisted I reach out to you immediately."

I rubbed my eyes and glanced at the time. It was four a.m. "Your . . . client? What client? Is it Sunny? Is she okay? Did something happen to her?"

"It's not Sunny," Marcus whispered. "I left her a few hours ago safe and sound in her bed. And thank you for not telling Shepherd about our situation, by the way."

I blinked trying to clear my head. Marcus wasn't saying anything that was making sense. "How do you know I haven't said anything to Shepherd?"

"Because I just spoke to him here at the station," he explained. "And if you'd told him about me and his sister, he probably would've arrested me on sight."

I snorted. "That sounds like him. Your secret will continue to be safe with me, Marcus. Now tell me what's going on."

"I've been retained by Siobhan Forsythe. She was arrested a few hours ago for the murder of William McMillen and Shepherd is attempting to also link her to the murder of her sister, Scarlet Rubi."

I nodded along, following the train of events better than I thought Marcus realized. "Yes, I'm aware of all that," I said.

"Good. Siobhan would like to speak with you.

She says that it's imperative to her case. She believes you can contribute to her alibi."

My brow furrowed. "In what way? I was here last night when McMillen was murdered. And I have witnesses." I didn't know why I said that last part—probably because I was nervous that Siobhan would somehow try to tie me to the murder, and I didn't want there to be any doubt as to my whereabouts the night before and the fact that three people could corroborate that—possibly including Shepherd given the timing of his call to me to let me know that McMillen had just been murdered.

"To my knowledge she's not suggesting that you were at the scene, Catherine," Marcus said. "I believe she's referencing something that took place earlier."

"What?"

"I don't know, but as her attorney, I'd sure like to. Can you come down here and speak with her before she's transferred?"

"They're transferring her already?"

"Not formally, but I have a feeling that even my skills at the bond hearing won't be enough to keep her from being denied bail and sent to Riverhead."

"Riverhead?"

"Riverhead Correctional. It's the county lockup."

"Ah," I said, my mind racing to figure out what Siobhan could possibly want to see me about.

"Yes, Marcus, I can come down. Will you be in the room with us?"

"I will," he assured me, obviously detecting the nervous note to my tone. I didn't especially *want* to be in the same room with a possible murderer—

mostly because I'd had that particular experience a few times before, and it never seemed to work out well for me.

"Great. Thank you. I'll be there in about half an hour."

"See you soon."

With a sigh I got out of bed, still sleepy and groggy as I got changed, brushed my teeth, and straightened my hair. Then I crept down the stairs to the front landing and winced when I realized my car was in the garage, which shared a wall with the guestroom where Gilley slept.

The man was one of the lightest sleepers I'd ever met and I knew I wouldn't be able to creep out at four a.m., so I tiptoed into the kitchen, foraged around in the dark for a pen and a piece of scrap paper, and was just writing him a quick note when the kitchen light flashed on, causing me to jump a full foot.

"Ohmigod!" I yelled.

"*Ahhhhhh!*" Gilley screamed, raising his fist clutching a dress shoe high in the air ready to bring it down on my head.

"*Gilley! What are you doing?!*"

"*What am I doing? What are* you *doing?!*"

"*I'm leaving you a note!*"

"*Why are we shouting?!*"

"*I have no idea!*"

"*We should stop!*"

"*I will if you will!*"

A loooooong stretch of silence ensued while we both clutched at our heaving chests and stared at each other wide-eyed.

"Where are you going at four in the morning?"

Gilley finally asked, sans Howler monkey level of screech.

"To the police station."

"To see Shepherd?"

"No," I said, wondering how to explain what I didn't yet fully understand. "Siobhan wants to speak with me."

Gilley shook his head as if he hadn't heard me right. "Siobhan what now?"

"She was arrested for killing McMillen," I said and Gilley waved his hand like he already knew that. "And she's retained Marcus to represent her."

Gilley's eyes widened. "Marcus *Brown*?"

"Yes," I said, thinking, *Who else could I be talking about?* "Anyway, Marcus called me and said that Siobhan wants to speak with me and supposedly it has to do with her alibi."

Gilley's face scrunched up in confusion. "I need to be more awake for this conversation. Absolutely nothing you've said makes sense."

I sighed and set the scrap piece of paper and pen aside. "I'll fill you in when I get back, but I gotta go."

"Not without me you're not," Gil said, already turning back toward the guestroom.

"Gilley," I called. "I don't have time to wait for you."

He didn't even pause or look over his shoulder. He merely sang, "Yes you do. Be out in a jiff."

I sighed again and rolled my eyes. I could've simply left right then and there, but I reasoned that I'd never hear the end of it when I got back, so I stayed put by the door to the garage until

Gilley came out fully clothed with a small bounce in his step to boot.

"That was quick," I said, grateful he'd only taken literally three minutes to get dressed.

"I'm practicing my fire alarm skills."

I opened the door leading to the garage and eyed him curiously. "Your what skills?"

"You know," he said, waving at me like I should know. "The get-dressed-in-a-flash-and-dash-out-the-door skills."

"Why would you be practicing them?"

Gilley paused by the passenger door on my car and rolled his eyes. Then he got in and so did I, starting the car and putting it in reverse. "Cat," Gilley said, as if I were simple. "Now that my divorce is final, I'll need to get out into the wilderness. Explore the terrain. Go on safari."

I paused to look at him meaningfully. "Are you talking about dating?"

"Duh, what else would I be talking about?"

"You're right. My bad," I said, shaking my head. "So, you're going to start dating again. What does that have to do with being a fireman?"

"Other than holding out the hope that I will *actually* date a fireman?"

I laughed, "Oh, you would loooove that."

"As God is my witness," Gil said, holding up his palm and donning a thick Southern drawl. "I'd slap my mama for a tall drink ah fire retardant!"

I giggled. "*Any*way, as you were saying about practicing your skills."

"Yes, I gotta practice my getaway skills. Gotta dress faster than he can say 'Can I call you?' and make my getaway!"

I gripped the steering wheel as I gave in to a full-on belly laugh. "Gilley, you're so bad!"

He shrugged. "I know you've always known me as a faithful and loving husband, but back in the day I had some *fun*, sugar."

"I bet. How long has it been since you were out there playing fireman, though?"

"Oh," he said, rubbing his chin as he thought about it. "Maybe five . . . six . . . ten years or so."

"That's a long time. Are you worried you might be a little rusty? A lot has probably changed on the dating scene in eight years. Especially after the pandemic turned everything on its ear."

Gilley eyed me with alarm. "I wasn't worried until you said *that*."

"Sorry."

"I'll need to do some research," he said. "Call up some single friends and pick their brains."

"Good idea," I told him, relieved to see the EHPD station just up ahead. Pointing to it I said, "Here we go."

"I'm surprised you agreed to meet with her, you know."

I turned left into the lot and slipped into a parking slot near the door. "Color me curious, but why exactly are you surprised?"

Gilley shrugged. "She probably murdered Scarlet. In cold blood. Execution style. That'd be just an awful way to die, Cat, and I'm surprised that you're willing to speak to the cold-blooded murderess who did that to your client."

"We don't know that for sure, Gilley. We merely suspect she did that and I want the chance to look her in the eye and ask her point blank if she pulled that trigger. I want to see if she can meet my gaze, and if I believe her."

Gilley was silent while we got out of the car and headed toward the front door. As I was reaching for the handle, he said, "Okay. I guess that's fair. But I want to be there with you when you ask her."

"You'll have to clear that with Marcus," I told him. "He's the one calling the shots here."

Marcus was in fact waiting next to the officer on duty at the front desk. They'd been having a boisterous conversation about football when we walked in. "Hello, Catherine," Marcus said smoothly when he spotted us. "Gilley," he said next, and I couldn't tell if he was annoyed or okay with my partner-in-crime also in attendance. If he was annoyed, he was covering it very well.

"Hi, Marcus!" Gilley said far too cheerfully for four thirty in the morning. "Have you ever thought about becoming a volunteer fireman?"

Marcus grinned and shook his head. "This way," he said, nodding to the officer and leading us around the intake desk to a secure door, which buzzed open when we got to it.

We went through the door and down a long corridor. I was familiar with this particular path. I'd been down this hallway both as a suspect and a witness and in neither case did I enjoy the experience.

The hallway was painted a sickly blue and it smelled of sour milk and bleach. I never understood what went on along that stretch of fifty feet to cause it to smell like that, but the odor was at least familiar.

We arrived at a door with a control panel to the

side. I knew this room too. Back in the day, Shepherd had once locked me in here to interrogate me after arresting me in front of a restaurant full of people. That incident remains one of my most humiliating, but Shep and I have come a long, long way since then, and I've forgiven him for it. Mostly.

Marcus entered a code on the panel and opened the door for us. We walked in to see Siobhan, sitting in a chair handcuffed to a table, her cheeks tearstained and her makeup runny and blotchy. Her hair was disheveled and I distinctly noticed that she seemed to be missing a shoe. I couldn't imagine what'd gone on during her arrest, but one look at her told me it hadn't been pretty.

"If you please," Marcus said to me, indicating the chair in front of Siobhan, which was the only other one in the room.

I took the chair and made a point to look directly at her. I wanted her to see that I wasn't intimidated either by this room or this circumstance and she could not count on me to be on her side. In fact, I hoped the look I conveyed was more accusatory than openminded. If she'd murdered my client—her very own sister—I wasn't about to become her ally in any way, manner, shape, or form.

"Thank you for coming," she said meekly.

"Don't," I told her. "What is it that you want from me in the middle of the night, Siobhan?"

She gulped and said, "First, I want you to know that I didn't murder anyone. I didn't murder my sister and I definitely didn't murder William."

Damn. She'd looked me dead in the eye when she'd said that. To my right and in my peripheral vision I could see Gilley cross his arms and lean against the far wall. His posture suggested that he was still skeptical, so I tried to be too.

"Those are just words," I told her. "They're easy to say. Why should I, or anyone else, believe you, Siobhan?"

"Catherine," she said, her gaze holding steady. "You saw us at the bakery when William proposed. You saw how *happy* we were! We were in love!"

My brow furrowed. She seemed so sincere. But was she? "You were in a public setting, Siobhan," I said. "You could've been putting on an act to create plausible doubt. If enough witnesses can come forward to say that they saw you as a happily engaged couple—"

"Engaged and then married," she interrupted me.

My mouth hung open, the words I was about to say catching in my throat. "Wait, what? You got married? When?"

"Right before the reading of the will," she said. "It was William's idea. He wanted to show the family that we were a team, and should any money fall my way, he'd be behind me if anyone contested the distribution of assets."

"But no money did come your way," I said. "It all went to William. Even the life insurance policy should the ME determine that Scarlet died before midnight, right, Siobhan?"

She sighed. "Catherine, William and I were already married. No court in the land would force us to get divorced simply so that William could inherit Scarlet's money." Turning to Marcus she added, "Right, Mr. Brown?"

Marcus cleared his throat and said, "She's right.

Legally, if Siobhan and William were already married, they couldn't be forced to divorce and a strong case could be made that the original stipulation would've been unenforceable as well."

I frowned, still unconvinced. "Siobhan, look at it from my perspective. You and William hated Scarlet—"

"I did *not* hate my sister," she snapped. "And neither did William. There were times when none of us got along, times when we even refused to speak to each other, but by the time William and I were growing close, all of that was water under the bridge."

"So you say," I told her. "But the fact of the matter remains that Scarlet died on *the* night her life insurance policy naming your dead husband the beneficiary expired. The timing seems just too perfect, doesn't it? If I were a betting woman, I'd say that you and William conspired to murder Scarlet and split the money."

Siobhan looked up at the ceiling, frustration etched into her expression. "William didn't care about the life insurance policy," she said. "He just wanted to be with me. My sister confronted him when she found out about us and she told him that she'd extend the terms of the life insurance policy if he stopped seeing me. He flat-out refused. She then asked him to name a price and he told her that she didn't have enough money to give him to stop seeing me. He was fine with the policy expiring, and he thought it had, until you and your associate woke him up and told him that Scarlet had been murdered."

"If he didn't care about the money, then why

the scene at the house during the reading of the will?" I pressed.

"He was caught by surprise. The minute he made bail he called me and told me what'd happened and insisted that he still loved me and didn't want our marriage to end. He wanted to fight the inheritance stipulation in Scarlet's will that demanded we separate and asked me to meet him at his home for dinner to talk it over and come up with a plan. I told him I'd be there around six thirty, but when I got there . . ."

Siobhan's voice fell away as her eyes welled with tears. She put a curled finger to her lips to hold back a sob, but she couldn't seem to talk without letting it out, so I said, "When you got there, William was already dead."

She nodded but then shook her head. "No," she choked out. Clearing her throat several times and wiping away fresh tears she finally added, "He was still alive. Barely, and I held him to me and begged him not to die. His last words to me were, 'It was always you.' "

"What does that mean?" I asked softly. I admit I was moved by her apparent heartbreak.

Siobhan looked down at the table. "It meant that he always loved me, even when he was with Scarlet and I was with my husband. I never knew he had feelings for me, of course, and I always thought of him as my bitter brother-in-law, but about three years ago, I finally hit rock bottom and it was William and my son who helped me into AA and William would take me to his group meeting every night to make sure I stuck with it. I naturally leaned on him for support as I worked my way through the program, and that's when we fell in love.

"Of course, Scarlet just assumed we'd been having an affair behind her back during her marriage, but that never happened. We didn't even go out on an official date together until a year after I was sober and then we were inseparable but very, very discreet. The last thing I wanted was for the family to get wind that I was with William. They'd go running to Scarlet and tell her about it the first chance they got and we didn't need her judgment or her disapproval."

"But you did need her money," I reminded her. "You did need to keep taking advantage and sponging off her."

A bit of fire lit behind Siobhan's eyes and she glared at me. "Okay," she said. "I get it. You don't want to let me off the hook."

"No," I said. "I really don't."

"I understand that, Catherine, but I still want you to consider that while you might be right about the fact that I leaned on my sister to make ends meet, I didn't murder her. Or William. And if you don't do something about it, you're going to let an innocent woman go to prison for a set of murders she didn't commit, and you're also going to allow the *real* murderer to collect their blood money."

Her statement set me back a moment. "What is it you think *I* can do, Siobhan?"

She looked intently at me, then her gaze flickered to Gilley and back again. "You and Mr. Gillespie have quite the reputation."

I crossed my arms, feeling defensive. "Meaning?"

"Meaning, whenever you two stick your noses

into an investigation, justice always seems to get served."

Crap. She was appealing to my thrill-seeking side. "We're not professional investigators," I told her. "And we've been lucky."

"Yes, I know all of that, and yet you always seem to apprehend the real murderer, even when the police are headed in a completely different direction."

I looked up at Marcus, who was listening intently and wearing a somewhat surprised expression. "Mrs. Forsythe, I can hire you a professional private investigator to look into the case," he said.

"I don't want a private investigator, Mr. Brown," she told him. "I want Catherine and Gilley.

"We'll do it," Gilley said, and I whipped my head toward him.

"Gil!" I said sternly.

"Cat!" he sassed back.

I held upturned palms to him. What was he possibly thinking?

"None of this is sitting right," Gilley said to me. "If Siobhan and William really did murder Scarlet, why wait until the last possible second to do it? I mean, even the ME is struggling to find a TOD, right? He can't decide if it was before or after midnight, and if I had five million dollars on the line and a criminal mindset, I'd make damn sure that I murdered Scarlet well before the midnight hour, just to ensure there was no doubt in anyone's mind about what day she died. And, come to think of it, I sure as heck wouldn't have pulled the trigger so close to said deadline because the *first* person the police would think of would be me. No, if

I were William and, by extension . . ."—he paused to wave a hand at Siobhan—"his girlfriend-slash-fiancée-slash-wife, I'd have killed Scarlet weeks ago. Maybe even months or years ago. And I would've made it look like an accident. I wouldn't have made it so obvious."

Siobhan regarded him like a damsel in distress, gazing at her knight in shining armor. Turning to me but pointing at Gilley she said, "Exactly. We might've been many things, Catherine, but neither William nor myself were stupid."

I pressed my lips together and shook my head slightly, thinking. On the one hand, Gilley made an excellent point, and I knew that if I didn't get involved, Shepherd would continue down the track of putting together enough evidence to bring the case against Siobhan to trial, and meanwhile the real person who murdered Scarlet and possibly William would get off scot-free *and* maybe even ultimately inherit some of Scarlet's riches.

If, on the other hand, I did get involved, I was risking personal safety, time I didn't really have when we were so close to going on our European trip, and my slightly, at present, shaky relationship with Shepherd. He'd be livid if/when he found out. And he'd think that I'd lied to him. That I'd betrayed him. That he couldn't trust me.

The choice felt impossible. "If I say no, Gilley, what will you do?" I asked.

"I'm going to look into it, Cat. With or without you. I want to find out who really murdered Scarlet. I know I didn't know her long, but I've been reading some of her books. She wrote with such heart and vulnerability that I feel like I knew her intimately. I can't let the wrong person go to jail while the real murderer gets to possibly enjoy an inheritance they don't deserve. Plus, if Siobhan really *isn't* the murderer, then the DeLeons could still be in danger. Real danger this time because someone is murdering all the named heirs to Scarlet's fortune."

I sucked in a breath. I had almost completely forgotten about the DeLeons. Gilley eyed me meaningfully. He knew I was starting to crack.

I dropped my chin and stared at my hands for a long moment, not wanting to be influenced by anything other than my conscience and logic. The trusting, relieved look on Shepherd's face when I told him that I was butting out of all future investigations, however, kept popping up in my mind's eye.

Finally, I looked up at Siobhan and said, "You must know I'm dating the detective assigned to keep you in prison, right?"

"I do," she said, and there was just the tiniest hint of a smile, and I understood immediately that that little fact had been an attractive incentive to get me to commit to helping her. If I became convinced she didn't murder Scarlet and William, then I might be able to convince Shepherd too.

I didn't like being played, but I was also now resigned to the task, so I swallowed my anger and said, "I'm going to talk it over with Shepherd, Siobhan. I want him to know that I'm going to be looking into the case." She appeared hopeful, so I was quick to add, "Know this: I will not lose my relationship with the best man I've ever known over someone like you. Someone who would treat her sister like trash. Someone who would actually get involved with her ex-husband *without first talking to her* about it. Someone who would even get physically abusive with Scarlet on occasion."

Siobhan's mouth formed a small O.

"Oh, yes," I said, narrowing my eyes at her. "I know all about the few times you beat your sister up."

"Catherine," she said quickly, her gaze now flickering to Marcus as well, who I was also sure was not pleased to discover his client had a history of physical violence toward Scarlet. "You have to understand—all those times I lost control with my sister, I was heavily intoxicated. I had a real problem back then, which I worked very hard to overcome. I've been sober for nearly three years and I apologized to Scarlet a dozen times. I even made a full amends to her almost a year and a half ago!"

"And yet," I said, not giving her an inch, "you still treated her like a doormat, and treated the gift of her financial support like it was something she *owed* you."

It was Siobhan's turn to drop her gaze. "You may not believe me, but ever since Scarlet was found murdered, I've felt terrible about my behavior toward her."

"Oh, a whole three days?" I mocked. I knew I was being especially unforgiving toward her, but I wanted her to know that someone in this world was still going to hold her accountable for treating a person as generous and kind as Scarlet Rubi like garbage.

Siobhan didn't say anything to that. Instead, she picked up her chin and simply said, "Thank you. I understand that you're only tentatively agreeing to look into the case, and I have no expectations for you to follow through."

I stood up and nodded toward Gilley. "We'll be in touch," I told her in parting.

Marcus followed Gilley and me out of the room and we huddled in a circle just down the corridor. "Thank you," he began.

I held up my hand. "Don't, Marcus. Don't thank me yet. I meant what I said. I'm going to talk this over with Shepherd and if he puts his foot down then I'm not going to get involved in any form."

"Understood," Marcus said.

"I'm still going to look into it," Gilley said softly.

I glared at him. He was putting me in a terrible position, because if Shepherd put his foot down and I told him that Gilley was still going to look into the case, I'd then have no choice but to defend Gilley's right to do that. As long as Gilley didn't actually cross the line into obstruction (and of course Gilley would cross that line, because . . . hello, it's Gilley!), then I'd stand firm in my efforts to champion his cause, even if I wasn't directly involved, and all of *that* would put pressure on my relationship with Shepherd. Something it definitely *didn't* need at the moment.

"Sorry," Gilley said to me, but he wasn't going to back down, I could tell.

"What do you need from me?" Marcus asked him, as if I weren't standing right there.

"What's the evidence Shepherd has against Siobhan?" I said, inserting myself back into the conversation.

Marcus's gaze drifted back to me, and damn him, but I swear he wore the hint of a grin. "It's not great but it's not bad. McMillen's next-door neighbor, Mike Erling, was chief of police in Dallas six years ago before retiring. He was out for a jog on the golf course when he heard the sound of a gunshot coming from the area near his condo and he ran toward it. He figures he was about a half mile away—"

"That's a long way away to hear a gunshot," I said.

"Not if you're on a golf course. Wide open spaces allow sound to travel, and this guy knew the sound of a weapon being discharged when he heard one."

"Point taken," I said.

Marcus continued, "Erling says it took him about four and a half minutes to reach the area where he heard the shot coming from and when he got there, he found McMillen's door wide open, and Siobhan's car peeling out of the driveway. He says as she passed the streetlight, he saw that she had blood on the front of her shirt."

"Okay, so far that's super circumstantial," Gilley said.

"It is, but, Erling also said that on a number of occasions he'd both witnessed and heard Siobhan and William arguing loudly. He'd even intervened in a recent argument when it looked like Siobhan was getting physical with McMillen."

"She does have a history of that," I said.

"And so does he," Marcus noted.

"What else does Shepherd have on her?" Gilley pressed.

"The murder weapon was found at the scene and the on-site tech pulled a set of prints that match Siobhan's.

"Yikes," Gil said.

"She claims that when she entered the condo, it was dark, and she was trying to find the switch when she kicked something on the floor that caused her to stumble. When she bent over to pick up whatever it was, she realized it was a gun, and the muzzle was still hot."

"Plausible," I said.

"It is," Marcus told me. "She says that she finally found a working light switch, and when she flicked it on, she saw McMillen, dying on the kitchen floor. She dropped down next to him, and pulled him to her—which is how she got blood on her blouse—and he died in her arms without ever revealing who'd shot him. Siobhan then panicked and ran out of the condo before good sense came back to her and she called the police from about two miles away."

"Did *she* hear the gunshot?" I asked.

Marcus shook his head. "In the four and a half minutes that passed between the time that Erling heard the shot and saw Siobhan fleeing the scene, it's possible that she could've been in her car, still driving over when McMillen was murdered and the real killer escaped. The timing would've been a little close, but it's possible that the killer could've fled the scene immediately after shooting McMillen and headed in the opposite direction from where Siobhan was coming from. I figure she was probably in the house a total of two and a half minutes before she panicked and ran, so there's likely about a minute and a half to two minutes of overlap time."

I shook my head. Even though all the evidence

was circumstantial, Shepherd still had a solid case against Siobhan.

"Who gets to inherit William's money now that he's dead?" Gilley asked.

"Unless he had a will that said otherwise, any assets would fall to his heirs," Marcus told him.

"His kids?" I asked. "Masie and Grayson?"

"Yes, and Siobhan. They were married at the time of his death, and if she's acquitted for his murder, then she'll definitely have a claim if he didn't leave a will."

"How do we know if he had a will?" Gilley asked.

"I'll do some digging in a couple of hours," Marcus said. "Siobhan doesn't think McMillen ever bothered to write one out, given that he expected Scarlet to leave her estate to their kids."

"Didn't quite work out that way, though, did it," I said.

Marcus shook his head and rocked back on his heels. "Nope, which opens the door to reasonable doubt."

"Okay," I said with a yawn. "Gilley, let's go get some coffee and some breakfast. We'll need to talk strategy before I have my talk with Shepherd."

"He's never going to let you investigate," Gilley said, and his expression was resigned.

"Probably true, but until I know that for sure, I'm free to talk the case over with you, and help in any way I can until he shuts me down."

"Good," Gilley said. "Good."

We left Marcus and headed out to get into some good trouble.

Chapter 10

Gilley and I ventured to the nearest Starbucks, which was the only place open at that hour. I was going to be up front and honest with Shepherd about wanting to get involved in Siobhan's case, and about the fact that if it was a dealbreaker between us, that Gilley would still pursue looking into things, but until I had that discussion with him, I could at least guide Gilley about where to look first.

"You're not eating?" Gil said, when we finished ordering at the counter and I'd only asked for a cup of herbal tea.

"I'm too nervous to eat. Telling Shepherd that I want to go back on my word isn't a discussion I'm looking forward to."

"I get it," Gilley said, and I could see a hint of

guilt in his eyes as he'd just ordered two slices of pumpkin bread and a couple of egg bites.

We took a seat near the window and waited for our names to be called in relative silence. I think we were both a little troubled by the heavy responsibility of getting deeply involved in a case that was proving far more complicated than we'd originally thought.

Which is why we both jumped a little when the barista called out to us. Gil got up and retrieved our orders, but before biting into his warm pumpkin bread he said, "We need to look at the next most obvious person for McMillen's murder."

"Why the next most obvious?"

"Because if Siobhan's telling the truth about not killing William, then she's being framed, and the only reason to make that kind of effort—and take that kind of risk—is because you don't want any attention to be drawn to yourself. You want your possible suspicion dismissed outright because the most obvious person has been caught."

I looked at him for a long moment and then said, "Sometimes, you are so brilliant, Gilley."

He made a face. "*Sometimes?*"

I laughed. "Okay, most times, but at present you are especially brilliant. That rationale makes total sense."

He chewed thoughtfully for a minute. "I have my moments. Anyway, next to Siobhan and William, who would be the most likely person to kill Scarlet?"

"Are we convinced that whoever killed Scarlet also killed William?"

Gilley shrugged. "I am. Aren't you?"

"I am. I wonder if they used the same gun?"

"I would," Gilley said. "It'd be a way of helping to tie Siobhan to both murders."

"But wasn't it risky leaving the gun behind for Siobhan to find? I mean, what if she hadn't touched it?"

"I'll bet you hers were the only prints they found on it," Gilley said. "And if she hadn't touched it, Shepherd would probably just say that she wiped the gun clean."

I nodded. "Still, it's a risk to leave the weapon behind at the scene. What if Siobhan had been a little quicker on her feet? What if she'd taken the gun with her and hid it somewhere before she was arrested?"

"I think the killer was counting on her to panic. Which is why it only makes sense that someone from the family killed both Scarlet and William."

"Why do you say that?" I asked.

"Because whoever staged the whole thing had to know them both very well to be able to predict their behavior like that."

I nodded slowly. "Yes, that's true, but who knew both of them the best?"

Gilley shrugged again. "Their kids," he said. "Masie, Grayson, and Luke."

"But would they murder a stepparent-slash-father and frame their own mother-slash-aunt?"

"For twenty-five million?" Gilley asked, while popping the last morsel of pumpkin bread into his mouth. "You bet that crowd would."

With a sigh I said, "You're right. They're hardly the Cleavers."

"They're hardly the Bundys," Gilley countered.

I chuckled but quickly sobered. "So, you're going to target those three first?"

"I think so. I'll dig around on their social media pages and see if there's anything that seems incriminating. I think I should also ask Siobhan herself who she might suspect could've been up to framing her and McMillen."

I palmed my forehead. "I wish I'd asked her that when we were at the station."

"You probably had Shepherd on the brain and weren't thinking it through," Gil said. "What're you gonna say to him, anyway?"

I took a deep breath and let it out slowly while I thought about it. Finally, I shrugged and replied, "I think I'll simply be open and honest and tell him what I *want* to do and if he tells me it's a deal-breaker for us, then, Gilley, I'm sorry but I'll have no choice other than to butt out."

Gilley nodded. "Guess I'm gonna go it alone then."

My shoulders sagged. "If you want to talk to me about anything you find out, I'm happy to weigh in. I mean, I won't *actively* investigate with you, but I can sure give an opinion if you need it."

Gilley offered me a sideways smile. "That'll have to be good enough, Cat."

A bit later I pulled into the driveway, intending to drop Gilley off before making my way over to Shepherd's place, when I noticed that the DeLeons' car was no longer in the driveway. "Wow," I said, noting that the time was just after seven a.m. "They left early!"

"We should reach out to them and let them know that Siobhan might've been framed."

I pointed to him. "You do that while I'm over talking with Shepherd."

"Will do," Gilley said, getting out of the car, but he paused to look back and add, "By the way, you're way overdressed for a talk with Shepherd."

My brow furrowed as I looked down at myself. I was wearing a black turtleneck, leather jacket, and jeans. "What're you talking about? I'm totally casual."

Gilley winked at me. "You're fully clothed, sugar. If I were you, I'd go in naked."

I rolled my eyes but added a smile, then waved him away.

To be honest, I sweated the drive over to Shepherd's, and I even considered Gilley's suggestion. Shep was going to be furious when I told him about my conversation with Siobhan and what she'd asked me to do. And he'd be absolutely livid when I told him I wanted to nose around a little. He'd then gravitate to apoplectic when I told him that, even if I didn't actively look into the case, I'd still back Gilley while he played gumshoe.

And that was the real issue with all this. I didn't know how I'd be able to repair what I was about to break. It all had to do with trust, and I didn't know if I could convince Shepherd that I was trustworthy if I continued to support Gilley while he did the thing that Shepherd forbade me to do.

When I pulled into his driveway, I hesitated for several minutes, trying to work up my courage.

It surprised me when the front door opened

and Shepherd stood there, wearing only pajama bottoms, holding a mug of coffee.

I blushed as I got out of the car. "Good morning, sweetheart."

"Cat," he said, lifting the mug in a silent toast. "You've been out here a while. Something up?"

I paused in front of him, marveling at his well-toned torso. Placing a hand on his chest and feeling the smoothness of his skin I regretted what I'd come over to say immensely. "Can we go inside and have a talk?"

Shep closed his free hand over mine. "Uh-oh," he said with a bit of a disarming grin. "Sounds serious." I nodded and he dropped the grin. "Come on in. I'll pour you a cup and we'll talk."

I took a seat at the kitchen counter and waited for him to bring me a cup of coffee and the creamer from the pantry. I stared at the black brew when he set it in front of me. My stomach was a mess of nerves and I didn't want coffee, but I wrapped my hands around the mug all the same, seeking out the warmth of the brew.

"Siobhan Rubi retained Marcus Brown last night."

Shepherd nodded, taking the seat next to me. "I'm aware."

"Marcus called me this morning and asked me to come meet Siobhan at her request."

"Uh-huh," he said, as if I'd casually mentioned today's weather.

I cleared my throat. "Anyway, I met with her and Marcus, and Siobhan has somewhat convinced me that she didn't murder her sister or McMillen."

Shepherd took a sip of his coffee, his expression

irritatingly relaxed. I couldn't tell what he was thinking as I told him all this.

"Anyway, she's made a special request of me and Gilley. She'd like us to snoop around a little, see if any family members might've had a reason to frame her for both murders."

Shepherd nodded with a lazy lilt to his eyes but didn't speak and I wanted to yell at him. Where was his immediate outrage? Where was the protest? The opening stanza for an epic argument between us?

"I'd like to do that, Shep," I said softly. "But I'd be going back on my word with you if I did, so I came here to ask your . . . forgiveness and understanding while Gilley and I nose around a little."

"Granted," he said.

I blinked. Then blinked again, and threw in a couple more for good measure. "Excuse me?"

He waved casually. "I think it's a good idea. Go for it."

"You . . . think it's a good idea?! What the hell is *that* supposed to mean?"

Why was I the one getting angry?

Shepherd laughed and got up to pour himself some more coffee. "It means that I'm fine with you nosing around in the family business, Cat."

"Wh-why?" I stammered. This man was confounding!

He turned back to me and leaned against the counter. "Because Siobhan *is* the murderer. She and William either cooked up a scheme to murder Scarlet, and then when William was about to back out of the agreement to split the dough with her after he inherited twenty-five million from his ex, she murdered him too, or, Siobhan acted on her own in both cases."

I opened my mouth to speak, but then closed it again. I didn't quite know what to say. Finally, I settled on, "But what if she didn't? What if she was framed?"

He shook his head. "My lab tech texted me a few minutes before you got here. We pulled a bullet out of the wall at McMillen's—the first shot missed. Anyway, it's a match to the one the ME pulled from the body of Scarlet Rubi. The same gun was used in both murders."

"Why does that mean Siobhan must be guilty?"

"The gun was registered to McMillen."

My jaw dropped. "Whoa."

"Yep."

I shook my head after thinking about it, however. "That's still pretty circumstantial, Shep. I mean, how can you convincingly tie Siobhan to a gun that McMillen owned?"

"You mean beyond having access to McMillen's house for the past year or two as his girlfriend, then his fiancée then his wife?"

"You heard they were married?"

Shepherd gave me one of those "Girl, please" looks and I remembered that his literal job was to ferret out details like that.

"Well," I said, still bent on arguing my point. "Just because they were a couple doesn't mean she *knew* about the gun."

Shepherd's grin was victorious. "We took a lengthy statement from McMillen's neighbor. He says he knew McMillen pretty well, the two liked to shoot and would often go to the shooting range together. He said that on several occasions, Siobhan went with them, and McMillen not only taught her to shoot, but taught her to shoot with *that* gun. She knew about it, Cat. And she also knew where McMillen kept it in the house, and how to shoot it."

"And yet the first shot missed," I said, pointing that fact back at him.

He shrugged. "They argued. She was emotional, her hand unsteady when she grabbed the gun. McMillen ducked the first shot but couldn't get away from the second. Case closed."

I frowned. "It just seems too pat, though, doesn't it?"

"No," Shepherd said. "It seems like what it is. She killed Scarlet, planning on having McMillen inherit the insurance money, then she killed him once they were married."

"What if *he* murdered Scarlet?" I tried, looking for holes.

"He had an airtight alibi for his whereabouts the night of her murder."

"Airtight?"

"Yeah, he and the neighbor—who's an ex-chief of police, I might add—were playing poker with a couple other friends from eight p.m. the night before until two in the morning the next day. The ME did a detailed analysis, trying to pinpoint Scarlet's TOD. His best estimate is a three-hour window between eleven p.m. and one a.m."

"That still doesn't mean *Siobhan* did it."

Shepherd flattened his lips. "Cat," he said. "Come on . . ."

I sighed. "Fine. I know it looks bad, but I still want to ask a few questions, poke around a little."

"Like I said, be my guest. And if you'd like to relay what you find out back to me, I'd appreciate it."

"Why aren't you protesting?" I asked him point blank.

"Because you'll be helping my case more than helping hers," he said. "We got the killer, Cat. Anything else you dig up will probably just cement that for us."

I studied him critically. "So, you won't be mad at me when I interview the family and a witness or two?"

"Nope," he said smugly.

"And you don't think of this as me going back on my word?"

He chuckled. "Of course it's you going back on your word—but you came to me and asked if I was okay with it, and that makes it good between us."

"Really?"

Shepherd pushed away from the counter he'd been leaning against and came over to where I sat. Setting down his mug he cupped my face tenderly and said, "Really, babe. We're good." And then he kissed me and I knew he was telling the truth.

An hour and a half later, I was back home, and found Gilley seated at my kitchen island, typing away on his computer. "Hi," I said jovially.

Gilley glanced over at me as I breezed into the room, setting my jacket on a chair. He then gave me one of those up-down looks and said, "Your shirt's inside out."

My face immediately flushed, but I tried to cover it. "I got dressed in the dark this morning."

Gilley smirked. "Yes. And then you got dressed again in broad daylight and put your shirt on inside out."

I rolled my eyes at him and headed to the fridge. Having worked up a bit of an appetite, I was hungry. "Ooh, you made quiche!"

"I did," he said. "It's probably still warm. Nuke a piece for thirty seconds and you'll be good to go."

I took the plastic-wrapped dish out of the fridge and began to slice myself a piece when Gilley said, "I'm assuming it went well with Shepherd?"

"It did."

"I'm also assuming you took to heart my suggestion to show up naked?"

I blushed again. "Gil, please!" I said. I'm a bit prudish when it comes to openly discussing my sex life—which I definitely, definitely don't do.

"Sorry," he said. "Tell me about your . . . er . . . discussion."

After popping the quiche into the microwave, I turned to him. "He said to go for it."

"Go for what?"

"The investigation."

"You're joking."

"I'm not."

"Was he high?"

I laughed and the microwave dinged. I took the delicious-smelling quiche out of the microwave, grabbed a fork and a napkin, and came around the island to take up a seat next to Gilley. "He's got some very damning evidence against Siobhan."

I then explained everything Shepherd had told me to Gilley, whose eyes widened with every new detail. "Whoa," he said. "That's bad. For Siobhan, I mean."

"It is."

"Maybe she *did* do it."

I shook my head. "Gilley, I think she's smarter than that. If she went to all the trouble to plot and murder her own sister without any of the clues pointing her way, why would she then be so impulsive and clumsy when she murdered McMillen?"

"Emotion," Gilley said. "She snapped when McMillen hesitated at the reading of the will."

"Did she?" I said. "I mean, if you're going to snap, you do it in the moment, right? Not hours and hours later. She had plenty of time to plan another murder—but this was impulsive. McMillen's murder wasn't premeditated. And she fled the house covered in his blood, remember? She did this after leaving no trace evidence at Scarlet's murder scene. If she committed both murders, then the second seems to be far too out of character for her to have pulled the trigger in both cases."

"You still think she was framed?"

I nodded. "I do. I think someone else knew about McMillen's gun and where he kept it and used that knowledge to steal the weapon, kill Scarlet, then went back to McMillen's house and murdered him, setting up Siobhan to take the fall for both murders."

"And you know who would've known about McMillen's gun other than Siobhan? His kids. And hers."

I made a face. "I'm beginning to hate these people," I said. "I mean, my parents were absolutely awful, abusive, even sociopathic, but even I couldn't imagine framing them for murder."

"Money does strange things to otherwise ordinary people," Gilley said.

I cocked my head at him. "That's both incredibly true and a little concerning. Do you think money has done strange things to me?"

"Definitely."

I rolled my eyes. "I'm serious."

"Ah, okay, then super definitely."

I put my hands on my hips. "Name one thing that money has done to me that's strange."

"One? That's not even a challenge! But here're just a few to chew on: you live in a house run by a state-of-the-art AI butler who isn't actually real but whom you think of as your friend; you have a permanent houseguest who doesn't pay you a dime in rent because you refuse to take any compensation for the use of your guesthouse, which could easily fetch you five grand a month on the rental market; you never—and I do mean *never*—open a bill because you've set up automatic payments for all utilities and credit cards and you're completely oblivious to your monthly expenses; you won't buy anything, and I do mean *anything*, on sale—even if it's by a designer you adore because you view something on sale as something unworthy of full price and therefore unworthy of hanging in your closet; you *literally* took a bath in three *hundred* bottles of champagne when you first moved in here just to celebrate; you—"

"Okay! Okay! I get it!" I yelled. "Geez, I had no idea you were keeping track like that, Gilley."

He stared at me with lowered lids. "You asked."

I scowled at him. "For the record, most of that champagne was a gift from the private equity group that bought my marketing firm, and I'd been saving all those cases to celebrate that way for over two years."

"You fly your freak flag high, sugar. I'm not judging."

I rolled my eyes again and said, "Can we get back to the business at hand, please?"

"Sure," Gil said, pulling his laptop close again. "I was looking into Luke's, Masie's, and Grayson's social media accounts and they all seem super self-involved and materialistic. Most of their posts involve designer duds, fast cars, and selfies of themselves in said designer duds and fast cars."

"Are any of them married?"

"All three were—all three are now divorced and single. Well, Masie seems to have a steady boyfriend, but I suspect that relationship is on the rocks."

"Why do you say that?"

"Because her boyfriend actually has two separate Instagram accounts—one featuring photos of them at various social functions, and one featuring him with a wide variety of younger, more attractive women cozying up to him."

"Ick," I said.

"Personified," Gilley agreed.

"What's the boyfriend do?"

Gilley raised his fingers to form air quotes. "He's a 'promoter.' "

I remembered Scarlet had described Grayson as a promoter but I wasn't sure I had a handle on what that was. "What does that mean, exactly?" I asked Gilley.

"He promotes."

"Promotes what?"

Gilley shrugged. "Clubs, concerts, restaurants, events, etcetera, etcetera."

"You can make a living at that?"

"Out here you can."

"Ah. Yes. Indeed, you probably could. Okay, so Masie is in a rocky relationship, and her mother just cut off her money. Do we think that maybe the boyfriend was sticking around Masie just for her access to loads of money?"

"We do, we do," Gilley sang.

"So once the money was cut off, the boyfriend would probably find out and he'd be out of that relationship quick, right?"

"I'd be out quick if I were him."

"In other words, Masie might've had a pretty good motive for killing her mother and father."

"She'd stand to inherit at least half of McMillen's money and that is a good motive but I kind of like Grayson's chances of being our killer better."

"Why do you say that?"

Gilley swiveled his computer around and I looked at the screen which showed Grayson at a gaming table with a stack of gambling chips and a happy grin on his face. "I'm still not getting your point, Gil."

"This was taken a year ago. He's posted almost nothing about gambling since, *but* prior to this post, there were plenty of photos of him in Las Vegas, Atlantic City, even Monte Carlo, but like I said, about a year ago, a lot of those posts stopped."

"Uh-huh, so you think he had a gambling problem?"

"No. I think he *has* a gambling problem, and about a year ago his luck started running out and the fun winner became the reclusive loser. I'm going to try to dig into his financials a little but I'm guessing he's in some deep debt and he might even be in deep debt to some not so nice people, which could make him desperate to get back in the black."

"I like it but it's pretty speculative. He could've also gotten some help for his addiction a year ago, and the lack of photos may be a product of his efforts to stay away from the tables."

Gilley shook his head, and he began to scroll through Grayson's Instagram photos. "See this?" he said, highlighting several photos of Grayson grinning from ear to ear as he held up a bounty of chips for the camera.

"Yeah," I said. "He's obviously good at the gaming tables."

"No, he *was* good at the gaming tables. Cat, you don't quit on a hot streak, and from what I can tell, his hot streak lasted about four months, and then nothing for about three months, then intermittent photos of him having a good night here and there, but even those have dwindled for the past few months. Trust me, the guy lost, and lost big."

"Okay, I trust you," I said, polishing off my quiche and setting the plate of crumbs down for Spooks to snuffle at and polish clean. "What about Luke? What's his deal?"

"You mean 'Chester the Investor,'" Gil said, using those air quotes again.

I laughed. "Uh-oh. Doesn't sound like Luke's in the clear, either."

"Nope. His social media account is chock-full of opportunities to invest in a sure thing!"

"There's no such thing as a sure thing," I told him. "But what's Luke's angle?"

"Beachfront condos, what else?"

I looked to the ceiling. "How did I not guess that right off the bat?"

"You didn't get much sleep. You're not as sharp as you usually are. Anyway, Luke and, from what I can tell, a silent partner are heavily invested in a decent-sized builder's lot that is, what I like to call 'water-adjacent.' "

"Will you stop with the air quotes?"

"Sorry," Gil said, lowering his fingers.

"What does water-adjacent mean, exactly?"

"It means that it would be on the beach if there weren't environmentally protected wetlands between it and the ocean."

"That's not beachfront," I said. "That's never-gonna-happen property."

I'd had to deal with a very, very minor drainage issue with the EPA when I built on this lot of mine and that had been an absolute nightmare. That agency never yielded when there was wildlife to protect.

"Exactly, but construction has already started and several of the condos have earnest money down on them, but from what I can gather on Zillow, several potential buyers have been backing out. I think they were promised a view of the beach and the smell of the ocean. Instead, they're getting a view of tall reeds and the smell of a swamp."

"Sounds charming."

"Practically sells itself," Gilley replied with a grin. "Anyway, with so many buyers backing out, Luke—aka Chester—is running out of money. Construction halted about a week and a half ago."

I squinted at him. "Interesting timing, don't you think?"

"Quite."

"In other words, he's looking for an infusion of cash to continue the construction, right?"

"And to fight the EPA," Gil said. "He's filed a claim against them in court, which takes money . . ."

"Money he doesn't have, but if he files a claim for a stake in Scarlet's estate, he'll potentially have cash for both endeavors."

"Correct," Gil said.

I made a swirling motion with my finger. "Okay, Gil. We've got three potential suspects to interview. Let's wrap this up and get going."

Gilley looked pointedly at me.

"What?" I asked.

"Before we go, you might want to turn your shirt right-side out, sugar."

My face went red-hot again. "Wise guy," I muttered, trotting toward the powder room. "We're leaving as soon as I pull myself together!"

"You might also want to run a comb through your hair, Cat. The back of your head looks like it's been pawed at by a group of monkeys . . . or one very passionate detective."

"One more crack out of you, Gillespie, and I'm gonna start charging you rent!"

Sure enough, that shut him up.

Chapter 11

Once we were on the road, Gilley and I talked about how to approach our three main suspects. "What's our angle?" I asked while I drove.

"I think we should go with the truth, Cat. I think we just tell everyone we talk to that Siobhan has asked us to talk to the family and see if anyone stands out to them as a possible alternative suspect in Scarlet's and William's murders."

I reached over to grab Gilley's arm. "I like that angle, but I think we should also remember that Masie and Grayson just lost both their parents, and if they aren't the killers, then this will be an especially difficult time for them."

"Oh, you're so right," he said. "Okay, change of plans; we start the conversation suggesting that we're there to express our sympathies and while we're expressing them, we could casually mention that Siobhan has asked us to speak to the family on her behalf to profess her innocence and also asked us to try to ferret out anyone who might've been willing to frame her for the crimes."

"Yes, good. We'll do that." I paused for a moment to think our plan through and still felt like it needed an adjustment. "We should stop at the flower shop. We'll load up on sympathy bouquets so that we don't show up empty-handed."

Gilley pointed at me. "Perfect! Buckley's is on the way to Masie's house, so it's not out of our way."

Buckley's was a local farm specializing in growing and arranging flowers and plants. It's where Gilley and I got our Christmas trees every year and luckily when we arrived there was no one else in the lot so there was no waiting.

We decided to get extra just in case we needed to interview more of the family, so I ordered six sympathy bouquets arranged in crystal vases, and I handed over my black card as the arrangements were being loaded into my car.

After signing the receipt, I looked at Gil and said, "Ready?"

"Sure," he said, "but just one question."

"Yes?"

He pointed to the receipt on the counter. "How much was the total?"

I blinked and felt a touch of blush hit my cheeks. "I don't know, Gilley," I said crisply. I knew he was tying his question to his earlier observation about my lack of attention to the pesky details of day-to-day finances.

"Sugar," he said gently, laying a hand on my arm. "I'm not picking on you. I simply want you to start recognizing the cost of things. I promise it'll make you more relatable and aware."

Glaring at him, because I was embarrassed, I turned back to the counter and eyed the receipt. I'd just spent over eight hundred and fifty dollars on flowers. "Whoa," I said. The arrangements had been nice—tasteful, elegant even, but to pay almost a thousand dollars on something so transient didn't seem to be an especially good use of my money.

Walking past Gilley, I said, "Point taken. Let's go."

We had already decided to start with Masie. We both felt she might be the easiest of the three to extract information—and a possible confession—out of.

We were very, very wrong.

But we didn't know that when we pulled up to her exquisite home with a driveway rimmed with rose trees and artfully shaped shrubs. The house itself was a classic shingle structure, painted a muddy brown with white trim and a triple garage bay marked by bright white doors.

We parked at the curb because the driveway was rather short and we didn't want to block anyone in—or out. Gilley carried the bouquet while we walked up to the front door and rang the bell. "Hope she's home," I said.

"It's nine thirty in the morning. She doesn't work. She's probably here."

Sure enough the door was pulled open a moment later by Scarlet's daughter, who stood there in red-and-black-checkered leggings, tucked into bright red patent leather boots, and she also wore a black blazer and matching silk blouse with a plunging neckline. Her long, blond, slightly curled hair tumbled down around her shoulders just so, and her makeup was freshly applied and powder perfect.

"Oh," she said, eyeing us with disappointment. "I thought you were someone else."

Gilley and I shoved toothy smiles onto our faces and he held forward the bouquet. "We wanted to stop by and offer our sympathies," he told her.

"For what?" she asked and then it was like she remembered a long-forgotten birthday. "Oh, yeah. Dad."

I nodded. "You must be devastated," I said, holding a hand over my heart.

"Sure," she said like she was bored. Taking the flowers she added, "Thanks. These are nice."

"It's the least we could do," I told her. "We feel terrible."

She eyed me suspiciously. "Why? You didn't murder him, did you?"

My eyes widened. "No!" I said quickly. "No. Of course not."

She sighed. "Yeah, well, someone did, and I doubt it was Aunt Siobhan, but what're you gonna do?"

I confess that I was taken aback by Masie's casual and somewhat dismissive demeanor. In the past several days she'd lost both parents and her aunt had been arrested for at least one of the murders. "Why do you say that you doubt it was your aunt who killed your father?" I asked.

She shrugged. "Siobhan's a manipulative, evil bitch, but she's not an impulsive idiot. If she wanted to kill Dad, she'd do it slowly to maximize the torture."

"Sounds like you two didn't get along very well," Gilley said. "Did that have to do with your mom?"

"What?" she asked him. "No. I've hated her long before she and Mom were at odds."

"Why?" I probed.

"Because Siobhan stole my ex-husband. That's what she does, you know. She goes after other women's husbands."

My jaw dropped, and a glance at Gilley told me he was equally surprised. "She had an affair with your ex?" Gilley asked.

Masie nodded. "I caught them in the act, if you can believe it. It'd been going on for months, and David talked about leaving me for her, but Siobhan dumped him when Mom threatened to cut off the money train over it."

"I'm surprised you didn't leave him," I said.

"Oh, I did. I dumped him the second he thought he'd won my forgiveness. It was a delicious revenge."

"Ah," I said. "And you've hated your aunt ever since?" Could Masie be outlining her motive for framing Siobhan for the murder of both her father and mother?

"Nah," she said, shaking her head. "I forgave Siobhan, but I never forgot. I've kept her at a distance ever since."

"Were you upset to learn that she was seeing your father?" I asked.

"I didn't even know they were a thing until they showed up at the reading of the will together. I was as surprised as anybody."

"You must've been furious," Gilley said, shaking his head in sympathy.

Masie made a face like she didn't much care. "What're you gonna do? They deserved each other."

"I'm sorry if we upset you by bringing you flowers, Masie. I didn't realize you weren't close to your dad."

"He was a jerk. And he was a drunk jerk for most of my childhood. The man was incapable of love. He never once told me he loved me or paid much attention to me, especially after Mom divorced him."

"What about your brother?" Gilley asked, and then pointed to our car parked at the curb. "We've got a bouquet for him as well."

Masie scoffed. "You should've saved your money. Grayson hated Dad. Like haaaated him."

I snuck a side look at Gilley. This is what we'd been hoping to hear. "Why?" I asked innocently.

"Dad borrowed a bunch of money from him, promising to pay it back, and he never did. That was the last straw for Grayson. Dad was always making promises he had no intention of keeping."

Behind us there was the sound of a car pulling into the driveway. Gilley and I turned to see a black Porsche convertible easing its way into the drive and behind it was another car—a sleek silver Cadillac.

Behind the wheel of the Porsche was a handsome-looking man in his midforties and he looked familiar to me. It took a moment but I finally placed him—he was the man Gilley had shown me from Masie's Instagram page.

The driver of the Cadillac was a woman of about

the same age, with chestnut brown hair shaped into a perfectly cut bob. She wore a stunningly tailored dark blue suit with a pink blouse that set off her porcelain complexion. She got out of the car carrying a briefcase and she wore a Realtor badge on her lapel.

"Hey!" Masie called to them, adding a wave.

"Mase," the boyfriend said, getting out of the car with a grocery bag. He came forward and nodded to his girlfriend, but his gaze landed and stayed on us. Or rather . . . on me. "Hi," he said as he reached the front step. Extending a hand out to me he added, "I'm Alexander."

I took his hand and shook it as briefly as possible without appearing impolite. "We were just leaving," I said, looping my arm through Gilley's.

Alexander nodded again to Masie. "I didn't know you were having company over." Shifting his attention back to me he said, "I've got plenty of champagne for mimosas. You should stay."

I could feel Masie's gaze land like a dagger on me and it was embarrassing and uncomfortable to be the object of this man's intense attention. "Oh, we couldn't possibly stay," I said. "We've got much to do today."

Pulling Gilley with me as we descended the steps I glanced back over my shoulder and said, "Thank you, Masie, and again, you have our deepest sympathies."

Alexander eyed me curiously, then he took note of the sympathy flower arrangement in Masie's hands and he actually scoffed. "Are they for real?" I heard him say.

"Yeah," she said. "The flowers are nice, though. They'll look good in the photos for the listing."

We passed the woman from the Cadillac and she gave us a perfunctory smile and said, "Are you interested in buying the house?"

"Uh . . . no," Gilley told her. "We were just expressing our sympathies."

The woman stopped and her eyes widened. "Your sympathies. Did someone die?"

"Yes," I said softly. "Masie lost her father yesterday."

The woman went from surprised to alarmed. Pointing to the house, she said, "In there?"

"No," I told her. "No. At his home."

"Oh, thank God," she said. "I hate having to disclose that someone died in a home."

Wow, I thought. Is everyone connected to this family so shallow?

"Have a nice day," Gilley said, and pulled us past the real estate agent.

We walked quickly to the car and got in around the same time that Masie was closing the front door after letting her guests inside. Once she was gone from view, I started the car but kept it in park for a moment. "Well, *that* was interesting!"

"You mean all the dirty laundry about her family, or the fact that Masie seems to be selling her house?"

"Yes," I said, and smirked.

"So true," Gilley agreed. "There's lots to digest from that talk."

I put the car into drive and pulled away from the curb. "Okay, so let's talk."

Gilley shook his head in wonder. "How about

first we simply acknowledge that, when we got here, I thought for sure we'd get info that would help point us away from Siobhan as the killer, but instead, I'm now wondering if she really did pull the trigger."

"That whole thing about Siobhan stealing Masie's ex-husband? How twisted and, frankly, *sick* is that?"

"And she goes from having an affair with Masie's ex to hopping into a relationship with Scarlet's ex," Gilley said.

I shuddered. "It's all so incestuous. I mean, there's a big wide world out there, why fish in waters that could only cause trouble?"

"Maybe that's the point, Cat. Maybe Siobhan likes to shake things up. Cause trouble. I mean, the woman didn't work and was limited to what her sister would provide her with financially. She had to be bored, and maybe that's why she was intent on causing trouble."

"Well, it's despicable," I said. My sister, Abby, and I are very close. I couldn't even *imagine* making a move on her husband—even if Abby had an ex that I was attracted to, there was still no circumstance that I would ever even consider showing an interest in him. It would be such a betrayal of trust.

"Scarlet's family is comprised of the most dreadful people," I mused.

"Agreed," Gil said. "And, lucky us, we get to talk to even more of them today."

I smirked. "Who should we call on next? Grayson or Luke?"

Gilley consulted his phone for a moment. "Luke's construction site isn't far away. It might be good to check it out in case we want to comment on it later."

"What if he's there?" I asked.

"All the better!"

"You're right," I agreed. "Okay, navigate me there."

"I got you, boo," he said, "But we also need to talk about the fact that Masie is putting her house up for sale."

I gave him a one-shoulder shrug. "Makes sense to me."

"How?"

"Well, she was cut out of the will, right? Which means she has no immediate access to cash, and her only asset is probably that house, which, let's face it, is worth . . ." I glanced at Gilley, who'd kept track of all the real estate values during the contract signing between Scarlet and her family.

"Ten-point-two million," he said. "It's off-season for home selling, but I think she'll probably clear eight to nine million after all the fees and taxes have been applied."

"That's a lot of cash to live on while she hashes out her stake in Scarlet's estate in court. And she'll have a really good claim, too, being the daughter of both the estate owner and the beneficiary."

"If she's careful with the house proceeds, it could last her all the rest of her life," Gil said. "If she invests it, even at a modest five to six percent return, she'd bring in between four and five hundred K a year, gross, without ever touching the principal."

I glanced over at him. "Lookit you with the math skills."

Gilley smirked. "Put a dollar sign on a figure and my brain acts like a supercomputer. Anyway, back to our encounter with Masie et al . . . what was up with that slick cat, Alexander? He was so into you, did you notice?"

I shuddered and made a face. "I did, and I don't know for sure what his angle is, but I'm assuming he thinks he can swindle Masie out of some of the cash she's about to come into."

"Why aren't men like him more obvious to you women?" Gilley asked me.

"Hey, don't lump me into that category, okay? I had his number the moment he pulled up."

"Yeah. Me too. I'd feel sorry for Masie if she weren't such an awful human being. Did you notice she seemed to have no grief for the murder of either of her parents? I expected her to be emotionally traumatized by the loss of her parents in the manner in which they were murdered, but she acted like it was just another day with nothing eventful going on."

"Agreed," I said. "It was weird."

"Was it ever. And it makes me think that she's cold-blooded enough to have done the deed."

I nodded but I didn't know that I was feeling it. Still, I kept that thought to myself as we wound our way through East Hampton, heading ever closer to the water.

"Take a left at that intersection," Gilley instructed. "And it'll be at the end of the street."

I did as he told me to do and immediately upon turning onto the street we could see the massive lot under construction.

Or, what had been under construction. The site was the shell of a five-story building that was little more than Sheetrock, two-by-fours, and electrical wiring.

"That's it?" I asked as we pulled to a stop in front of the site.

"Yep," Gil said. "Let's take a closer look."

We got out of the car and walked over to the site. The area just in front of the building was all wetlands, and the smell of rotting vegetation was pungent, especially since the wind—coming from the west—was carrying it in. "Good Lord, in the spring and summer they'll never be able to get away from that stench," I said.

"Just think of the mosquitoes in July," Gil said. "It'd be intense."

"For sure."

We walked around the site in silence, taking it all in, then ventured inside the building, which looked like it hadn't seen any work done on it in at least a month. "Wow," I finally said. "He's in deeper hot water than I thought."

"Yeah," Gil agreed.

"Hello?" we heard from outside.

I grabbed Gilley's arm and froze. He went stiff as well.

"Who's here?" the voice demanded. "You're trespassing on private property!"

I bit my lip and motioned toward the direction of the voice. We had no choice, really, but to reveal ourselves and try to explain our presence. But Gilley shook his head. He seemed to want to make a run for it. I rolled my eyes at him because, where was he going to run? Into the swamp? No way was I going to ruin my best Kate Spade mules.

"Hello!" I called, pulling Gilley with me around the corner only to come up short when we practically bumped right into Luke.

"You're trespassing," he said angrily.

"I'm so sorry, Luke," I told him in the most innocent voice I could manage. "We meant no harm."

"What'er you doing here?" he asked, and I could tell he was trying to place us but having a little trouble.

"Well, we were looking for you," I said.

"Me? Why?" he asked warily, and then it seemed to dawn on him who we were, because he pointed to us and said, "You two again? Why are you harassing me and my family?"

I shook my head. "I swear we meant no harm. We actually have something for you back at the car and—"

"You have something for me?" he interrupted, anger still present in his voice. "What?"

"A bouquet of flowers," Gilley told him and I was quite proud of the way he puffed up his chest and raised his chin, almost in challenge to the brutish attitude of Scarlet's nephew.

Luke simply stared slack-jawed at Gilley.

"They're sympathy flowers," I explained. "We wanted to express our condolences."

Luke scrunched up his face. "Why?"

"Because you recently lost both your aunt and your uncle, and we thought it was the right thing to do to drop in on some of your family members and express our deepest sympathies."

"That's just . . . weird," he said.

And of course I knew it was weird, but to be called out on it like that insulted me. Still, I managed to keep my temper in check and said, "Perhaps where you come from, Mr. Forsythe, but we also heard that you were looking for investors on this piece of property, and as it happens, I've got some money I'd like to invest and beachfront condos seem like a sure thing."

Luke's entire attitude changed in an instant, and it was then that he seemed to take me in, like really take me in. Even though I was dressed casually, I still wore a Gucci leather jacket and had a Birkin on my arm and the five-karat sapphire on my right ring finger.

People with money can always spot high-end material when they see it.

"Oh," he said in a much softer tone. "Sorry for coming on a little strong. We've had a bunch of trespassers in the area and I'm trying to keep the property safe from vandals."

"That's so wise," I told him with a smile. I then pointed to a nearby beam. "Solid construction, though."

He nodded eagerly. "Yeah, I only hire the best contractors."

I walked a little away from him, pretending to inspect the area. "What's the projected completion date?"

"We're looking at next spring," he said. "Just in time for the tourist season and with it all those potential Hampton vacation home buyers."

I pointed a finger gun at him. "Smart."

"How much were you looking for to complete the project?" Gilley asked, taking out his phone as if he were about to crunch some numbers.

Without blinking Luke said, "We're looking at an initial investment of twenty million for a fifteen percent stake."

Gilley scoffed, and I could tell it was simply a reaction to that absolutely absurd offer, and not an intentional effort to laugh off the terms.

I quickly said, "My partner and I would need twenty-five to thirty percent for a twenty-million-dollar offer—assuming you've sold at least twenty-percent of these already?"

"We have," Luke said and I couldn't tell if that was a lie or not, but I suspected it was. "I'd have to talk it over with the other investors—I mean investor. Our third partner recently . . . left the project."

I nodded. "Of course, of course," I said, knowing there was no way that, if Luke had a partner in this scheme, he or she would be willing to give up so much equity simply to finish the project unless their bank accounts were completely empty and they owed people—which was highly possible.

Stepping back up to him I offered him my card. "Call me when you've discussed it with your partner and we'll get to work on the details."

"Terrific," he said, taking my card and holding it tight like it was liquid gold.

"Follow us out to the car, Luke, so that we can give you your flowers," I told him.

"Oh, uh, sure," he said.

On the way to the car I said, "And we really are so sorry about the loss of your aunt and uncle."

"Thanks," he replied, much more conciliatory than before. "Yeah, it's a real tragedy."

"It must've been such a shock when Scarlet left so much of her estate to her ex-husband," Gilley said boldly.

Luke's guard was down, which was exactly what we'd wanted, so I wasn't surprised when he seemed to answer us honestly. "Those two were always playing games with each other. Once Aunt Scarlet divorced Uncle Bill, she had all the power because she controlled the alimony checks. If he stepped out of line, she'd stop sending the checks and force him to go back to court which would cost him even more money and he hated her for that.

"When she found out that he was taking up with my mom, she tried to get him to stop seeing her, but I guess Uncle Bill had had enough by then and he told her he wasn't going to let her dictate his life anymore."

I paused once we reached the car. "How do you know all of that?" I asked.

Luke's expression turned embarrassed. "I was there when Aunt Scarlet confronted him about Mom."

"You were?" Gilley and I both said together.

Luke nodded. "I was at his house when she showed up out of the blue. I don't know how she found out about Mom and Bill, but she was hopping mad about it."

"Can you blame her though?" Gilley asked.

Luke shrugged. "There was so much hate between those two that I didn't understand it. I mean, the stories he told us about living with Aunt Scarlet . . . they weren't pretty. Everyone thinks that it was Bill who was the bad guy, and I'm not saying that he was a saint or anything, but she was just as abusive to him over the years."

"Why would he share all of that with you?" I asked, curious about the intimate relationship Luke seemed to have with his ex-uncle.

He shrugged again. "We kept in touch after the divorce and it was Bill who helped me get Mom into rehab and also helped her stay sober once she got out. The two of them worked the program together and that's when they fell for each other. It was kind of nice to see them both happy, to be honest.

"And Bill and I were buds. He treated me like a son, and I appreciated that, because my own dad was a deadbeat."

"Was?" I asked.

Luke nodded. "Yeah, Dad died a decade ago. Liver cancer. It took him quick. I didn't really know him that well—he and Mom split when I was four, and he never made an effort with me over the years, so by the time he died, he was more a stranger than a dad. Bill filled that void, though. Even when I was young, he would take me on the golf course with him all the time during the summer. What can I say? We got along really well."

"Then you *are* sad about your uncle," I said, reaching into the car to bring out an arrangement of the sympathy flowers.

Luke took it from me and nodded while looking down at the ground. "I am. I guess I loved that old geezer. To be honest, I'm still in shock about it. And I'm worried about Mom too. There's no way she killed him."

Gilley cocked his head and said, "Do you think it's possible that your mom was framed?"

"Of course she was framed," he said flatly.

"By who?" I asked.

Luke shook his head. "If I had to guess, I'd say by my cousin Grayson."

I stole another one of those knowing quick glances at Gilley, who looked back wearing the same expression. "Would Grayson be capable of such a thing?" I asked, pretending to sound well and truly shocked.

Luke snorted. "Yeah. He'd be capable of that and a whole lot more if you get my meaning."

"I don't," I said.

"Let's just say he had no love for his dad or his mom. Grayson only has love for one thing, and that's gambling."

"Wow," Gilley said. "That's a lot to deal with in one family."

Luke ran a hand through his silver-tipped hair. "Growing up as part of the Rubi family was no picnic—trust me."

"We do," I told him, hoping to continue to ingratiate myself to him. But truth be told, I sort of *did* trust him. To a point. I mean, I certainly wasn't going to give him any money to invest in his disaster of a real estate deal, but I believed him when he'd spoken about how he and William got along well and liked each other.

Thinking we'd spent enough time picking his brain, I said, "Thank you for speaking to me about the condominium project, Luke. I look forward to hearing from you soon and we'll begin to work through the details."

He nodded and held up my card to me. "I'll be in touch soon."

With that, we set off and something told me we were getting closer and closer to discovering the true murderer.

Chapter 12

"Do you have Grayson's address?" I asked Gilley as we drove away from Luke's condo project.

"I do. But it's almost noon. Can we stop for lunch?"

"Of course!" I said. "Where would you like to eat?"

"I could really go for a burger, Cat."

I looked over at him with a slack jaw. "A burger? You? You who eats only rabbit food for lunch?"

Gil smiled sideways. "What can I say? Luke was a hottie. He got my home fires burning and when my home fires burn, Gilley needs some protein!"

I laughed. "You thought he was hot?"

"You didn't?"

I shrugged my shoulders while I thought about it. "I guess I see him through suspicious goggles. To me, everyone we talk to is a potential murderer."

"True, but I didn't get that vibe from him, Cat. I mean, he's the *only* one that talked about his mom and uncle with even a hint of affection. That says a lot."

"Agreed, but Gilley, he's *so* underwater on that condo complex. If he's looking for twenty million, he's out of money. That's probably even more than he needs to complete the project, which means he's not just out of money, he owes people."

"Yeah, like maybe that third partner he referenced. It's bad when the initial partners are jumping ship."

"See? So maybe he's a little less hot-looking to you now that you know he's a terrible businessperson."

"Oh, please, like I'd let a little thing like business acumen get in the way of a good time."

I laughed. "You are so bad!"

"Do you think it's a good sign?" he asked me after a long moment of silence.

"A good sign? What specifically are you referring to?"

"That all the time we were grilling Luke, I was imagining him dressed in a crisp black tux, ready to say 'I do.' "

"Whoa! Gilley, that escalated quickly! First you admit you're attracted and now you're fantasizing about marrying him?"

"Oh, like you didn't fantasize about marrying Shepherd the minute you two met."

"I didn't," I said firmly.

"Liar."

"Gilley, the man was insufferable back then! Don't you remember? Don't you remember how he *arrested* me? In *public*? And had me tossed in *jail* on suspicion of *murder*?"

Gilley waved his hand at me. "Oh, please. You still had the hots for him even from the words, 'You have the right to remain silent.' "

I laughed in spite of myself. The truth—if I'm being totally honest—is that I *did* have the hots for Shepherd from the very first time I opened the door to him. That feeling lessened a few degrees when he trotted me out of a packed restaurant with my wrists handcuffed behind my back—but, to Gilley's point, it was a bit of love at first sight with Shep.

Still, I wasn't going to admit that to Gilley. "Whatever," I said, waving my own hand back at him. "My point is that Luke could be real trouble, so I wouldn't take the risk. Even if he plays for your team."

"Oh, he plays," Gilley said knowingly.

"You sure?" I didn't exactly get that vibe from him, but what did I know?

"Positive. We know our kind, sistah."

I rolled my eyes, then pointed to the East Hampton Grill. "There?"

"Ooh!" Gilley said, clapping his hands. "Yes, please!"

We took our time eating lunch together, and spoke more about our trip to Europe than about the case, but then an older couple walked by our table and I asked Gil, "Hey, have you heard from the DeLeons? They were gone by the time I got back from Shepherd's this morning and I want to make sure they're okay."

Gilley took out his phone and scrolled through

a few screens. "Carlos hasn't responded to my text. Should I call him?"

"Yes," I said, a tiny spark of worry igniting in my solar plexus.

Gilley hit a button, then put the phone to his ear. I waited for him to speak, but after several seconds he merely shook his head, then he waited another few seconds and said, "Hi, Carlos! It's Gilley. Cat and I want to make sure you and Mariana are okay. We met with Siobhan and her attorney very early this morning, and we're concerned that maybe she's not the murderer the police think she is. Because of that, we think it'd be best if you two came back to Chez Kitty, so . . . yeah, give me a call when you get this message and I'll explain a little more, okay? Okay, bye."

He hung up the call and I smirked at him. "Isn't it funny how we ask questions that can't be answered on someone's voice mail?"

"What do you mean?"

"You said to give you a call and you'd explain, 'okay?' "

Gilley smiled. "I know, that's weird, right? I get uncomfortable with the silence. I think I say that to make myself feel better about talking into the void. Speaking to no one directly is weird."

"For sure. You ready to hit the road?"

"I am!" Gil said.

We paid the tab and headed out. Once we were on our way, Gilley again played the role of navigator, guiding us over to Grayson's place. His home was a bit unexpected, actually. The architecture was modern and sleek with teal-blue stucco walls, both black and brown trim, and a bright orange door, which took the interesting structure to a whole other level approaching actual art.

"Cool," Gilley said when he got out of the car to stare up at the house.

"It is, isn't it?" I agreed, then motioned back to the car. "Don't forget the flowers."

"Oh, right," Gil said, and quickly got out one of the arrangements from the back seat.

We'd begun to approach the house when the front door opened and out stepped a middle-aged bald man, wearing an ill-fitting pair of khaki pants and a blue polo shirt—who definitely wasn't Grayson McMillen. "Can I help you?" he said when he saw us walking toward him.

"Hi," I said with a wave. "We're looking for Grayson."

The man scowled. "You're not the only one."

"Oh?" Gilley asked, pointing to the door. "He's not inside?"

"No," the guy said. "But I wish he were. The sink has been backed up for three days and I keep calling to tell him he needs to fix it or I'll notify Airbnb about it and it'll hurt his ranking."

"Hold on," I said. "You're *renting* his house?"

"Yeah," he said. "Why?"

I looked at Gilley and he shook his head and shrugged. He hadn't known that, either.

"For how long?" I asked the man.

The man narrowed his eyes suspiciously. "Why is that any of your business, lady?"

I held up my hands in apology and said, "I'm so sorry. I don't mean to be confrontational, it's just . . . well, a family member has died unexpectedly, and we're trying to find Grayson to tell him in person."

"Oh," the man said, his gaze roving to the flowers in Gilley's hands. He immediately dropped the suspicious attitude. "Sorry. I didn't know. And I also don't know where to find Grayson. The last time I saw him was on the first when he came to collect my check."

"Okay," I told him. "Has he mentioned at all where he might be living?"

"Nope," he said before pointing to his car. "And I'm sorry but I have to get back to work."

"Ah," I said. "Sorry. I'm boxing you in. Thank you for your time, sir."

When we got back to the car I backed us out of the driveway and began to make my way down the road, allowing the tenant from Grayson's house to pass me before I pulled over and turned to Gilley. "If Grayson's renting out his house, where the heck is he living?"

Gilley pulled out his phone and began to tap at it. "I'll see what I can find on public records. If he bothered to change his mailing address so all his mail could be forwarded, we might be able to narrow it down."

I waited while Gilley poked at his phone. My gaze drifted back toward Grayson's house and I thought about all the generosity Scarlet had granted to her family over the years, and how almost all of them appeared to be absolute financial disasters, unable to make a decent living, invest their money, or contribute meaningfully to society. They'd been given freedom from financial worry and they'd squandered it.

And then I felt a pang of guilt and my gaze traveled back to Gilley. While it was true that Gilley worked for me, he didn't make a huge salary, and even there he was grossly overpaid. He didn't contribute a dime of rent for Chez Kitty—not that he hadn't tried, but I'd refused to take a penny from him, preferring to spoil him and see to most of his financial needs.

Whatever money he had in the bank was money that Michel had likely made and Gilley wasn't going to get alimony. No, they'd split the finances fifty-fifty and at most I figured Gilley had two hundred thousand in savings. That wasn't a lot for a forty-year-old man to have saved for retirement. I suddenly wondered if I was actually doing Gilley the favor I thought I was, and I realized, in my effort to help Gilley get ahead, I was actually holding him back.

"Gil," I said, wondering how to even broach the topic.

"Nuts," he said, staring at his phone. "The only other address for Grayson listed is Scarlet's address."

Abandoning the topic of financial responsibility with Gilley, I said, "If he's listed his mother's home as his mailing address, then his mail must still be delivered there, right?"

"Probably," Gilley said.

I tapped my lip. "I have an idea."

Gilley shimmied in his seat. "Do tell."

"Do you have Grayson's cell number?"

"No, but I can get it in about three seconds."

"Perfect. Let's call him and if he picks up or he doesn't we still offer him the same message."

Gilley made a rolling motion with his hand. "Which is?"

"We tell him that we're calling about his mother's life insurance policy. As his father is now deceased, the policy reverts to him and his sister, we've sent him some paperwork in the mail to fill out and sign, and if after doing that he'd like to expedite a check, he'll simply need to scan the completed forms and email them to us and we'll get a check out in the next forty-eight hours."

Gilley grinned at me. "You are a clever girl. No addicted gambler would waste time getting his hands on free money. He'll beeline it over to his mom's house to retrieve the forms and we can ambush him then, right?"

I saluted. "That's the plan, Stan."

"It's freaking brilliant, Cat!" Gilley gushed.

And seeing the excitement in his eyes and the way he lit up whenever he was jazzed about one of my ideas caused that little pang of guilt to rise up and hit me like a gut punch.

"Let's get over to Scarlet's and find someplace out of view where we can scope out her mailbox," I said.

Gilley pointed to the road ahead. "Tallyho, madame!"

We sat in the car for nearly an hour after placing the call to Grayson. "I don't think he's gonna show," Gilley said, lying his head back against the headrest and giving in to a big yawn.

"Who knows where he'll be coming from," I said. "He might've been in Atlantic City for all we know and it'll be hours before he can get here."

But then something curious happened. I noticed movement out of the corner of my eye and turned to see Scarlet's garage door lift up. From inside, out strolled none other than Grayson McMillen, wearing a thick hooded sweatshirt and wrinkled jeans.

Behind him in the garage was a ladder extending down from the attic and I slapped Gilley's arm in surprise and excitement.

"Ow!" he complained.

"Sorry!" I told him, quickly pointing to where Grayson was walking down the driveway. "Look, Gilley!"

Gil sat forward. "Ohmigod, how did he get past us?"

"He didn't," I said. "He came *from* the garage and I'd bet dollars to doughnuts he came down from the attic!"

"What?" Gil said, squinting toward Scarlet's garage.

"See that?" I said, pointing again. "The ladder is down. We went through the garage a couple of times, Gilley. Do you ever remember the ladder being down like that?"

"No," he said staring at it, before turning to me and adding, "Do you think he's been *living* there?"

I was almost too excited to speak. Grayson had reached the mailbox by now and he pulled the little door open to look inside. Even from here I could see that the mailbox was stuffed full. It probably hadn't been checked in a week.

"I think it's definitely possible he's been squatting in Scarlet's attic," I told Gilley. "And if he's been secretly living there, then he could've easily bypassed the alarm system and been in the house all alone with Scarlet."

"Ohmigod!" Gilley said as we both watched Grayson fish around in the mailbox, pulling out leaflets and junk mail on a quest to find paperwork that was never sent to him.

We watched in silence as Grayson emptied the mailbox of its contents and he continued to sort through all the flyers, junk mail, and regular mail. As he disqualified each piece, he chucked it to the ground, not caring one whit if he was breaking the no-littering law.

"Well, that's just uncalled for," Gilley said as Grayson continued to throw away the mail.

"He's obviously desperate," I said. "Do you see that his hands are shaking?"

"I do. That boy needs some *help*!"

"He needs to be arrested," I replied. "Gilley, I think we've found our number one murder suspect."

"Agreed. And as such I don't think we should attempt to interview him. It'd be obvious that we know his secret and we don't need to put ourselves in danger like that."

I nodded vigorously. "We should definitely steer clear of him."

Grayson finished sorting through the mail, then stood there empty-handed for a moment and uttered some expletives that we couldn't hear, but we could definitely read his lips. And then he pulled his phone out of his back pocket, scrolled for a bit, and placed a call.

"Wonder who he's calling?" Gil asked.

In the next second my phone began to ring.

Gil and I looked at each other with wide eyes. "What do I do?"

Gilley waved frantically at me. "Answer it! It'll go to your voice mail if you don't and he'll know it's us!"

I answered the call on its last ring. "Riverside Insurance, Peggy speaking," I said. "How may I help you?"

"Yeah," Grayson said. "This is Grayson McMillen. I got a message from you about some paperwork and I just checked my mailbox and it's not here."

I had confirmed Scarlet's address when I'd left Grayson the message, so that we could make sure to lure him here off his property without a chance to run back into his house and shut us out.

"Oh, Mr. McMillen, I'm so sorry to hear that. We sent it certified mail. Did you perhaps miss your postman?"

Grayson looked up and down the street, using his free hand to swipe his long bangs out of his eyes. "Yeah, probably."

"Well, he should bring it to you on his next round."

"Can't you just email it to me? I mean, don't you guys have a DocuSign system set up for stuff like this?"

That caught me off guard and I had to think fast. "Of course we do, sir, we just didn't have your email address on file and were only able to secure your mailing address from a search on the web."

"Oh, well it's grayday-one-four-seven-two at me dot com."

"Right," I said. "Got it. I'll get those forms right out to you."

"Thanks," he said. "And how soon can I get the money? I mean, can you wire it to me?"

"Of course we can," I said. "That process takes three business days, however it still might be faster than mailing you a check. To wire you the funds, we'll just need your account number and the routing number to your bank. Include that in the email reply back to me, all right?

"Cool," he said. "Thanks."

And with that he hung up.

I wiped my brow as I set the phone down. I'd been so nervous while I was on the call with him, and Gilley mopped at his brow too. "That was close," he said.

Grayson was already walking back down the driveway and we waited while he headed into the garage and punched the button to lower the door. Just before it closed, we could see his feet walk over to the ladder and begin their ascent up into the attic.

"He *is* living there!" I said.

Gilley nodded excitedly. "We need to tell someone."

"Marcus first. Shepherd second," I said.

"And I need to send out some fake insurance forms," Gilley said. "Otherwise, Grayson is going to be calling your phone nonstop."

"Sorry," I told him. "I didn't mean for you to have to do extra work. It seemed like a good idea at the time."

"It was a great idea, Cat, don't worry. It'll take

me a half hour at most, and you can call Marcus and Shepherd while I take care of that loose end."

"Good," I said. "Home then?"

Gilley pointed out the windshield. "Yeah, Peggy. Let's get home."

I smiled and we set off.

An hour later Gilley had finished creating a fictitious website for our Riverside Insurance company, and he'd sent Grayson a bunch of legal-looking forms to fill out. "That was fun!" he said when he'd finished.

I grinned at him just as a call from Marcus came through to my cell. "Catherine," he said in that smooth baritone of his. "Sorry I couldn't pick up earlier. We were in court."

"Oh?"

"Yes. Siobhan made bail."

"She did?" I said, completely surprised.

"She did," Marcus confirmed. "It was a high bond, but she put her house up as collateral and was able to convince a bail bondsman that she's not a flight risk."

"I guess that's good news," I said, not really sure how I felt about the fact that Siobhan was out amongst the masses again. I mean, I was somewhat convinced Grayson murdered both his parents, but of all the circumstantial evidence I'd seen, Siobhan was still probably higher on the suspect list.

"What do you have for me?" Marcus asked.

"A lot," I said. I'd spent the time waiting for Marcus's return phone call to jot myself several pages of notes about each suspect. Slowly and methodically, I went through each page for Marcus, so that he could decide for himself how best to use what we'd discovered to defend his client.

When I got to the part about Grayson living in Scarlet's attic, Marcus interrupted me for the first time. "He's *what*?"

"He's living in Scarlet's attic," I told him. "He's rented out his house on Airbnb, and somehow he's managed to figure out the alarm code to the garage and let himself in and out. We saw him climb the ladder to the attic once he'd checked the mailbox."

"That's good, Catherine," Marcus said, practically purring with victory. "That's very, very good."

"I have to call Shepherd and tell him about everything we learned today too, Marcus."

"Of course," he said, and I could practically hear the smirk in his voice. "Are you two going to keep investigating?"

"Do you think we need to?"

"I'll take everything you and Gilley can dig up. It'll only strengthen our defense."

I tugged on a lock of my hair. I have to admit that I was feeling a tiny bit uneasy helping Siobhan's case. I couldn't decide if I was doing a good thing or a bad thing by possibly allowing a killer to avoid justice.

"Marcus?"

"Yes."

"Do you think Siobhan is guilty?"

He was quiet for a moment before he said, "That's a question I never ponder when it comes to defending my clients, Catherine."

"Why not?"

"I don't want my opinion to color my effort to give the strongest defense possible. Everyone deserves a vigorous defense, the guilty and the innocent, because sometimes there's simply no way to tell the difference."

"So how do you deal with the guilt when, in the course of discovery, it becomes clear that your client committed the crime?"

"You're feeling guilty?"

"Maybe," I said. "I don't know. I can't tell."

"Good," he said. "That's good."

"Why is that good?"

"It means you're still open to Siobhan's innocence, and you've already seen and heard enough to entertain reasonable doubt. You're like my test case for the jury, and if she is in fact guilty, trust me, the jury will see it. Even with my mad lawyer skills."

He chuckled as he said that last part and I was able to laugh a little too. "Thanks, Marcus," I told him. "We'll keep working the case for the next few days until we leave for Europe."

"Excellent. Have a good night," he said.

I glanced out the kitchen window, realizing that the sun was starting to set. "Good night," I replied, and disconnected the call.

I then immediately called Shepherd, who answered on the first ring. "Hey, beautiful," he said in greeting.

I blushed. "Hi there, love."

"What's up?"

"Gilley and I have been at it all day, and we have much to share."

"Shoot," he said.

"Actually, would you like to come over for dinner?"

"As a matter of fact, I would. Should I head your way now?"

"Yes, please."

"See you in twenty," he said.

After I hung up with Shepherd I turned to Gilley. "What can you whip up for dinner in twenty minutes?"

Gilley dropped his chin and leveled a look at me. Then he said, "Well, I suppose I could rustle up some carryout."

I scrunched up my face. "Really? There aren't any leftovers of that amazing pesto dish you made last night?"

"The dish you never came home for?"

"Yeah. That one."

"Nope. Mariana, Carlos, and I demolished it, and later on, I had your portion as a midnight snack."

"Okay," I said. I'd been hoping to greet Shepherd with a homemade meal.

"He'll be happy with pizza and beer," Gilley said, reading my mind.

"Do we have beer?"

"Sebastian," Gil said.

"Yes, Master Gilley?"

"Do we have any stout in the fridge?"

I made another face at him and waved toward the refrigerator. He couldn't just get up and take a look?

"Yes, Master Gilley. There are four bottles left from the six that were delivered two weeks ago."

"I love it that Sebastian is connected to the fridge!" Gilley squeaked. "He can scan its contents and tell us exactly what's in there at a moment's notice."

"Okay, so now all we need is the pizza."

"Shall I be ordering that for you?" Sebastian said.

"Yes, please," Gilley and I both sang.

"If Master Shepherd is to attend, shall I order his favorite? Or yours, Lady Catherine."

"Both," I told him. I liked pineapple on my pizza and Shepherd thought it an abomination.

"Consider it done," Sebastian said.

Shepherd arrived before the pizza, and seemed happy about our plans for pizza and beer. Or pizza and wine for Gil and me.

We chatted about Shepherd's home renovation project, and I urged him to share photos of that gorgeous fireplace and countertop with Gilley, which he did. I stood back and watched Shep scroll through the photos on his phone for Gil, and the pride for a job well done was so evident on his face. I deeply regretted trying to butt in and take over by hiring a contractor for the job, and made myself a solemn vow not to do that again.

When our pizza arrived, we took the pies and drinks over to Gilley's, as Chez Kitty had an actual kitchen table and chairs, making it far more intimate and cozier than my kitchen island with everyone seated in a row.

After getting settled at the table, Shepherd asked, "How did the amateur sleuthing go today?"

I offered a plate of pizza to Gilley and said, "It went very, very well. We discovered some things that might even make *you* rethink Siobhan's guilt."

Shepherd chewed the bite of his pizza, then said, "This I gotta hear."

I did the same for Shep as I had done for Marcus, going through my notes methodically, revealing one dirty family secret after another. When I got to the part about Grayson living in Scarlet's attic, Shep actually leaned forward and said, "He's what now?"

"Living in the attic," I said.

"You're sure?"

"Positive."

Shepherd wiped his mouth and pulled out his phone. Placing a call he said, "Hey, Bosco. I've got a possible trespass at the scene of the Rubi murder. Can you get Frank or one of the other unis to go check it out? The intruder was the victim's son, but as far as I know, he's not allowed on the premises. Have Bosco or the uni check the attic, that's where he might be hiding and he's accessing that through the garage. We should still have the garage code on file from when we processed the scene." Shepherd paused, then said, "Great. Call me when you get this guy in cuffs, okay?"

Shepherd hung up the phone and smiled at me. "Thanks for the tip," he said.

"Are you going to interrogate him about McMillen's murder? And his mother's? If he was in the attic the night she was murdered, he could've killed her and gotten away with it. I mean, it explains how he bypassed her alarm code, right?"

"I'm going to talk to him," Shepherd said vaguely.

When I stared pointedly at him, he said, "Hey, come on. Let me do my job, Cat. I'll shake the tree and see what falls out."

"We're worried that you won't have an open mind," Gilley said.

Shepherd held his palms up. "I have an open mind, Gilley. I follow the evidence, and until I have more convincing evidence regarding either murder, then I'm going to stick with the most likely suspect, and that's Siobhan Forsythe."

"You have evidence that she murdered Scarlet?" I asked.

"Not yet," Shepherd said. "But I like her for it. Scarlet wanted to break up her engagement to McMillen, and she'd just cut her off financially. That's a hell of a motive if you ask me.

"Besides, it doesn't really matter if we can't pin her for Scarlet's murder. We're building a solid case against her for McMillen's murder."

I squinted at Shepherd. There was something in his eyes . . . something that troubled him. I leaned in and asked, "What aren't you telling us?"

Shepherd lifted another slice of pizza onto his plate, clearly avoiding my gaze. "Nothing," he said.

I cocked an eyebrow at him and lifted his chin so that he could see I wasn't buying it.

He sighed. "The ME has had several calls about McMillen's death certificate."

I looked at Gilley and he seemed just as confused by that statement as I was. "Why does that matter?" he asked Shepherd.

"It normally wouldn't, except that the person who keeps calling about it is Luke Forsythe."

"Chester the Investor?" Gilley said.

It was now Shepherd's turn to appear confused. "Who's Chester?"

I waved my hand impatiently. "Gilley's nickname for Luke, because he's invested in this failed condo complex."

"Ah," Shepherd said. "Got it."

"Why would that concern you?" I asked.

Shepherd took a big bite of his pizza and chewed aggravatingly slowly before answering me. "It's less of a concern and more of a question."

I rolled my eyes. "Would you please stop stalling and just tell us?"

Shepherd wiped his mouth and set his napkin back in his lap. "The only reason I can think of to request a death cert so soon after McMillen died is to send it in to file an insurance claim."

"An insurance claim," I repeated, still not quite following. "You mean, a *life* insurance claim?"

He pointed at me. "That's the one."

"But how could Luke claim a life insurance payout for McMillen. They weren't even related."

"Technically, they were," Gilley reminded me. "I'm not sure on the law, but I bet Luke's lawyer would argue that he became McMillen's stepson the same day the old guy was murdered."

I scratched my head. This was getting tangled. "Wait, so Luke wanted to file a claim on Scarlet's insurance payout? The one that would've gone to McMillen if it could be proven that Scarlet died before midnight?"

"Maybe," Shepherd said. "But he's got to know it's a long shot, and it doesn't really explain the sense of urgency he's shown the ME about wanting the death cert."

"Could Luke have taken out a separate insurance policy on McMillen?"

Shepherd nodded. "That's what I'm thinking."

"Then he knew McMillen was going to die?" I said.

"That's what I'm thinking," Shepherd repeated. "And I don't like that thought."

I glanced at Gilley and he was just as wide-eyed as I was. "Wow," he said. "This case gets weirder and creepier by the second."

Shepherd's phone rang and he picked it up to look at the caller ID. Holding up his index finger to us he answered the phone with, "Bosco! Buddy, tell me you got this guy in the back of a squad car—"

Shepherd's voice cut off as he listened intently, his expression turning from eager expectance to super serious in a flash. "What's their status?" he asked after a long moment. "Got it. I'm on my way."

Shepherd pocketed his phone and stood up. We got up with him. "What's happened?" I asked.

"It's the DeLeons," he whispered, reaching out to grab my hand.

I gasped and put my free hand to my mouth. "No!" I cried as tears immediately stung my eyes. "Oh, God. Please, don't say it!"

"Hey, hey," he said gently. "Cat, they're alive. At least for the moment."

"What does that mean?" Gilley demanded, just as rattled and upset as I was.

"Someone tried to blow them up tonight," Shepherd said.

The three of us stood there for a good ten seconds, two of us stunned into silence, the third probably thinking through the implications of what he'd just told us.

At last, Gilley said, "You're going to have to be more specific, Detective."

Shepherd motioned toward the door, never letting go of my hand. "Come on. I'll explain what I know on the way."

Chapter 13

"They were both found passed out on their front lawn," Shepherd explained on the drive to the DeLeons' home. "Someone had cut the central line from the furnace and filled the house with gas. The DeLeons were overcome by the fumes and barely got out of the house before it blew up."

"Ohmigod!" I gasped. "Their house *actually* blew up?"

Shepherd nodded. "I don't know how bad it is, but fire trucks were on scene, waiting for the gas company to turn off the gas to that street."

"How far away are we from their house?" I asked.

"It's after rush hour, so twenty minutes or so."

"Can you turn on a siren or something?" Gilley asked from the back seat.

Shepherd eyed him in the rearview. "No, Gilley. I can't." Shep's tone was clipped and curt.

"What good is being a big bad detective if you can't put a strobe light on top of your car to run all the red lights with?" Gilley pouted.

Shepherd sighed. "How about we just go the rest of the way in silence, eh?"

I put a hand on Shepherd's arm. I could feel the tension radiating through him. "Cut him some slack, Shep," I said softly. "We're all very worried about the DeLeons."

"I get it," he replied, then he glanced at Gilley in the rearview again. "Sorry, bud."

"It's okay," Gil said. "Just get us there as fast as you can, okay?"

"Doing my best, my friend."

We finally turned onto the street where the DeLeons lived, and I knew that because of the orange glow at the end of the block coming from the smoldering remains of their home. Shepherd had to flash his badge to get us through two levels of cops and firemen, set out to protect the area from lookie-loos. He managed to pull over at the curb about four houses down, and I could see that paramedics were on the scene, tending to someone shrouded in a thick blanket wearing an oxygen mask. "There!" Gilley said, extending his arm across my face to point out the windshield. "That's Carlos!"

We hurried out of the car and quickly walked directly over to the open bay of the ambulance. Carlos was struggling to breathe even with the mask, and paramedics were talking to him and taking his vitals.

As we stepped forward, I let Shepherd take the lead, grabbing Gilley's arm to hold him back. Shepherd eased over to one of the medics and flashed his badge. The pair spoke softly and it was around then that Carlos seemed to see us. He pulled his mask down and said, "Miss Catherine! Mr. Gilley!" Immediately after speaking to us, the poor man devolved into a fit of coughing and wheezy breathing and I bit my lip. The last thing I wanted to do was cause him any more physical discomfort, so I held up my hand to show him I didn't want him to speak.

"Carlos," I said. "I'm so glad to see you're alive. We don't want to get in the way, but we did want to rush over to see if there's anything we can do for you."

Carlos began to pull down his mask but I shook my head vigorously. "Don't speak," I told him. "Let us talk to these people and assess what we can do, okay?"

He nodded and pointed behind him. *Mariana,* he mouthed.

I leaned out around the ambulance to see another one also with its bay doors open and a disheveled, soot-stained, but seemingly okay Mariana sat, taking whiffs of oxygen every now and again.

There was only one paramedic attending to her, so I held up a finger to Carlos and said, "I'll be right back. I'm going to check on her for you."

He pressed his palms together to form a thank-you and I slipped away around the vehicle and over to her. Gilley followed close behind.

"Oh!" she cried when she saw us. "You came!"

I hurried to her side and clasped her hand in

mine. "The moment we heard," I said. The emotion of knowing she and her husband had come so close to death caught up with me and my eyes welled while I stood there, looking her over.

She seemed in better shape than her husband, although there was a patch of hair that was singed right off, and a few cuts on her face told me she might've been hit with flying debris from the explosion.

"Have you seen Carlos?" she asked, almost frantically.

Gilley pointed to the ambulance behind us. "He's okay," he assured her. "He's sucking down some oxygen, but otherwise he looks okay."

It was Mariana's turn to well up. "I don't know what I'd do if something happened to him," she said. "He's my whole world."

"We understand," I said, cradling her hand. "What can we do for you, Mariana?"

She shook her head. "I don't know, Miss Catherine." Sadly she glanced at the remnants of her smoldering house. "Everything we owned was in there."

As she said that, Mariana burst into tears, and Gilley stepped forward, gently nudging me aside to wrap her in his arms and comfort her. "There, there, sugar," he cooed. "Let it all out. I got you."

I patted him on the back and whispered, "I'm going to find Shepherd. You stay with her. If Carlos needs to go to the hospital, then she's coming home with us. If he doesn't need to go to the hospital, then they're *both* coming home with us."

"Got it," he whispered in reply.

I retraced my steps and found Carlos being

placed on a stretcher and loaded into the ambulance. "Are you taking him to the hospital?" I asked one of the medics.

"Yeah. His oxygen levels are hovering in the low nineties and he needs to be checked out by a doctor."

"Good," I said. Moving a little closer to Carlos, I said, "Hey, guy. We're going to bring Mariana home with us and take good care of her, so don't you worry. You just focus on getting better, okay?"

Carlos removed his mask and croaked out, "Thank you."

I smiled at him. He was such a sweet man.

I left him and went in search of Shepherd, finding him talking with another plain-clothed detective. He saw me out of the corner of his eye and waved me in, wrapping his arm around me as I got close.

With his free hand he reached into his jacket pocket and pulled out a business card. Handing it to the detective he said, "Thanks, Wyatt. Here's my card. Call me if you get any further updates from the fire marshal."

"Will do," the detective said, using Shepherd's card to salute him, then moved away from us.

"What's the deal?" I asked after he'd gone.

"Mariana and Carlos were in the house sorting through their belongings. Get this, they were worried—if the will is contested and they lose—that they'll be kicked out of their home, so they thought it best to start sorting and packing, just in case."

I put a hand on my heart. "Oh my God, these are just the *sweetest* people!"

"Agreed. Anyway, Mariana told Navarro—that's

the detective I was just talking to—she told him that she and Carlos were in the basement and they started hearing a weird, muffled pounding outside their house. She says the far wall where the gas line is was vibrating a little. She and Carlos didn't know what to make of it, so they went upstairs and looked out the windows, but didn't see anything, so they went back downstairs to continue their project.

"She told Navarro that about fifteen minutes later, Carlos said he smelled gas and went racing upstairs. The house had filled up pretty good by then, and he yelled downstairs for Mariana to get out. She exited out the basement door into the garage, and he ran for the front door. He got out first and the house blew. Thinking his wife was still inside, he tried to go back in to save her. She saw him go into the front door and had to scream her head off to get him to come out again. He inhaled a lot of smoke in just the minute or two he tried to look for her."

"I don't know what he was thinking!" I said. "He could've been killed!"

"He was thinking it was well worth the risk to save the woman he loves. I'd do the same."

I looked up at him and cupped his cheek. "You would?"

He wrapped me in his arms and hugged me tight. "In a heartbeat."

We held each other for a moment, the smell of smoke clinging heavily in the air, and people all around shouting orders to each other, but inside Shepherd's hug, I felt safe and sound and whole.

"Hey, guys," Gilley said. I looked up from where

my head was resting against Shepherd's chest to see Gil standing awkwardly to one side. "I put Mariana in your car, Shep. She's cold and covered in soot and wants a shower and a comfortable bed. We should get her home."

I nodded. "Yes. Let's go." We started to head toward Shepherd's car, then I paused and pulled back on his hand. "She won't have any clothes," I said, nodding toward the car.

Gilley flashed his teeth in a "yikes" expression. "You're right. Nothing in your closet is likely to fit her," he said. Mariana was a little taller than me and definitely bigger around the middle. All I had in my closet were petite sizes. "We could stop at a Target on the way home and get her a few things," I said.

"Not a problem," Shepherd said, and I smiled gratefully at him.

We all got settled into the car—Mariana and Shepherd up front and me and Gil in the back—and headed off. No one spoke much, but Mariana could be heard sniffling now and then. I wanted badly to hug her, and it did my heart good when I saw Shepherd reach over and take her hand to squeeze it in reassurance.

Once we got to Target I said, "Shep, would you mind driving Mariana and me to Chez Kitty so that I can get her some clean towels and heat up some tea and dinner for her while Gilley goes in and buys both her and Carlos some clothes and essentials."

"Ooh, a shopping spree," Gilley said, trying to sound upbeat for Mariana. "I like it." Tapping her on the shoulder he said, "What's your size, sugar?"

"I'm a size twelve," she said. "But please don't spend too much, Mr. Gilley. Just one pair of sweatpants and a sweatshirt and maybe the same for Carlos would be good."

"You got it, honey," Gil said, winking conspiratorially at me. I smiled at him and nodded. No *way* were either of us going to settle for one pair of sweats for these two.

I handed Gilley my credit card and he climbed out of the car. "I'll be back to pick you up in forty-five minutes to an hour," Shepherd called to him.

Gilley waved over his shoulder—he was already trotting into the store.

True to his word, Shep drove us to my home and dropped us off, then turned right around to go pick up Gilley and bring him back.

When we came through the door of Chez Kitty, Mariana looked toward the kitchen table where our dinner plates and half-eaten pizza were still littering the table. Instinctively she moved right toward the mess as if she were going to begin cleaning it up, and I stopped her by gently taking her by the arm and wheeling her around. "You are not on duty, Mariana. Especially not while you're a guest in my house. Now, let's get you to the shower. I'll find some clean towels and a robe for you, okay?"

"Thank you, Miss Catherine," she said and she wobbled on her feet a little, probably exhausted from the day's events.

While she headed to the bathroom, I hurried to the linen closet and found her some towels and a washcloth, then I dashed across the courtyard to Chez Cat and hurried up the stairs. My son Matt had gotten his growth spurt this past summer and he now stood nearly six feet tall and had filled out nicely in the shoulders. I'd bought him a new robe to wear, hoping he'd take it to boarding school, but it had hung on the back of his bathroom door since the day I'd purchased it. He'd never once used it and the tag was still on the lapel.

Tearing off the tag I took it back to Chez Kitty and discreetly slipped into the bathroom while Mariana showered, then gathered up her sooty clothing, laid the bathrobe on the counter, and hurried out before she even noticed I'd come in.

I then dumped all her clothes into the washer, added a little extra soap, and started the cycle. She'd have clean, dry clothes in about an hour and a half.

I moved on to tidy up the kitchen and did a thorough inspection of Gilley's pantry and refrigerator. Locating shallots, coconut milk, an orange, some chicken, and rice, I began a simple curry dish using a sweet curry spice Gilley kept in his spice rack.

By the time Mariana was out of the shower, ensconced in Matthew's robe, I was plating her dinner. "Come," I ordered. "Sit and eat. Gilley and Shepherd should be back any minute."

Mariana sat down and stared at the plate. I could tell she wasn't hungry and there was a haunted look in her eyes that I didn't like one bit. "Should we call the hospital and check on Carlos?" I asked.

A tear slid down her cheek. "Yes, please, Miss Catherine."

I found the number for the closest hospital to

the DeLeons' home—guessing that's where they'd taken Carlos—and was relieved to hear he'd been checked in. I handed the phone to Mariana so that she could get an update on his condition and the tense set to her shoulders relaxed a bit when she heard that he was stable, asleep, and likely would be released in the morning once his O_2 levels normalized.

Once she hung up, she tried a bite of my curry and smiled. "It's delicious," she said.

I poured her a glass of white wine and sat down next to her.

"Oh, I don't really drink, Miss Catherine," she said, eyeing the wine skeptically.

I pushed the glass toward her. "Try a sip, Mariana. If you don't like it I'll get you some water or some lemonade, but I think you could use a little something to take the edge off tonight."

She smiled shyly at me and lifted the glass to take the smallest sip, and her brows rose. "Oh," she said. "That's nice."

I nodded knowingly. "Good wine isn't something to be underestimated."

She took another longer sip and smiled again. "Thank you," she said softly. "You're so kind."

"The least we can do," I told her.

The front door opened and in came Gilley, completely loaded down with shopping bags. He was followed by Shepherd, who was also loaded down with perhaps even more bags.

I laughed as they entered. "Did you buy out the store?"

Gilley grinned triumphantly. "Not quite, but I only had forty-five minutes."

"Oh my goodness!" Mariana gasped. "Mr. Gilley, what have you done?"

"I've gotten you enough clothes for a month, Mariana," he said. Then he pointed to Shepherd's load. "And I did the same for Carlos."

"Oh, you shouldn't have!" she protested and she really did look upset, as if she was taking advantage of us or something.

I reached out for her hand and drew her attention to me. "Mariana," I said. "It's okay to accept a little kindness when you've given the world so much of it already."

She stared at me and her eyes welled with tears. "It's too much," she whispered.

"It's not," I assured her. "Now, finish your dinner and then sort through the bags for something to wear to bed." Looking up at Gilley I added, "You got her something to sleep in, right?"

Gilley set down the last of the bags, popped a hand on his hip, and said, "Gurl, please. What do I look like? An amateur?"

I laughed and was relieved to see Mariana smile too.

We then gathered around the table and spoke in gentle tones until she'd finished her dinner. She looked asleep on her feet so Gilley jumped up and grabbed a bag. Handing it to her he said, "Here, sugar. You should find something comfortable to wear to bed in there."

"Thank you, Mr. Gilley," she said, but then looked toward the bedroom and bit her lip. "I've never slept away from Carlos before."

I rubbed her shoulder, the poor dear.

Gilley said, "Would you like to sleep with Spooks tonight?"

Mariana's brow shot up. "May I?"

"Of course!" he said. "Spooks is a wonderful bedwarmer. And he'll make sure you're safe and secure tonight."

Mariana looked so relieved, and I wanted to hug Gilley for his quick thinking. "I'll just take him out for a quick walk and bring him back to you," he said.

"He's at Chez Cat, Gil," I said. "I left him snoozing by the door when I came back over here."

Gilley grabbed the leash and set off to find his pup. Mariana thanked me and Shepherd with a hug, then she trotted off toward the bedroom.

Shepherd took my hand and motioned toward the door. "Let's talk," he said.

We went across the courtyard and into the house, heading to the kitchen where I got him out a bottle of beer and I poured myself a glass of the same wine I'd given to Mariana.

"What're you thinking?" I asked him, seeing the troubled look on his face.

"I'm thinking that Siobhan makes bail and a few hours later the gas line to the DeLeons' house gets cut? That might be too much of a coincidence."

"Or," I said. "It could be that the real killer was never arrested."

"Speaking of which," Shepherd said, pulling out his phone and dialing a number. "Bosco," he said, holding the phone to his ear. "What's the status on that intruder from earlier?"

I watched him while he listened, trying to read

in his expression what had taken place. "Uh-huh," he said, flattening his lips into a thin line. "Okay, keep me posted." Hanging up the call he shook his head. "The uni didn't find your guy. He searched the attic and found a sleeping bag and a bunch of food wrappers and other garbage that suggests someone's been living there a couple of weeks, but there's no sign of Grayson McMillen on the premises."

"He must've seen your uni coming," I said.

Shepherd shrugged. "We'll keep tabs on the house and see if he shows up again, but right now he's not trespassing so there's nothing to arrest him for."

"Unless of course *he* was the one who cut the DeLeons' gas line."

"You mean to get them out of the way?"

"Yep. If they're dead before the estate is transferred over, it reverts back to next of kin. Every single member of Scarlet's immediate family could stake a claim. And as it is now, all of McMillen's inheritance is back in the pool."

"Yeah, I got that," he said. "So what's the endgame here then, do you think?"

"What do you mean?"

"Is this killer going to murder every person who stands to inherit something from Scarlet's estate?"

I shrugged. "I doubt it. I think the central targets were the estate holder herself, Scarlet, and the two largest inheritors of her extensive fortune, meaning the DeLeons. If Scarlet truly was worth a hundred million, split between all the members of the family, any one of them would still be looking at, what? Ten million dollars or more?"

"That's a lot of motive," Shepherd said.

"Not to mention the life insurance policy if that ever pays out. That's another five mill to Scarlet and McMillen's children, and Grayson is desperate for cash. I really think you should consider him a major suspect, Shep."

Shepherd reached out to circle his arms around my waist and pull me in close. Kissing me tenderly he said, "I promise you I'll follow the evidence in this case, babe. And if it leads away from Siobhan and toward someone else, I won't hesitate to follow that thread, okay?"

"Okay," I said. "That's all I'm asking."

He bounced his brow and said, "Is it *all* you're asking?"

I giggled. "Well, I *could* ask for a backrub if you're up for it. But I have to take a shower. I smell like smoke."

"Backrub in the shower it is!" he said with enthusiasm. I laughed again and he took my hand and led me upstairs.

The next morning Shepherd left early. He said he wanted to track down Grayson and have a chat with him about trespassing on his mother's property, and of course, ask about an alibi for the nights of his parents' murders.

I wished him luck and got a little more sleep before the smell of coffee and something delicious baking in the oven downstairs enticed me to get out of bed.

"Hi," I said, coming into my kitchen to find Gilley at the stove.

"Hey, shug," Gil said.

"Hello, Miss Catherine," Mariana said, and I jumped a little because I didn't know she was in the house. Turning my head, I saw that she was curled up on the couch with Spooks, who was using her lap for a pillow.

"How'd you sleep?" I asked her. She looked pale, exhausted, and sad, and my heart went out to her.

She shook her head. "I don't think I slept longer than fifteen minutes."

"Did Spooks keep you up?" Gilley asked, pouring me a cup of coffee and setting it on the kitchen island.

At the mention of his name, the pup's ears perked, but otherwise he didn't move from his comfy spot on the couch with Mariana. "No, no, Mr. Gilley," she said. "Your dog was so good. He didn't hog the bed at all. He just leaned against me all night, and it was nice. It almost felt like Carlos. . . ." Mariana's voice caught and she put a finger to her lips, trying to hold in a sob.

Spooks picked his head up and sniffed at her, then he licked her wrist and wagged his tail.

I made a mental note to myself to offer the pooch an extra dog biscuit later. He was such a good boy.

We held the silence in the room until Mariana was able to speak again. "It was almost like Carlos was right there next to me," she said at last.

"We'll have breakfast and then we'll go see him," Gilley told her.

Her expression lifted immediately. "Really?"

"Of course!" I said, taking a seat at the island. "He's going to be discharged today anyway, right? We can all head to the hospital and wait for them to release him."

Mariana shook her head, though, and her expression went back to worried. "I talked to the doctor this morning. He said Carlos's lungs aren't in good shape and he may have to stay another day."

"Oh, no," I said. "That's tough news. Still, Mariana, I'm sure he's in the best care. We'll go over to the hospital and visit for a bit, then we'll leave you there if you like and pick you up later so you can spend the day with your husband."

"Oh, Miss Catherine, I'd like that very much!"

"You got it," I said, adding a wink.

"Breakfast is served," Gilley announced, opening the door to the oven and pulling out a large cast-iron skillet.

"Frittata?"

"You know it," Gil said, swaying his hips over to the island to set the skillet on a bamboo cooling rack. "Come get it while it's hot so we can fuel up for the ride to the hospital."

The three of us walked into Carlos's hospital room and came up short. He was in bed, still on oxygen, and next to him was Carson, sitting in his chair, bent forward with a hand on Carlos's shoulder.

"Mr. Carson!" Mariana exclaimed when she saw him.

"Mariana!" he replied, just as enthused, and the pair hugged.

"It's so good to see you!" she said. "We missed you!"

"I've been missing you too!" he said.

"Hello, *mi vida*," Carlos croaked out.

Mariana let go of Carson and went to Carlos's side. She curled up on the bed next to him and cradled him in her arms so sweetly and so tenderly that—honestly?—it made my eyes well up!

"Is there pollen in here?" Gilley asked, turning away to wipe his eye.

I rubbed his shoulder while Carson looked on with a sweet smile.

"Carlos," I said as he gazed into his wife's face with such love that I didn't know if my heart could take it. "We just wanted to drop Mariana off to you for the day. We'll be back later to pick her up or the both of you if the doctor releases you, okay?"

He nodded but I could tell he'd likely only half heard me. I crooked my finger to the other two and we headed out of the room and into the hall.

"Carson," I said when we were out of earshot. "It's so good to see you're all right."

"Why?" he asked, his expression turning alarmed. "Is there a threat out there I don't know about?"

"Possibly," Gilley said to him. "Did you know that your cousin Grayson has been living in your aunt's attic?"

The color drained from Carson's face and he stared at Gilley with big wide eyes. "He's been living in the attic? For how long?"

"We think for quite a while," I said, remembering that the uniformed officer dispatched to Scarlet's to check out the attic found food wrappers and other garbage that made it appear that Gray–son had been there at least a few weeks.

Carson shook his head, clearly unnerved by the revelation. "Grayson isn't someone I'd like living in my attic," he said softly. "Or within ten miles of me."

I cocked my head curiously. "You two didn't get along?"

"Nobody gets along with Grayson. He's the pariah of the family. He's been to rehab four times for his gambling addictions, and burned through a *lot* of his mother's money. But, besides all that, he's cruel. Like sociopathic."

"Why do you say that?" Gilley asked.

Carson offered us a one-shoulder shrug. "About a year ago, Grayson did something that made me afraid for my life."

"What?" I asked, riveted by the turn the topic had taken.

"We were at the country club for my aunt's birthday. She'd rented out the ballroom and it was a pretty private affair—only about a hundred guests were invited and of course the whole family. I got stuck on a call with Scarlet's publicist, so I was one of the last people to arrive.

"Anyway, I got out of my van and handed the keys to the valet—there were only two working that night and the other one had to take care of Grayson's car, because he'd come in behind me. So, while they're off parking our cars, I had to wheel myself over to the ramp which was uphill and off to the side of the building."

"Uphill?" I said. "Who puts a wheelchair ramp uphill?"

"That place is so pretentious, they cringe whenever I show up in my chair. I think they did it on purpose to discourage other people with disabilities from coming to the club. It ruins the visual and all."

"Reason number eleventy why I never joined that establishment," I sneered. I hated the country club scene.

"So," Carson continued, "as I was trying to maneuver over to the wheelchair ramp, Grayson came up behind me and took my chair by the handles. He said he was going to help me up the stairs, because it would be faster. I told him to let go, that I didn't need or want his help, but he wouldn't let go and he was stronger than me. He kept tilting the chair forward to make me almost fall out so I couldn't fight him as he pushed me toward the stairs.

"He then whips me around and starts pulling me backward up the steps, and there were a lot of them, so each one was a jolt and I was barely able to stay in my seat. He finally gets us to the top, then spins me around again to face him and I couldn't help it. I yelled at him. He just stood there and smiled, the way a crocodile smiles at a zebra, and then when I stopped yelling, he said, 'You know what you are, Carson? You're ungrateful,' and that's when he kicked my chair and I went down the steps backward."

"Ohmigod!" Gilley gasped. "That's terrible!"

"Were you badly hurt?" I asked, reaching out to touch his arm. The poor man was obviously still traumatized by the incident.

"The chair stayed upright until the last step, and

then it tipped over backward. I got my hands up just in time, otherwise I probably would've broken my neck, but I hit the ground on my right side and fractured my hip. The problem was that I couldn't feel it, so, other than being banged up, I thought I was okay. I tried calling for help, but everybody was inside—including Grayson. He just left me there."

"What a terrible, despicable, awful, hateful man!" Gilley exclaimed.

I couldn't have agreed more. What kind of human would do that to a paraplegic?

"What happened after that?" I asked.

Carson shook his head. "I crawled over to my chair and right about then the first valet came back and helped me get into it. He's the one who said my hip was sticking out at a bad angle. Long story short, I ended up in the hospital and they had to do surgery on my hip, which was broken in two places."

"Did you report the assault to the police?" I asked, already guessing the answer.

Carson pressed his lips together and with no shortage of anger said, "Nope. The family talked me out of it."

"Why would they want to do that?" I asked. "I mean, he *did* assault you!"

"Aunt Scarlet was afraid of the bad publicity. She said it would cause a scandal, and she paid for a brand-new van for me as a thank-you for not reporting him. She also sent him right back to rehab and made him take anger management classes. After that, she wouldn't let him come near me if she wasn't in the room."

"I'm so sorry that happened to you," I told him. "What a dreadful experience."

Carson nodded. "So you can see why it freaks me out that he's been living in Aunt Scarlet's attic. If she were still alive and knew about it, she'd have him removed from the property like that!" Carson snapped his fingers for effect.

"Carson," I said. "We suspect Grayson might've had something to do with his mother's death. Do you think he'd be capable of something like that?"

Carson snorted derisively. "Yes," he said without further comment. And it was the way he so quickly agreed with me that sent a chill up my spine.

"Thank you for telling us that story," I said next. "Would you mind if I shared it with the detective assigned to your aunt's murder?"

"Feel free," he said. "And if he wants me to elaborate on any of those details, just tell him to call me."

"I will."

Gilley then said, "An officer was dispatched last night to arrest your cousin on the trespass charge and bring him in for questioning. The officer had no luck locating Grayson, so he's still out there. Lurking."

Carson gulped. "Yeah, got it, Gilley. Carlos told me a little bit about what happened to him and Mariana, and it really bothers me that someone seems to be targeting anyone who stands to gain a piece of the inheritance. Knowing that Grayson found a way into Scarlet's attic, I think I should stay away from her house until all of this is over."

"Good idea," I said. And then I thought of something else. "Say, Carson, how did you know to find Carlos here?"

"Siobhan called me," he said.

My brow rose and Gilley's did as well. "Oh?" I said. "How did *she* know?"

"Her lawyer told her."

"Ahhh," I said. "Yeah, Marcus probably would've heard about it right around the time Shepherd did." Marcus had ears all over the place, the better to assist him as a criminal defense attorney.

Reaching out to squeeze Carson's arm a final time I said, "We've got to be off, but I want to make sure you stay safe. Can we call you later to check on you?"

"Sure," he said, patting my hand. "I'd like that."

"Perfect," I said and we waved goodbye.

Chapter 14

When we drove out of the hospital parking lot I called Shepherd. "Hey!" he said when he answered the phone. "I was just about to call you."

"Can we meet?" I asked.

"What's wrong?"

"I have a disturbing story to tell you and I want to tell you in person."

"How disturbing?"

"It sheds more light on Grayson's character."

Shepherd grunted. "Yeah, okay. I just left the Southampton fire marshal's office."

"What'd he have to say?"

"I'll explain when we meet. Where are you?"

"Just leaving the hospital. We brought Mariana out here so that she could be with her husband for the day."

"He hasn't been discharged yet?"

"No. They might want to keep him one more day."

"Makes sense. Carlos isn't a young man anymore. It's better to be cautious with him."

"Agreed. Since we're not far from each other, do you want to grab coffee with me and Gilley someplace close?"

"Sounds like a plan. I've got to follow up with the Southampton PD later this morning but I have about an hour to kill and I've had a cup of joe at the Hampton Coffee shop. It's pretty good."

"Where's that?"

"It's just off the Southampton Bypass, near the BMW dealership."

"Oh, I think I know exactly where you're talking about. We'll meet you there."

We arrived at the coffee shop just five minutes later, beating Shepherd by thirty seconds. We all got coffee and settled into a booth together to exchange information.

Shepherd allowed us to go first, and Gilley and I—but mostly Gilley—repeated Carson's story about Grayson. Shepherd seemed angered by the story. "What a son of a bitch," he muttered. "Who would do that to a crippled person?"

"Grayson McMillen," I said flatly. "And if he'd do that to his crippled cousin, imagine what he'd do to his own mother if she cut him off permanently from the money train."

Shepherd pointed at me with a finger gun and made a clicking sound with his tongue. "Good point."

"What'd the fire marshal say?" Gilley asked.

"Well, it was definitely arson. The gas line leading into the house was punctured, and a hose was duct-taped to the line and fed in through a window. He found the melted plastic of the hose and thinks the window might've been broken when the hose was fed through it."

"Wouldn't the DeLeons have heard the sound of breaking glass?" I wondered.

Shepherd held his palms up. "You'd think, but they were in the basement and the window was at the opposite end of the house, near the front door, so maybe they didn't hear it."

I nodded. It was plausible that they didn't hear the breaking of glass when they were down in the basement.

"What about the thumping noises they heard, though?" I asked, remembering that detail.

Shepherd scratched his head. "That's a puzzler, Cat. I don't know what that was about, but, my guy at the SHPD—"

"Detective Navarro?" I asked, recalling the man's name from the night before.

Shepherd pointed at me again. "Good memory. Yeah, him, he said his tech pulled some large footprints from the area around that window. He says the arsonist wore at least a size twelve shoe and guesses they were steel-tipped working boots."

"Wow, that's a big dude," Gilley said.

I had no idea about men's shoe sizes. I had tiny feet—size sixes. Abby always joked about my shoes being toddler size. Of course, *she* wore a gigantic size ten, so those in glass houses . . .

"Yeah," Shepherd said. "And the CSI estimates that he was also around two hundred thirty to two hundred fifty pounds."

"A seriously big dude," Gilley said.

"Who in the family fits *that* bill?" I asked.

"No one I can figure," Shepherd said. "Which is why I'm wondering if maybe it was a contract hit."

"You mean someone hired to murder the DeLeons?"

Shepherd nodded. "I think that whichever one of the family members is responsible for murdering Scarlet and McMillen has had enough of getting their own hands dirty, and maybe wants to throw us off the scent by hiring out the next set of murders."

A chill went up my spine. "That . . . is seriously scary, Shep."

"It is. Which is why I want you and Gilley to take extra precautions while the DeLeons stay with you."

"We've got Sebastian and Spooks," Gilley said. "Do you think that's enough?"

He grimaced as he thought about it, then he eyed me and said, "I'm gonna be hanging out with you for the next couple of days, okay?"

"Of course," I said, the tension across my shoulders easing a little. "We'd love that, actually."

"We would," Gilley said. "Especially if you walk around shirtless."

I slapped his arm and he giggled. Shepherd grinned and flexed an arm muscle. "Always happy to put on a gun show, Gilley."

"And I am always appreciative!" Gil replied.

I shook my head, but I was giggling as well. "You two are terrible."

Gilley leaned in and gave me a kiss on the cheek. "And you love it."

Shepherd did the same on my other cheek and for a moment I was the middle layer in a kissing sandwich. "Stop!" I laughed, pushing them away.

Those two brats grinned at each other like they'd just got my goat.

After leaving the coffee shop, Gilley and I sat in the car, waved at Shepherd, and then tried to think of what to do next. "Should we interview any more of the family?" Gilley asked.

"I think—" I began, but was interrupted by my ringing telephone. "Well, look who it is," I said, holding it up for Gilley to see.

"Luke Forsythe," he said. "Innnnteresting."

I answered the call. "Hello, Luke, nice to hear from you."

"Catherine," he said, sounding relieved to have reached me. "Listen, I met with my co-investor and he'd actually like to meet with you. Do you have some free time this afternoon?"

"As a matter of fact, I do," I said. "When and where would you like to meet?"

"Mike would like it if you came to his place. He's right off the golf course."

My eyes widened and I stared out the windshield for a good ten seconds.

"Cat?" Gilley whispered.

I ignored him.

"Hello?" Luke said. "Catherine, are you there?"

"I'm here, Luke, sorry, I dropped my phone. Where did you say your partner is located?"

"His condo is right off the East Hampton Golf Club."

"Isn't that where your uncle lived?" I said, and I

turned my wide-eyed stare at Gilley, whose brow was good and furrowed.

"It is," Luke said softly. "Mike was his next-door neighbor. But how did you know that?"

"I . . . remember reading about it in the paper." It did me no good to admit how I knew exactly where McMillen lived.

"Ah, okay, I'll text you his address. We can meet in . . . about an hour if that's good for you?"

"That's perfect," I said in my most pleasant tone, while mouthing *Ohmigod!* to Gilley.

"What? What?" he whispered back anxiously.

"See you soon!" I told Luke, and clicked off the call. Turning to Gilley I said, "*Guess* who Luke's other investor is!"

Gilley shook his head. "I only caught about a quarter of that conversation."

"Mike Erling!"

"Mike Erling . . . Mike Erling . . ." Gil repeated.

"McMillen's neighbor! Gil, the guy who called the police and gave a witness statement naming Siobhan as the primary suspect!"

"Whoa," Gilley said. "And Luke is still friends with him? I mean, the guy turned in Luke's mom, right?"

"Technically, he only told Shepherd what he saw, and as a former police chief, I could see why he'd want to be truthful."

"Yeah, but still," Gilley said. "I mean . . ."

"Oh, I get it. This whole case just keeps getting more and more tangled. But I think Luke needs to keep on Erling's good side because he's in a massive amount of debt and it does no good to blame the guy who discovered his neighbor's dead body and saw his mom fleeing the scene."

"True," Gilley conceded. "But what does that mean for our case?"

I shook my head. "I have no idea. One minute I'm convinced Grayson McMillen did the deed, and the next we find out a really juicy tidbit that throws a little curveball into the mix."

"So are you really going to meet with him?"

"Of course! And you're coming with."

"Okay, but I gotta feed Spooks first."

"Good," I said, backing us out of the parking slot at the coffee shop. "It'll give me time to reach out to my broker and tell him he's going to be telling a big fat fib today."

"What's the big fat fib?"

"That I've got twenty million in liquidity to invest in a condominium project."

"*Don't* you have twenty million in liquidity?"

"No," I said. "Most of my money is in investments. And besides, there's no way my broker would allow me to liquidate so much money to invest in something as risky as a construction project. But I need him to lie to Erling because I'm positive he'll ask to speak to my financial guy to make sure I'm not full of baloney."

"Ah," Gil said. "The ruse continues."

Putting the car into drive I pointed at the windshield and the road beyond. "Tallyho!"

We pulled up to McMillen's condo and I asked Gil, "Which one is his neighbor in? The one on the right or the one on the left?" It had begun to rain and by the time we got to our destination, it was really coming down hard, making reading the addresses on the sides of the condo nearly impossible.

"I'm assuming it's that one," Gil said. "Isn't that the same silver F150 we saw at the construction site? I assumed it belonged to Luke."

I nodded. "Yeah, I think you're right. Okay, grab an umbrella from the side well of your door and let's see what Mr. Erling has to say."

Gilley and I got out of the car, huddled under our separate umbrellas, and hurried to the door. I rang the bell and bemoaned the fact that my new suede shoes were wet. I hadn't had a chance to waterproof them, so they were likely now ruined.

"Crap," I said. Gilley looked at me and I pointed to my shoes.

"You didn't waterproof them, did you?"

I sighed. "No."

Gilley shook his head and I knew what he was thinking. The shoes had been pricey, and here I was being irresponsible again. It irked me that he'd called me out on that.

The door opened as I was about to sneer at Gil, and I quickly changed my expression and faced forward. I found myself staring at a chest. Slowly my chin rose up, and up, and up to finally take in Mike Erling's complete form.

He stood just a little under the top of the doorway, which I knew was seven feet tall, so I was guessing he was maybe six-foot-six or six-foot-seven. And he was a tall man with a fair amount of flesh on that frame. No way was he the kind of person you messed with, and I made a mental note to watch myself.

"Wow," Gilley whispered, and I knew he was looking way up too. Gil and I are on the shorter side, so most people look tall to us, but this man. He was a whole other level.

"Catherine?" Erling said.

"Yes! Hello, Mike. This is Gilley Gillespie, my . . . partner."

"Come on in," Erling said, opening the door wide. "It's raining cats and dogs out there."

We came into his home and I took in the heavy use of brown and muddy yellow in the place. It definitely wasn't my style, but it evoked a sort of masculinity that suggested Mike didn't have a spouse, or he didn't have a spouse that had a say in the home's décor.

"Let's move into my den," Mike said.

We followed behind him to the rear of the condo, coming into another room that was a tiny bit brighter, painted a more muted brown, with a massive window at the far end that looked out onto the golf course. "How lovely," I said, making a sweeping motion with my hand.

"Thanks," Mike said.

"Hey!" a voice behind us said, and Gilley and I both jumped.

"Oh! Hello, Luke," I said with a hand over my heart.

"Sorry," he said. "I was in the loo when you guys pulled in. Didn't mean to scare you."

"It's all right," I told him. Gilley and I moved to

the distressed tan sofa and took a seat. "So! Tell me about this construction project," I said to them.

For the next hour—which I swear was one of the longest of my life—Mike and Luke went through their "big" plan to convince the EPA to allow them to rip out the swamp and put in a beach so that selling the condos would be a total breeze.

I listened and nodded along like I totally believed them, but in my mind, I wondered how two grown men could be so stupid. They'd be lucky to even get a meeting with someone from the EPA, let alone get the agency to agree to let them rip out a protected wetland.

At the end of their pitch, I smiled gamely and said, "You two have really thought this through!"

They eyed each other in that way that said they'd just won twenty million of my dollars. "We have," Luke said, beaming at me.

I nodded and an awkward silence followed. Luckily, Gilley—who miraculously hadn't fallen asleep during the pitch—was quick on his feet and said, "Luke mentioned that there was a third investor that pulled out of the deal. Could you please outline the reason for his exit?"

Luke and Mike exchanged another look. This one was less confident. This one said, *Uh-oh.*

"The truth is," Luke began, "he passed away unexpectedly."

"Oh my!" I said, putting on an act. I'd immediately guessed who the mysterious third investor was. "That's terrible! I'm so sorry!"

"Thank you," Luke said, making an effort to appear sad.

"Well, I hope you had an insurance policy on him," I said. "You know, to protect your investment should his family come looking for an inheritance."

For a third time, Luke and Erling exchanged a look—this one was hesitant—but finally Luke said, "We did."

"Oh, good," I said. "I'd hate to put my money into a project that could lose its investments over an estate case."

"We'll be collecting that insurance money soon," Luke said.

"Is it enough to cover his investment?" I prodded, hoping that these two were just naïve enough to think I was a sound businesswoman who'd invested in lots of projects like theirs.

Luke's lips pressed together and he unconsciously crossed his legs. "It is. Don't worry," he said.

So that's a lie, I thought, wondering how much the policy was actually for. Maybe it was enough to keep them from having to declare bankruptcy, but I doubted it was much more than something to buy them a few months of payments on the construction loan. They were simply too eager to get their hands on my money.

"Well, that's given me peace of mind, Luke. Thank you," I said. Getting to my feet I added, "You boys gave such a great pitch that I think I'm very interested. I'm assuming you'd like to speak with my financial advisor to confirm the funds are in hand?"

Mike nodded vigorously. "Yes, Catherine. That would be great."

I offered him my card and turned it over to display a handwritten note on the back. "That's him. He can be reached at that number. Call me after you've spoken with him and we'll have our attorneys draw up the papers, okay?"

Mike and Luke each got to their feet, practically falling all over themselves to shake my hand. With that, Gilley and I took our leave.

Once we were outside I looked up at the sky. The intense rainstorm had settled into a steady drizzle. "Good Lord, I'm sick of these cold wet days."

"It's supposed to rain all through tonight, but tomorrow it's gonna be clear, sunny, and sixty-five degrees."

"Good, we've had too many cold and cloudy days of late."

On the way to the car, I was purposely keeping the chatter light and about the weather because I assumed that Mike might have a window cracked to listen in on our conversation.

Once we were in the car, Gilley said, "Can I say what I'm thinking?"

"That Mike Erling has mighty big feet?"

"And that he probably wears a size twelve construction boot?"

I nodded. "My God, Gilley. Did we just find our murderer?"

"Maybe," he said. "I mean, it's super plausible that he murdered McMillen and framed Siobhan for it, coming up with a fake story about being on the golf course jogging when he heard the gun go off."

"And don't forget the guy's a retired cop," I said

as we sped away. I wanted to put some distance between the two men and us.

"Right," Gilley said, but then frowned. "Why is that important?"

"It's important for two reasons: one, Erling would know how to get away with murder—right? I mean, who better than a cop to come up with a foolproof plan like that?"

"Yeah," Gilley said, nodding his head. "Yeah, you're so right. What's the other reason?"

"Well, a cop would probably also know how to get inside a house without setting off an alarm. I mean, in his career he probably came across a burglar or two that'd pulled that off. Maybe he learned from the masters."

Gilley pointed at me. "Yes!" he said. "Yes, that is so true! What do we do now, though?"

"After we pick Mariana up from the hospital, we call Shep," I said. "I think he'll be very interested in Mike Erling's shoe size."

As it turned out, Shepherd was less enthused than I'd expected. "So he's tall. Cat, lots of people are tall. Hired hitmen can be tall," he said that evening when he came over for dinner.

"Okay, but what about the fact that Erling *literally* owns a construction site?"

"You mean the work boot angle?"

"Yes."

Shepherd ran a hand through his hair. "Listen," he said, "I know you're excited about what you've discovered, but I can't see a motive here."

"*What do you mean you can't see a motive here?*" I

yelled. I was getting angry and Gilley reached across the kitchen island to put a gentle hand on my arm.

"Shug," he said, and I immediately calmed down.

Still, I wanted to hear why Shepherd wouldn't take Erling as a suspect seriously. "His motive was to murder McMillen to collect the insurance policy he and Luke took out on him in order to stave off either bankruptcy or foreclosure on the construction site."

Shepherd took a bite of the chicken cordon bleu that Gilley had made and said, "Mmmm. Gil, this is outstanding."

"Stop trying to get him on your side!" I snapped.

Shepherd set down his fork and turned to face me. "Babe," he said. "I'm not trying to get anyone on my side. I'm not on the opposite side of you. I'm actually *on* your side. But I have to take into account that this guy wasn't just a cop who took an oath to protect and serve and did that for forty-plus years—he was also *chief of police* for the entire city of Dallas. The guy is a *big* deal. He's a legend, even, with a sterling reputation, and trust me, I've already looked into him."

"You have?" Gilley asked, still beaming over Shepherd's compliment.

"Yeah, Gil. I looked into him after I took his statement, because I always vet every witness that comes forward with information. That's what we do in an investigation. We investigate—everyone—so that we don't miss a detail that could be the difference between a criminal walking or seeing justice done."

"Or send the wrong woman to jail, right, Shep?" I said with a small sneer.

He sighed again and took my hand. "Cat," he said. "I'm still working this case, okay? In fact, I'm now working *three* cases. Scarlet's, McMillen's, and, even though it's not my jurisdiction, I'm also looking into the DeLeons' near brush with death. So cut me a little slack and let me see this whole thing through, okay?"

It was my turn to sigh. "He did it, Shep," I said softly. "Everything fits. At least for the McMillen murder and the attempted murder at the DeLeons'."

"Maybe it looks like it fits," he said. "But from my angle, it doesn't track. It's too out of character for this guy."

"Suddenly finding yourself financially ruined can do strange things to people," Gilley said.

I pointed to him but looked at Shepherd. "He's right. If Erling sunk most of his funds into the project, then he could be wiped out and desperate."

Shepherd ran that same hand through his hair again. "Okay," he said. "I'll look into the guy's financials."

"That's all I'm asking," I said.

"And, babe, can we not fight for the rest of the night?"

I softened. "Okay. Sorry."

"Don't be. You're pushing me to get to the truth on this case or cases, and that's not a bad thing."

I took his hand and squeezed it. He squeezed mine back and said, "How's Mariana doing?"

"She's worried about Carlos," Gilley said. "But the docs all say he can go home tomorrow morning. His oxygen levels have slowly been climbing back into the normal range, so it looks really good."

"We're going to go early tomorrow to pick him up."

"Great," Shep said. "And you two should start packing, shouldn't you? Your flight takes off in a few days."

"It does," I said, feeling some tension creep back into my shoulders. We'd been paying so much attention to the case that we were now crunched for time to pack and get ready for our European trip.

"I'll drive you to the airport, so you don't have to worry about parking."

"Thank you," I said. "And would you check in on the DeLeons while we're away? I told them they could stay here as long as they need to."

"I will, Cat. Promise."

We enjoyed each other's company for the rest of the evening and I was heartened by the fact that Shep went over to Chez Kitty to check on Mariana, who'd chosen to rest instead of eat dinner with us. He reported back that she was asleep on the couch with Spooks, and he simply laid an afghan over the pair and left.

That night, I think I had the first good night's sleep I'd had in ages.

Chapter 15

We picked Carlos up from the hospital around ten the next morning. He was wheeled out to the front exit, but when the nurse's aide stopped to allow him to get up from the chair, he bounced up and hurried into the arms of his wife.

It was adorable.

As we were driving home, Gilley was telling Carlos and Mariana all about the case and our suspicion that Mike Erling could be the person who'd set their house on fire.

"But why would he try to kill us?" Mariana said.

I shook my head. "The only thing I can think of is that maybe he and Luke are working together to eliminate the beneficiaries of Scarlet's estate. You remember that Terry told us that, should you two be unable to receive your allotted portion of Scarlet's estate, then the entire thing reverts back to being evenly distributed among the rest of her family members."

"As far as we can tell," Gilley said, "Luke and Erling are in a mountain of debt, and they need a mountain of money to help them dig their way out."

"But won't they come after us again?" Carlos asked, his voice a bit shaky. "I don't want them to try to blow up your house, Miss Catherine."

"Carlos," I said, eyeing him in the rearview mirror where he sat cuddling his wife. "Please. It's just Catherine. And I think that the absolute safest place for you to be right now is my guesthouse. I mean, remember, I'm supposedly about to offer them a twenty-million-dollar check. No way would they mess with the opportunity for a short-term windfall when, even if you two were out of the way, it would take months and months for Luke to get his hands on any kind of inheritance."

"Oh," Carlos said. "I hadn't thought about it like that."

Mariana then asked, "Do you think they murdered Miss Scarlet?"

I glanced at Gilley, who shrugged and answered her by saying, "That we don't know. It seems to me that Grayson's a more probable candidate as he'd had access to the attic around the time that she was murdered."

"And remember what he did to Carson," Gilley said.

"What's happened to Mr. Carson?" Carlos asked with alarm in his voice.

"Nothing!" I assured him. "He's fine as far as we know. Gilley was referring to what Grayson did to

Carson at Scarlet's birthday party at the country club."

"Ohhhh," Carlos said. "Yes, that was terrible. Miss Scarlet was furious with him for that."

"It was such a mess," Mariana said. "Mr. Carson's hip took a long time to heal. It's a blessing that he couldn't feel it, though. He would've been in so much pain."

I nodded. "Broken hips aren't fun. Still, we think that Grayson was perfectly capable of murdering his mother."

"Do you think that Grayson, Luke, and Erling could be working together?" Gilley suddenly asked.

I shook my head, but then hesitated. "Anything's possible. I just *wish* Shepherd would listen to us and go interrogate Erling, and while he's at it, get a mold of any construction boots he might own."

"He'd need a warrant for that," Gilley replied. "No way would Erling let him anywhere near his closet. Being a former cop, he'd be totally suspicious of the request."

I sighed. "It's just so frustrating that the one piece of evidence that we really need to get a warrant for is Erling's work boots, which is also the one piece of evidence that we'd need to be able to get that warrant for in the first place."

"Why don't you just take a picture of his footprint?" Mariana said.

"How do we do that?" Gilley asked, looking grouchy. "Ask him to put on his construction boots, then lure him out of his house with candy and onto a shoe mold?"

A thought came to mind and I slapped Gilley on the arm in my excitement. "Ow!" he said. "Be careful, Cat. You know I bruise like a tender, ripe peach!"

"Gil," I said softly, trying to keep myself calm while I offered up my idea. "What if we got Erling to come out to the construction site on the premise of having another discussion about investing in the project. It rained all day yesterday. No way would he wear a pair of good shoes to that muddy environment! We could have an innocent little talk with him, and you could discreetly record him with your phone, and then we could take a picture of his muddy footprint when he left and send that to Shepherd!"

"Oh . . . my . . . God! Cat! That's brilliant!"

From the back seat, Carlos protested, "Miss . . . I mean, Catherine, I don't want you to do that. It will be too dangerous!"

"But it won't, Carlos!" I said. "Which is the beauty of the plan! No *way* is Erling going to mess up his chance at my twenty million, especially after he talked to my financial broker yesterday and was told I'm good for the money. He'd never hurt me, even if he were a tiny bit suspicious, because he needs that infusion of cash so desperately."

"I don't like it," Carlos muttered. "Please, don't do it."

I looked at Gilley and he grinned back at me. "We're doing it," we both said.

"Please, please be careful," Mariana said. "I don't want anything to happen to you or Mr. Gilley. Too many people have already been hurt."

"We'll be careful," I assured her.

"Pinky swear," Gil said, holding up his pinky for her.

"I don't like it," Carlos said again, but my mind was already made up. This was the perfect plan.

Mike and Luke agreed to meet us at noon at the construction site to answer a few "questions" I had about the project. After setting the time with them, I called the contractor I'd hired to build Chez Kitty and Chez Cat to ask him what kinds of questions I could ask about the condo project to help me vet if it's a good investment or not.

"Oh, yeah," he said when I had him on the phone. "That's a junk project, Ms. Cooper. You don't want to put a thin dime into it."

"All the same, Trevor," I said. "I need to at least ask them a few questions so it looks like I'm legitimately interested."

"Just tell them you talked to me and I told you not to commit."

I sighed. Why were men so difficult? "Trevor," I tried again. "This is the nephew of a dear friend of mine who asked me to hear her son out. I owe her and him at least that, so can you give me some questions that sound like I know what I'm talking about?"

He sighed. "Okay. I'd start with the soil. They constructed that thing mostly on swamp soil, and it's gonna shift and sink pretty rapidly unless they put in some deep pylons, at least fifteen feet down. If they put anything shorter than that in, then they're looking for trouble because they're trying to build it on the cheap. One really good nor'easter and the building will be uninhabitable. Or worse."

"What's worse?"

"It'll collapse."

"Yikes. Okay, so I definitely want to ask questions about the foundation and the soil, right?"

"You do."

"Good, what else?"

Trevor led me through a long list of questions to ask Luke and Mike, which would give Gilley and me plenty of time to get some footage of Mike's shoes.

"We'll need to lead him through the mud," Gil said, while I searched the cluttered front hall closet for a pair of wellies to wear.

"Agreed," I said, triumphantly emerging from the closet with my boots.

"I'll also make sure to get footage of Luke's footprints, just to cover all our bases," Gil vowed.

"Excellent," I told him, sitting down on the bottom step of my staircase to shimmy into the boots. Standing tall again I pointed to Gilley's feet. "You're wearing those?"

Gilley looked down at his shoes. "What's wrong with these?"

"They're sneakers."

He rolled his eyes. "They're not *sneakers* and who says that anymore, anyway?"

I glared at him. "It's a word!"

"Yes, but it is soooooo yesterday." Lifting the leg of his jeans, Gilley revealed that his shoes weren't actually sport shoes, but a leather boot. "See? And they're GORE-TEX. Totally waterproof."

"I stand corrected," I said.

Just then the front door opened and in came Spooks first, then Mariana, and Carlos, who was toting some of the Target bags Gilley had brought home. "Is it okay to move over now?" Mariana asked.

We'd discussed it earlier, and I had told them that I felt better if they'd move into Chez Cat where they could benefit from the protection of Shepherd and the rest of us.

"Of course! Gilley has moved his things out of the guest bedroom down the hall and to the left. We also put fresh sheets on the bed, and I've given you some extra towels in there as well. The bedroom has an en suite so you can claim that bathroom as your own. Please make yourselves at home, and also feel free to raid the fridge if you're hungry."

"You're too kind, Miss . . . Catherine," Carlos said. He took my hand and squeezed it. I smiled at the kindly man.

I motioned to Gilley then and said, "We're off to catch a killer!"

I'd said that lightly but both Mariana and Carlos seemed rattled by it. "Please don't go," Mariana said. "I have a bad feeling, Miss Catherine."

I pushed a smile to my face, but I'll admit that she caused me a moment of pause with that phrase. My sister is a professional psychic, so I'm not one to shirk off anyone's "bad feeling" about something, but I had set my mind to the task, and Gilley and I *would* be careful.

"We'll be fine," I assured her. "I promise."

A few minutes later we were in the car and hustling it over to the condo construction site.

"Is this a smart idea?" Gilley asked when we were about halfway there. We'd been driving in silence, alone in our thoughts until he'd spoken.

"I don't know if it's smart per se," I said. "But it's the only way I can think of to get Shepherd to take our hunch about Mike Erling seriously."

"Still," Gil said softly. "Cat, are we walking into a trap?"

I glanced over at him with a furrowed brow. "How could we be doing that?"

Gilley shrugged. "Maybe they know we're looking into the case?"

"How?" I asked again.

"What if Siobhan said something to Luke about asking us to snoop around?"

I bit my lip. That hadn't occurred to me. "Well," I said, "that wouldn't be good. But I doubt Siobhan said anything, I mean, she *is* trying to clear her own name, right?"

"But what if she did, Cat?" he asked nervously.

I tapped the steering wheel with my finger while I thought that through. "We don't know, Gil. We don't know that we're not walking into a trap, but the odds are in our favor and if either of us senses trouble, then we should have a code word to use and a story to get us out of there."

"You mean like, 'banana,' and, 'Oh gee! Lookit the time! I must rush off to have my hair done!' "

I rolled my eyes. "Maybe not quite that obvious. I was thinking along the lines of something like I'll need to wrap up the discussion because I have a meeting with my broker to discuss moving some investments around so that I can cut them a check."

Gilley pointed at me. "Ooh, yeah. That's a better angle."

"Good. I'm glad that's settled."

Gilley was silent for another minute or two, then said, "Should we call Shepherd and tell him what we're up to?"

I opened my mouth prepared to emphatically tell him no, because Shepherd made such a big deal out of anything we did that had a sneaky side to it, but then I thought better of it. Closing my mouth, I weighed the pros and cons and finally said, "Yeah. I think we better. But I don't want to alarm him by telling him we're meeting with Luke and Erling, so let me do the talking, okay?"

"You got it," Gilley said.

After telling Siri to call Shep, I played the call on speaker and we waited through the rings until he answered. "Hey, babe," he said. "I can't really talk right now. I'm meeting with Detective Navarro in two minutes."

"I don't want to keep you," I began, "but Shep, I want you to know that Gilley and I are headed over to the condo construction site to take some pictures of any footprints we find."

"What? Why?"

"Because we think that one of them might be a match for the footprints found at the DeLeons'."

"This again?" he said, and there was a little irritation in his voice.

"Yes, this again," I said crisply. "At the very least, if only to eliminate Erling as a suspect."

Shepherd was quiet for a moment, then, "How're you going to know which prints are Erling's?"

I looked at Gilley and he held up his palms. He

didn't know how to answer that without getting us into sticky water, either. "We . . . won't," I said simply. "But we plan on taking photos of any that we find, especially some of the bigger ones, and maybe the tread or something will give us more information."

"It rained last night, Cat," Shepherd said. "In fact, it rained all day yesterday. Any prints you find will probably have been washed away."

"On the outside of the building, for sure. But maybe there're some on the ground floor inside that'll be interesting."

Shepherd sighed. "Well, I think you're wasting your time, but I can't argue about it right now. I gotta get to my meeting with Navarro."

"Of course," I said. "I'll see you tonight."

A few minutes later we arrived at the construction site. At the end of the road were two big trucks, nearly identical except that one was black and the other silver, and next to them stood Luke and Mike, obviously waiting for us.

I waved to them and turned my car at an angle before backing into the space next to the black truck—which I assumed was Erling's.

"We're backing into the space?" Gil said as I made the maneuver.

"Yeah," I said. "In case we need to make a quick getaway."

"Good thinking," Gil said.

We hopped out of the car and greeted the two men warmly, smiling and shaking their hands. I snuck a quick peek at both of their shoes and was thrilled to see both men wearing work boots.

"Shall we?" Luke said, waving me forward toward the pathway that led to the building.

"We shall," I said, thrilled to take the lead. Scanning the ground as I walked, I made sure to lead us through the muddiest route, noting that Gilley was bringing up the rear and had hopefully turned the video camera on his iPhone on.

"Such a muddy mess!" I exclaimed as we walked. "I'm glad I wore my wellies today."

Just as I said that I slipped a little and Mike, who was behind me, caught my arm. "Whoa, careful there," he said.

I blushed in spite of myself, embarrassed for almost ending up on my keester. "Thank you, Mike," I said.

We got to the building then and stepped inside the cool, totally silent interior. I made a show of walking around in a circle, inspecting the floor, and started right in on the questions that Trevor had supplied me with.

"I have a dear friend who's a licensed contractor," I began. "And he—"

"Oh, yeah?" Mike asked, interrupting me. "Who?"

"Trevor Hays," I said. "Do you know him?"

Luke nodded. "I've never met him, but I do know of him. He's a good guy. Great reputation."

"He is and he does," I agreed.

"Would he be interested in taking over the construction?" Luke asked next.

That was a question I wasn't prepared for, but I saw how I could use it to my advantage. "Trevor and I go way back," I said. "I'm sure I could convince him to take this project on and see it to completion."

Mike and Luke both smiled in that way that told

me I'd just taken a worrisome fear off their shoulders, and had I not been convinced that one or both of them were killers, I would've felt a little bad. Recalling Mariana's soot-stained and tear-streaked face from the night her house exploded actually helped me feel a little glee that I was duping these two men so well.

"Anyway," I said to them to get us back on track. "As I was saying, Trevor told me to inquire about the pylons used to secure the building's foundation. I understand that the soil out here near the wetlands can be problematic to build on if the building isn't secure to the bedrock."

"We drove twelve-foot pylons into the ground at all four corners of the building and six more throughout the base foundation," Mike was quick to assure me, and he didn't know that he was actually three feet shy of the recommended depth.

"Oh, that's excellent," I said, nodding both to him and Gilley, who also nodded in enthusiasm like that was *just* what we wanted to hear. "Trevor suggested that if the building weren't properly secure, not only could it damage the interior of the condos with cracked walls and ceilings, but that it could make the elevator unusable if it shifted more than ten degrees."

Mike began to walk forward toward a boxlike structure in the middle of the space. "If you'll join me over here, Catherine, I can show you how we've accommodated for that by increasing the size of the interior frame of the—holy cow!"

Mike had walked around the interior boxed structure ahead of us and he jumped back three full feet when he looked inside the box. We all rushed forward and each one of us gasped and came up short when we saw what was inside.

"Oh my God!" I whispered, shaking as I took in the sight. Looking up at Luke, who was deathly pale and trembling, I said, "It's Grayson, right?"

The battered and beaten body of a clearly dead Grayson McMillen lay crumpled in the middle of the elevator shaft. It looked like he'd been pummeled with a baseball bat and there was no mistaking that he was dead.

Luke nodded to answer my question, and then he opened his mouth to speak, but before he could even get a word out, something made a sound from outside that took all of us by surprise.

A series of *Whump! Whump! Whump!* noises approached and even those were interspersed with a high-pitched whining sound—almost like a hydraulic mechanism.

The bottoms of my feet could feel the reverberation with each new *Whump!*

"What the hell?" Luke said, and he moved away from us in the direction of the sound while we stood and stared at each other and the area outside where the sound was coming from.

Abruptly, the noise stopped and then we heard Luke cry out, "No! Don't!" followed by the unmistakable sound of a gunshot and something dropping to the ground like a large sack of flour.

And then the *Whump! Whump! Whump!* started up again.

Gilley turned to me and whispered, "Banana! Banana, Cat!"

He didn't have to tell me twice. The three of us bolted.

Mike led us around the above-ground pylons over to the back left corner of the building. We skirted a rusty-looking wheelbarrow, some plastic sheeting, leftover Sheetrock, and various piles of bricks making our way to what I could now see was a back exit.

Mike reached it first and smashed his large frame into the release lever to get it to open, but it only opened up about two inches, revealing a thick chain that kept us locked in.

Meanwhile, the heavy sound of machinery continued to approach and Gilley whined in panic. "We're sitting ducks!"

Mike whirled around, his eyes darting here and there, and then he pointed up the stairs right next to us. "Get up there!" he ordered.

Gilley and I exchanged looks of panic before darting up the staircase toward the second floor. We were about to crest the midpoint landing when a gunshot rang out and the Sheetrock next to my ear exploded outward, pelting me with little splinters of material.

"He's shooting at us!" I cried, trying to pick my feet up faster.

"Get up there!" Mike yelled from right behind me.

But then another shot rang out and Mike grunted, falling to his hands and knees on the staircase.

"*Mike*!" I cried out, pausing to reach behind me to him.

"Go!" he choked out before coughing up blood. "Go!" he urged when I hesitated.

And all the while, below us the *Whump! Whump! Whump!* never let up.

Grabbing Mike by the lapel and using the kind of strength forged in pure adrenaline, I pulled him up to a doubled-over posture and got him to stumble up the stairs.

Another gunshot rang out, and Gilley squealed.

"*Gilley!*" I screamed when he also sank to his knees.

I feared the worst but then he got up and continued up the stairs, reaching the second floor and relative safety.

After lugging Mike up the last few steps we'd collapsed onto the cement floor, when another round of bullets hit the area near the top of the stairs.

Mike pulled up his knees to keep his feet from the gunfire and he looked at me with a grave, pained expression. "You two get to the top floor," he gasped. He then pulled up his iPhone with a shaking hand. "I'll call for help."

Gilley crawled to me, and down below the whumping sounds came closer and closer to the staircase. "*Who is shooting at us?*" he hissed.

I shook my head. I had no clue as I hadn't even paused to look, fearing it would be the extra second I needed to get away.

"It's . . . Robocop," Mike gasped and then he coughed and spit up more blood. Handing me his phone he said, "Can you dial? I can't get my hands to stop shaking."

I took his phone and dialed 911, but then the whumping sounds got too close to the staircase and another shot rang out. This time, the bullet hit the wall right above Gilley's head.

"Nine-one-one, what is your emergency?" the operator asked.

I lowered the phone and grabbed Mike by the lapel again. "*Send help!*" I screamed, pulling Mike away from the open staircase.

"Ma'am?" the operator said. "Ma'am? What is your location please?"

Another shot was fired and searing pain lit up across my upper arm. The pain was so sudden and impactful that it sent me reeling backward, dropping my hold on Mike and his phone. I screamed in pain and clamped my hand over my arm. "I'm hit!" I cried. "*I'm hit!*"

"Ma'am!" I could hear the dispatcher yell out. Mike's phone had dropped down a few stairs but I could still hear the 911 operator trying to help me. "Ma'am! Where is your location?!"

Gilley grabbed me under the shoulder and hauled me to the side. Mike rolled with us to get clear of the opening, but his phone was still at the top of the stairwell, out of reach if we didn't want to get shot at again.

"Cat! Let me see!" Gilley commanded as I continued to clamp my right hand over my upper left arm, which felt like it was on fire.

I shook my head, hissing out through my teeth. Getting shot *hurt*!

"You've got to get up the stairs," Mike said, his voice no louder than a strained whisper. "Get up there and hide till the cops get here!"

"We're not leaving you!" Gilley told him.

"We can't use the stairs anymore," I said. "He's got a clear path to shoot us again."

The palm of my hand felt slick and wet, and I

glanced at it and could see the blood seeping down my arm in little trickles. I felt woozy and shaken and so scared I couldn't seem to think of a strategy to stay alive until help arrived.

If it arrived. Mike's phone was still on the staircase, and no way could we get to it. Turning to Gilley I said, "Call nine-one-one and tell them our location!"

Gilley held up his phone. The front of the screen was completely smashed and bits of glass seemed to be clinging to life but many had already dropped from the screen, which was totally black.

"I landed on it when he shot at me," Gilley said, trying to tap at the broken glass, then turning the screen toward me to show me that his phone wasn't even lighting up. "It's dead."

"Just like we'll be if we don't *think* of something!" I snapped.

"Where's your phone?" he asked, his eyes roving over me trying to find it.

"I left it in the damn car!" I growled. I'd set it in the well between our seats while it was connected to the Bluetooth in my car and had completely forgotten to bring it with me. "I can't believe I was so stupid!" I whispered.

And then, from below came another *Whump!*

We all froze. The whumping sounds had stopped when the gunman—or gunwoman—reached the staircase. But now they started up again, and as the staircase shook with each new *Whump!* we all knew that the killer was beginning to make his or her way up the stairs.

I looked all around the second floor for someplace to hide, but the place was basically barren except for some bricks and loose lumber.

Getting to my feet I motioned to Gilley. He got up too and followed me over to the scattered bricks. "Grab as many as you can!" I told him, while also releasing the hold I had on my upper arm.

Gil's eyes widened as he took in the wound, exposed through the hole in my shirt, torn away by the bullet.

"Cat," he said, his complexion pale as he pointed to it.

"No time!" I yelled. "Come on, Gil!"

Setting aside the pain I felt radiating down my arm, I gathered as many bricks to myself as I could and hauled them over to the top of the landing near the stairs. The whumping sound was getting closer, but it was also much slower than it had been down below on the first floor.

When we had our two small piles of bricks I said to Gilley, "Give me your coat."

He shrugged out of it and handed it to me. I turned toward the stairs and threw it out into the open. Three shots rang out as the gunman put three bullets into Gilley's coat. He whimpered but I didn't have time to be sympathetic. Instead, I took two of the bricks, leaned over the opening just a little bit, and threw them down at the gunman.

"Ow!" Carson yelled when a brick hit him in the head. He was almost completely encased in some kind of exoskeleton that looked like it was incredibly heavy. He was strapped into the contraption and I could see that his feet were encased in large leather boots, which were strapped to the legs of the exoskeleton. They looked to be a size twelve.

He locked eyes with me and raised his gun. I ducked back just in time; the bullet narrowly missed hitting me in the head. "You'll pay for that!" he yelled.

"Why are you doing this?" I shouted. I was terrified, scared out of my mind because, even if we somehow managed to throw all of our bricks at him, his exoskeleton would probably protect most of his body. I didn't think I'd get lucky again and strike him square in the head, and that made our chances for survival all the more tenuous.

"Because you two wouldn't leave it alone!" he yelled, obviously answering my question. "I didn't *want* to kill you! I just wanted everyone else out of the way!"

Gilley was staring at me, shaking in fear as another *Whump!* sounded on the staircase.

"You'll never get away with it!" Gilley yelled, and tossed his brick in the air in the general direction of the staircase. We heard the brick hit metal and bounce away.

"Go ahead," Carson taunted. "Throw all the bricks you want. You're still gonna die."

I looked around for another weapon, anything we could use, but only a few of the two-by-fours offered any kind of option.

And then I had an idea. Motioning to Gilley I got up and we hurried over to the two-by-fours, which were about six feet long. With my injury I could hardly lift one, but Gilley grabbed one for himself and helped me with mine and we hustled back toward the opening of the stairwell, sitting just out of sight. To distract Carson I said, "How do you think you're going to inherit everything, Carson? You'll never get away with killing your whole family off, and you can't inherit the money or the property if you're convicted for murdering the rest of your relatives!"

"Oh, I'll get away with it," he said confidently. "No one ever suspects the cripple. And getting rid of William, Grayson, and Luke are really all I needed. I'll take the twenty-five million split between the remaining four of us. Siobhan's going to go away for the murder of her husband, and Grayson will be blamed for his mother's murder.

"Thanks for that tip by the way," he said. "When the police discover this murder scene, I can tell them all about how my cousin hated his mother, and once told me he wished she were dead so he could get his hands on her money. He owes some bad people for his gambling debts, so I'm pretty sure the police will just assume he was murdered because of them and you four were simply collateral damage."

By this time Carson had almost reached the point of the staircase where he could look over the lip of the landing and take aim at us. I motioned to Gilley and we got to our feet, and then I motioned that I was going to maneuver around the stairwell opening to the opposite side.

"I can put a bullet in Grayson's head to tie all the murders together too," Carson said. "But I have to confess, it was *so* good kicking his ass to death. The look in his eyes when he saw me show up in this thing—man. That was definitely worth the price of this suit."

"But why?" Gilley said, hoping to stall Carson. We'd both noticed that the exoskeleton would stop climbing when Carson paused to speak to us. It wasn't buying us much time, but it was buying us a little. "Why murder Scarlet in the first place? She was so good to you!"

"Good to me?" he replied. "*Good to me*? That woman tortured me! She blamed me for her beloved brother's death, even though it was an accident! Dad *made* me drive the car that night! He said it would be good for me to get in some practice, and he *knew* I didn't like driving in the dark!"

"But she employed you!" Gilley yelled down. "She gave you a job, and your own place to live! And a few million on top of that!"

Carson snorted derisively. "I was her slave, Gilley. She paid me minimum wage. Did you know that? *Minimum wage*! She knew I'd never be able to land another job with my disability. And I never complained to her about it. No, I just kept working harder and harder for her, hoping she would see how valuable I was. But she didn't! She only saw me as the guy who'd killed her favorite relative. And she left me that four million just to rub my face in it while rewarding her ex and two *servants*? I mean, come on!"

By this time, I'd made it to the other side of the opening and I crouched there, holding the two-by-four up like a lance. I nodded to Gilley to do the same and he copied my posture. I then pantomimed what I had in mind, which was to jab the pieces of lumber into Carson's chest and if we were very lucky, it would tip him back and he might drop the gun as he reached out to steady himself.

I thought if we could just get him to drop his weapon, we'd have a chance to fly down the stairs, retrieve the gun, and hold him until the police arrived.

Carson paused just before his head would crest the landing, and I knew he suspected a trap. "If you cooperate," he said, "I promise to make it quick. But if you try to pull anything on me, I'll beat you all to a pulp like I did Grayson. Trust me. He suffered."

I stifled a shudder and allowed some anger and venom into my voice when I said, "You want us, you sick sociopath? Then come get us!"

The high whine of hydraulics told me he was taking a chance and coming the rest of the way. I nodded to Gilley to get his attention. *Whump!* came the sound of the exoskeleton's foot on the staircase. *Three!* I mouthed.

Gilley nodded.

The hydraulics started up again.

Two!

Gil nodded again.

The hydraulics continued and the tip of a gun began to crest the top of the opening.

"*One!*" I shouted, and Gilley and I stood tall, leaned forward, and used our makeshift lances to strike Carson in the chest.

Our weapons hit metal, and Carson did indeed reach out wildly to steady himself, and he managed to do that without dropping his weapon, leaving Gilley and me totally exposed and easily dispatched. "Dammit!" Carson swore as he gained his balance.

Then he began to draw the gun up toward me.

Our eyes met.

His were filled with murder.

Mine were filled with regret, because I knew that in the next second, I'd be dead.

"Carson!" someone shouted below. A voice I recognized.

Carson immediately switched targets and pointed his gun downward, and in that moment, when I didn't even realize what I was doing, I stepped forward and jumped feet first onto his torso.

I landed with a thud on the metal barrel protecting his chest, and rebounded away back against the hard cement stair, banging my elbows and back so hard that the blow took the breath from me, but still I watched Carson tip backward and flail wildly again, only this time, he could gain no purchase. This time, he tumbled backward down the whole flight of stairs.

Chapter 16

Luke survived the shooting.

Shepherd found him at the entrance to the condo and immediately radioed for help before making his way inside, only to come up behind Carson quietly and stealthily, ready to take him out. But he had no clear shot with that giant exoskeleton protecting most of Carson's soft spots.

The only thing he could do when Carson aimed his gun at me was shout out, and it was just the distraction I'd needed.

Shepherd didn't even bother to check Carson's condition when he raced up the stairs, kicking the gun Carson had dropped down the open staircase where it landed with a clatter. Shep reached me and bundled me into his arms, cradling me like a lost puppy.

"Why?" he whispered into my ear. "Why do you

do this to me, Cat? Why do you scare me when you know I'd be lost without you?"

I reached around to hug him slowly. I felt banged and bruised but mostly okay. In rebounding off Carson, I'd been very, very lucky, because I could've easily broken my neck. "How did you find us?" I asked.

"I met with Navarro. He showed me a couple of photos of some tracks they found near the footprints at the DeLeons' house. The tracks were weird, and we couldn't figure out what'd caused them, but our best guess was maybe some kind of wagon. And then I remembered something one of the techs who'd worked the McMillen murder scene had pointed out. He'd said that he found a set of tracks on the front lawn and he didn't know what they were from, but he'd taken a picture and a mold. When I looked at the mold, I knew it was a wheelchair. That's when I started putting the pieces together that it was probably Carson's chair that'd made those marks.

"I called over to Carlos to ask him if he'd ever seen Carson navigate his chair through the soggy ground, and instead, he tells me that you've gone to the construction site to meet Luke, and that shortly after you left, Carson called him, looking for Luke, and Carlos told him where he could find his cousin, and you and Gilley.

"I didn't know Carson owned an exoskeleton, but it makes sense now how he managed to corner his terrified aunt and shoot her from a standing position. I had a bad feeling and came out to this construction site, and thank God I did," he said. "Thank God I did."

In the distance, the sound of sirens cut through the quiet of the shell of the building. And then there was the sound of hydraulics again, but it was a feeble sound, like a broken toy.

"He's alive," I said, looking over Shepherd's shoulder, where Carson was laid sprawled face-down on the concrete while his legs were giving little kicks but nothing even remotely more threatening.

"Shep," Gilley said as he crouched down on the stair above me. "We've got a man down up here."

Shep nodded but he wasn't quick to let go of me. Instead, he pulled back and said, "How bad are you hurt?"

"I'm really not," I assured him. His gaze traveled to my upper arm and I suddenly remembered being shot. Merely the remembrance of that was enough to engulf my arm in fire again. "Oh, yeah," I said, feeling woozy. "Except for that."

Shep tugged a little at the cloth surrounding my wound and I hissed through my teeth. "Sorry," he said. "It looks like the bullet just grazed you, babe. There's no hole here, but it did take a notch out of your arm."

"Oh, God," I said, feeling like I was going to lose my lunch.

By now the cavalry had arrived and there was a hoopla coming from the front of the building. "Shepherd?" someone shouted.

"Over here, Bosco!" he called out. "The scene is secure, but we need paramedics up here immediately."

"Got it," Bosco called back.

Shepherd kept me wrapped in his arms as he

got to his feet. "Let's get you checked out," he said, carrying me down.

"I can walk, you know."

He grinned at me. "Don't want you to step on that big cockroach on the stairs," he said, taking care to step over one of Carson's legs.

"Help me," Carson said feebly. I looked down at him and he was bleeding from his nose, which was clearly broken, along with one arm that was splayed out at an odd angle, but otherwise, he seemed much better off than he'd left Luke or Mike.

Shepherd cut sharp eyes toward him. "You'll be last in line, buddy. You just lie there for now and we'll get to you when we take care of everybody you hurt."

Gilley stayed with Mike, who'd fallen unconscious, until the paramedics got to his side. Mike also survived the shooting, but his complexion was gray and his lips were tinged in blue. I kept my fingers crossed that he'd make it.

Gilley joined me in the bay of the ambulance where a third paramedic worked to make sure I didn't go into shock.

"That was a wild day," Gil said.

I smirked. "Why, what happened?"

He laughed. "Nothing unusual," he said, "given that it is *us*, after all."

"Magnets for trouble," I agreed with a sigh.

Gilley grinned. "You'd think we'd learn by now."

"You'd think."

"Have we?" he asked.

I shook my head but kept the smile on my lips. "Oh, I doubt it."

"Well, at least life will never be boring for us."

"You know, right about now, Gilley, I could use a little boredom."

"Well, let's find some in Europe," he said. "Something tamer than this hot mess at least."

My smile went to full grill. "Deal."

Just a few days later, Shepherd was waiting patiently for me to finish packing so that he could take Gilley and me to the airport.

While we were gone, the DeLeons were still willing to house-sit, and we'd given them the lowdown on Michel's impending arrival in the next few days. They'd gone off to the market to buy some groceries to stock the fridge, and Gilley was at Chez Kitty, frantically rethinking the wardrobe he'd packed for Europe.

"We gotta get going soon, babe," Shep said.

I glanced at him, then at my watch. "We've got time. I'll be good to go in ten minutes or so."

Shepherd got up from the chair where he'd been sitting, in the far corner of my bedroom. He seemed fidgety and nervous and I couldn't understand what was going on with him.

"Is it hot in here?" he asked.

I eyed him dully. "Well, you do have your jacket on and a sweater on under that. Maybe lose a layer or something."

Shepherd started to wiggle his way out of his jacket, then seemed to think better on it, and pulled it back up around his shoulders. I cocked an eyebrow at him and the layer of perspiration across his brow. He scowled in annoyance and took the jacket off, laying it ever so carefully over the chair.

I shook my head and got back to focusing on what items to put into my suitcase.

"I'm gonna get some water," Shep announced. "Want some?"

"Sure," I said without turning toward him. I was counting shoes and wondering if eleven pairs would be enough.

"Okay," he said, and headed out of the room.

"That man is so weird," I whispered.

Five minutes later I closed the lid of my suitcase and sighed in relief, happy with all of my wardrobe choices.

"Cat!" Shepherd called up from downstairs.

"I'm coming!" I called back impatiently. We still had twenty minutes or so before we absolutely *had* to leave for the airport.

"No," he said from the bottom of the stairwell. "I gotta go."

I came to the banister and looked down. "We've still got twenty minutes before it'll get dicey, Shep."

He shook his head. "No, what I mean is that *I* have to go. There's been a hit-and-run and my sergeant just called to assign it to me. I'm sorry, babe, but I can't take you to the airport."

"Oh, gosh," I said. "Okay. You go take care of police business and I'll figure something out."

"I've already figured it out for you," Shep said. "I called Carlos. He and Mariana are on their way back here, and he'd be happy to drive you. And I'll pick you up in three weeks, okay?"

I rushed down the stairs and threw my arms

around him. "I am going to miss you so much!" I said, squeezing him and kissing him with gusto.

"Hey, hey," he said, laughing. "Save some of that for when I can take advantage of you."

I laughed too, and swatted him lightly on the bum. "Go," I ordered. "Be someone else's hero today."

He saluted and off he went.

Just as he went out the door, Gilley came through it, tugging several pieces of luggage. "We ready?" he asked Shep as he darted past him.

"Almost," Shep said, then pointed back at me. "She'll explain."

Gilley shut the door behind Shepherd and looked at me expectantly. "There's been a hit-and-run. Shep got called to take the case and Carlos is going to drive us to the airport instead."

"Great," Gilley said. "I'm glad we have a backup plan. Spooks is all packed and ready to be dropped off at Sunny's place."

"Good," I said, then crooked a finger at Gilley. "Come on upstairs and help me with my luggage, will you?"

"Sure," Gil said. "I don't want you to overuse that arm."

I placed a palm over the bandaged section of my arm that'd been grazed by the bullet. "It hurts a little less today."

We headed upstairs and Gilley began to gather the biggest bags first. "You don't lift anything heavy," he ordered. "I'll come back up for the second load."

As he was leaving I noticed Shepherd's jacket still draped over the chair. "Oh, no!" I said.

"What?"

"Shep left his jacket. It's cold and windy outside. I've got to try to catch him and give it to him."

Grabbing the jacket I began to race from the room when something fell out of the pocket with a loud thump.

I paused and so did Gilley and we both looked to the source of the noise.

"Oh. My. *GAWD!*" Gilley exclaimed. "Cat! Is that what I *think* it is?"

I didn't answer because I really couldn't. I was totally speechless, in fact. My body moved toward the object on the floor like a magnet drawn to metal. Bending down I picked up the blue velvet ring box and stared at Gilley with wide eyes.

Neither one of us spoke. My heart racing, I opened the lid and there, inside, was the most perfect pear-shaped two-karat diamond I'd ever seen. It was mounted in platinum, with diamond baguettes in a channel down the ring.

"Whoa," Gilley said when I turned it toward him. "Cat! What're you going to say when we get back from Europe and he pops the question?"

I blinked several times and my mind simply emptied. "I . . . I . . ."

"Do?" he said eagerly. "You do?"

I shook my head, then nodded. Finally, I said, "I don't know, Gilley. I just . . . don't know."

In the midst of their European vacation, life coach Cat Cooper and best friend Gilley Gillespie take a detour to Northeast Texas to support Gilley's new beau at the famous Texas Rose Festival, but their trip hits a snag when a murderer strikes days before the big event . . .

Gilley's whirlwind romance with creative director Stuart Jacobs began in Paris, where Stuart was sourcing fabric for the world-renowned Texas Rose Festival, which he is heading-up for the first time. The festival is nothing short of spectacular, bringing in half a million people (and their wallets) to see the artistic displays, and exquisite gowns and jewels worn by the Rose Queen and her court. Stuart and his crew seem to have it all under control. But the night Cat arrives in Texas, someone is shot in cold blood, and a member of Stuart's staff is named the prime suspect!

The Rose Festival is too important to the city's economy to cancel, so while Stuart scrambles to prevent the festival from derailing, Cat and Gilley launch their own investigation into the murder. With a parade of potential suspects to parse, and an even longer list of motives, they bring in East Hampton Police Detective Steve Shepherd to help. As rumors of arson, burglary, and professional sabotage swirl around the already fraught festival planning; Cat and her team immerse themselves in the cutthroat pageantry to identify the killer, who has already picked their next victim . . .

Please turn the page for an exciting sneak peek of the next Cat & Gilley Life Coach mystery coming soon wherever print and e-books are sold!

Chapter One

"*Now* will you call him?" Gilley pleaded.

"And tell him what?" I snapped, waving wildly to the giant wall of flames coming from the warehouse where we'd barely escaped being burned alive.

"I don't know, Cat, maybe something like, 'Gee, Shepherd, I sure do miss you by golly! Also, I've been a fool to stay away this long. Of course I'll marry you! Especially since I was nearly made into barbecue brisket tonight, which has me questioning all my life's choices and I've been a fool to run away from the man I love! And, also, could you come down here and help us solve this hot case we're looking into that just got a *whole* lot hotter?' "

I scowled at him and adopted a droll tone. "Wow. That sounds just like something I'd say."

"Cat," Gilley said, sighing dramatically. "I'm serious."

"Of that I'm sure, my friend."

Gilley glared at me.

I glared back.

"We need his help," he said.

"Do we though?"

"*Yes,* Cat, we *do*! Plus, you could lose him over what happened at the airport. This could be your one chance to repair the damage."

My stomach muscles clenched. He was right. I could lose Shepherd over the stunt I'd pulled. "It's impossible," I said softly, wiping a big fluff of ash from Gilley's sideburn. "I can't face him until I know what I'm going to say."

"Why is saying 'yes' so hard, Cat?"

I sighed and glanced again at the flames roaring out of the open door to the warehouse, and I thought it was the perfect metaphor for my life right now and what a mess I'd made of things. My mind immediately flashed to that moment when Shepherd had met me at the airport, looking more handsome than I'd ever seen him, dressed in gray slacks, a navy blazer, crisp white shirt, and a megawatt smile. He'd emerged from the limo that had come to pick me up after the European vacation Gilley and I had been on, and as he got out of the car my heart had leapt at the sight of him and then he'd ruined the moment by getting down on bended knee and producing a little blue velvet box.

The same little blue velvet box which I'd discovered just before embarking on that very same vacation, and the reason why I'd avoided talking to him for much of our trip.

So, I hadn't told him about Stuart Jacob, the fabulously talented designer Gilley and I had met on our first day in Paris, and how, when Stuart had caught Gilley's eye, they had gravitated toward each other like two fireflies on a dark night and had been nearly inseparable since.

I'd never witnessed love at first sight, but it was the only way to describe Gilley's reaction to Stuart, and Stuart's reaction to Gilley.

Stuart had been in Paris to select some fabric for a massive and world-famous event—the Texas Rose Festival, and he and Gilley had spent all the days we were in Paris together and then as we moved on with our itinerary, Gilley simply couldn't stop talking about Stuart and he couldn't stop talking *to* him either. The two chatted on the phone incessantly. Finally, as we landed in Amsterdam with six days left on our trip, I looked at how unenthused Gilley seemed about the last week of our vacation and secretly purchased him a ticket to Texas, which I handed to him over dinner that night.

Gilley had practically sprinted back to our hotel to repack his things and head to the airport, and I'd stayed to finish the trip on my own, which hadn't been nearly as fun as I'd expected.

At last I'd boarded my own flight back to New York—where, as I mentioned, Shepherd had met me—and I'd been so happy to see him until he did that whole proposal thing.

Truthfully, my reaction had been poor. Terrible, even. Before he could even say the words, "Will you . . . " I'd blurted out, "Nope!" And then I'd turned on my heel and ran back inside the airport to dart into the nearest ladies' room, where I knew he couldn't follow.

I'd waited twenty minutes trembling at the sink, and then I'd cautiously made my way out of the lavatory and walked to the nearest ticket agent. "I need to get to Dallas, Texas, please. As soon as possible."

There was one seat available on a flight that'd left twenty minutes later for Dallas, and once I arrived there I'd called Gilley and confessed what I'd done.

"You *what?*" he'd screeched. "Cat! Please tell me you did *not* leave that poor man kneeling on a public sidewalk without even an explanation!"

I didn't reply and the silence had stretched out between us for a long, awkward moment, until the sob I'd held in for the past six hours escaped from my throat and I dissolved into a puddle of tears.

"Stay put," Gilley ordered. "I'm sending you a limo."

An hour or so later I emerged from the Town Car an absolute emotional mess. Gilley had been waiting in the circular drive of whatever stately home we'd pulled into, and he rushed forward to hug me tightly.

I wept none too quietly on his shoulder for a long, long time. The tears and sadness were much heavier than I'd expected them to be and I knew as soon as I'd come to my senses on the plane to Dallas that I'd done a horrible, horrible thing. A thing that I deeply regretted and absolutely should've handled better.

Shepherd would probably never forgive me.

Or speak to me again.

I'd absolutely humiliated him and he was the last person on the planet I ever wanted to do that to. "I've made such a mess!" I wailed.

Gilley patted my back and cooed, "It'll be okay, Cat."

"He'll never forgive me, Gilley!"

"He will."

"I panicked!"

"I know, sugar."

"I . . . I . . . I knew he was going to propose—but not at the *airport*!"

"The excitement of your return probably overrode all good reason," Gilley assured.

I nodded into his shoulder and tried to wipe my eyes with the back of my hand. I was an unkempt puddle of misery.

"How's she doing?" I heard a voice behind me say. It sounded like Stuart.

"She'll rally," Gilley said.

His confidence in that statement helped tremendously. I swallowed hard, sniffled, and stepped back out of our hug. Wiping my eyes again I turned to look back at Stuart and felt so embarrassed by my emotional display. "Hi," I said shyly. "I'm so sorry to crash your party, Stuart."

"Oh, pish!" he said, waving his hand. "Honey, we've *all* been there. I can't tell you the number of hearts I've had to break over the years. Men always fall too hard and too fast for this bag of goodies." He added a shimmy for effect and a wicked smile.

I forced a smile to my own lips, but my gaze drifted to Gilley. He looked alarmed, and I again regretted inserting myself into this budding romance between the two of them that was now likely layers more complicated than Gilley had expected.

"Do tell," Gil said, and Stuart seemed to realize what he'd just admitted.

Stuart's smile held a hint of regret. "Gilley," he said. "You had me at hello. Your heart is safe with me."

Gilley all but swooned and the two had a little magical moment between them before Stuart broke eye contact and waved at me again. "Come inside, woman, and we'll fix you something to eat and pour you a glass of wine, which, I suspect, you badly need."

"I do, I do," I said.

"Too bad Shepherd didn't pop the question with an open bottle of chardonnay," Gilley quipped. "He'd have been a *much* happier man right about now."

I glared at him.

"Too soon?"

"You're a scoundrel, Gilley Gillespie," I told him, walking around him to follow after Stuart.

As we approached the front door, I had to marvel at the home I'd been standing in front of for several minutes, but hadn't quite taken in. The place was as large as my own home back in East Hampton, but of a much different architectural style.

Sand-colored limestone brick lined the two story structure, with windows and the front door framed in a dark espresso wood. Succulents lined the red brick driveway and beautiful hot fuchsia crape myrtles gave a glorious pop of color to the side of the main entrance.

Once we were through the door, the heavy scent of gardenia and sandalwood wafted down the hallway to greet my nose in the front foyer.

Someone was obviously burning the most delicious scented candle nearby. The front hall was large and mostly bare, save for a brass iron railing that ran along an off-white carpeted staircase and, in the middle of the staircase, hung a seven to eight-foot tall abstract painting, composed of layered, long brushstrokes of brilliant Klein Blue, black, and gold leaf which was so striking that I had to pause, simply to marvel at it.

Waving my hand toward it I said, "*That's* breathtaking."

"You like?" Stuart asked, sidling up next to me.

"I *love*," I said. "Who's the artist?" Like many of my peers who've been fortunate in life, I had a growing art collection that I was immensely proud of.

Stuart chuckled. "It's one of mine."

I gaped at him. "You really painted that?"

Stuart shrugged, as if it were no big deal. "When I'm not sketching costume designs, I like to unwind by creating abstracts. The bigger the canvas the better."

"He has another one upstairs," Gilley said, and I detected a note of pride in his voice. "Every bit as beautiful as that one."

"Is this your house, Stuart?" I asked.

"No, love. This house is owned by Nigel Bloomfield. He's one of the five."

"One of the five?"

Gilley said, "Stuart means that Nigel is one of the five families that've been growing roses in this town since the eleventies, and they're all rich, rich, *rich*!"

I giggled. "The eleventies, eh?"

"A long, long time ago," Gilley said.

I laughed again and rolled my eyes. "Well, that clarifies things."

"The point is," Gilley continued, "that Nigel and the other family heads are some of the top rose growers in the world. They grow *millions* of roses, Cat. Mill-eh-yons."

"Wow," I said. "I had no idea."

"Nigel's company is the biggest producer," Stuart said. "And he grows some of the rarest varieties."

"He's *loaded*!" Gilley exclaimed.

"What's gotten into you, Gilley?" I asked. "You're literally surrounded by vast fortunes back home—why is Nigel's money making you so giddy?"

"Cat," he said, as if I were simple. "There's money, and then there's *money*, and these people have the latter."

"Well good for them," I said. Wanting to get off such a superficial topic I switched my focus back to Stuart.

"You were saying, Stuart?"

He waved his hand airily. "This is Nigel's guesthouse and this is the house the Costume and Scenic designer each year gets to use as their personal quarters for the two weeks leading up to the festival."

"This is his *guesthouse*?" I gasped. The place had to be five-thousand square feet if it was an inch and I couldn't help but compare it to my own guesthouse, where Gilley lived, which was just over fourteen-hundred square feet.

Gilley wagged his brows at me. He knew what I was thinking, and he was enjoying my reaction. "Wait till you get a load of the main residence," he said. "It's as big as the Entwistle estate."

"Wow," I said. Wealth doesn't usually impress me unless it's someone like Julia Entwistle who was just our local neighborhood billionaire. She floated in circles no one without an extra set of zeros was invited to, which probably meant that, like Julia, Nigel Bloomfield was not only wealthy—but powerful.

Gilley took my hand and tugged me down the hallway then around the corner to the kitchen. As I took in the pink granite countertop with honey colored cabinets and appliances which I knew quite well cost a fortune, I realized that, in my haste to escape answering Steve's proposal, I might've overstepped on the side of imposing. "I should get a hotel room," I said as Gil let go of my hand and pointed to one of the light brown leather-back chairs at the counter.

Gilley pointedly rolled his eyes. "Don't even, Cat," he said, as if the very thought were absurd.

"This house has five bedrooms," Stuart said. "All have an en suite and only one of those is currently being occupied." Stuart eyed Gilley and the pair traded nearly identical wicked smiles.

I felt my own cheeks flush. "I really should've booked a room," I insisted. "Clearly you two were about to have a marvelous, romantic time together and here I am, the third wheel, crashing your party."

This time Stuart rolled his eyes. "You're not going anywhere, miss. And I don't want to hear another word about it. Gilley and I are upstairs. There's a lovely little suite down here that faces the garden and has its own private sitting room." Stuart then came to sit down next to me while Gilley poured us each a glass of wine.

"How's the festival preparation coming along, Stuart?" I asked.

He shook his head. "As you know, Catherine, this is my first rodeo, which means there's a lot at stake for me, and my crew and I have been working on these designs since January, but pulling this whole thing together is like trying to corral a tornado."

"Yikes," I said. "That bad?"

"It's not that it's bad, necessarily, so much as there are so many moving parts that all have to coordinate together to maximize the time we have left to create and finish all forty-six gowns for the court and the costumes for the twelve attendants, plus there're the hats, the shoes, the scepters and crowns, and parts of the added scenery that will need to be secured to the float for any individual member of the Queen's court."

Gilley set a plate of sliced apples and caramel dip in front of me. I smiled at him, took up a slice of apple, and then went back to my conversation with Stuart. "Tell me about the festival itself, Stuart. What is the makeup of the court and what themes are you creating this year?"

"Our theme this year is Enchanted Twilight."

"Ooooh," I said. "That sounds so dreamy."

"It is," Gilley gushed. "Cat, some of Stuart's designs are a vision!"

"Can I see some of your designs, Stuart?"

He smiled and got up from his chair, disappearing out into the hallway. I sipped my wine and nibbled on an apple while Gilley began to pull items out of the refrigerator that I suspected were the ingredients for a marvelous dinner.

In short order Stuart returned with a large sketchpad. Placing it on the counter next to me, he then got settled and opened the cover to reveal a breathtaking gown of the same Klein blue—a shockingly vivid blue that popped out against any background. Mingled at the bottom of the skirt of the gown were large stars made out of crystals and the bodice was a mixture of warm yellows, oranges, and reds. The dress gave the effect of the setting sun and it was absolutely spectacular.

In the rendition of the woman wearing the gown was a large scepter of gold, white and sapphire blue crystals and topped with a three-dimensional star.

As for her crown, it was a wishbone tiara with three rows, peaking in a point that formed the shape of a star. Overall, Stuart's design was elegant and regal.

"I love it," I said. "Who's wearing this dress?"

"The Queen," he said. "It's her coronation, after all."

I flipped the page and found a gown shaped like a crescent moon, in cool colors of mint green, light blue, and white. It was whimsical and wonderful. "And who wears this one?" I asked.

"The princess," Stuart said. "For every coronation there's always one queen but only sometimes is there a princess. This year we're blessed to have both."

"How is the court structured?" I asked, continuing to flip through the sketchpad, delighting in the fantastical designs on every page.

Stuart crossed his legs and rested an elbow on one knee while holding aloft his wine glass. Perfectly relaxed and perfectly poised. "This year, as I said, there's one queen and one princess but there is also one Duchess of the Rose Growers.

"The Duchess of the Rose Growers is a direct descendant of one of the five original rose grower families. Melissa is a lovely girl, and her mother was also the Duchess thirty years ago, and her grandmother was the Rose Queen twenty-two years before that."

"Wow. That's incredible that these families have been so tied to this event for so many generations."

"It is," Stuart agreed, taking a sip of his wine. Then he continued. "Most of the rest of the gowns belong to the Ladies in Waiting and the regular Duchesses. The Ladies in Waiting are all local women who grew up in town and are now juniors in college. In fact the entire court is made up of college juniors, so they're all about twenty years old and they're a tight-knit group. The Duchesses are girls who didn't grow up here—they come from all over. They can be sorority sisters of one of the Ladies in Waiting or simply just college friends. And there are about twenty in each group. At least this year there are twenty. Some years it's more, some years it's less. Rounding out the court are the attendants—these are young boys and girls in middle school and they are placed on the floats to give the appearance of attending to the queen, princess, and the rest of the court. Their costumes need to reflect the colors and styles of the young lady they'll be attending so there's an additional twelve costumes to add to the list."

"My goodness," I said. "I had no idea there was so much work involved."

"This is a *project*," Stuart said. "We hit the ground running ten months ago and we haven't slowed down since."

"Amazing," I said. I so admired Stuart's work ethic, but I was still curious about the makeup of the festival's court. "How are the young women chosen, Stuart?"

"The queen and princess are chosen by the president of the Rose Festival. The president is part of a four-person committee and the roles rotate through year-to-year so that no one person is president for more than one year in a four-year period. And there is also a committee made up of about twelve members. The Rose Festival is such a large affair that it requires quite a bit of planning, preparation, and effort to execute. The other women are nominated by members of the committee and other influential citizens in town."

I got to the last sketch and marveled at it. It was so incredibly imaginative. "These are amazing, Stuart and I can't wait to see these designs come to life," I said.

Stuart smiled. "I'm glad you like them, Catherine."

Something that smelled delicious came wafting

to my nose from the stove. "What're you making, Gilley?" He'd been largely silent during the conversation.

Gilley stepped back from the stove, holding the handle of a large pan, swirling and flipping the contents. "We didn't have a lot on hand," he said, reaching for one of the stacked plates on the counter. "So I threw some odds and ends together and voila!" With a flourish he portioned out a plate for me and set it down on my placemat before reaching for another plate for Stuart and then himself.

I looked down at the mound of food. It was a pasta dish with chicken and English peas, all covered in a creamy looking sauce that smelled heavenly. I swirled some linguini onto my fork and tried a bite. "Oh, my God," I said, closing my eyes to relish in the flavor. "This is incredible. What *is* this sauce?"

Gilley beamed a smile at me and said, "We didn't have any cream so I used the next best thing. The sauce is a fair amount of butter, Bailey's Irish Cream, Kailua, and a splash of bourbon."

"Get out!" I said. "I don't taste the alcohol at all."

"The alcohol is used to emulsify the butter," he said. "You burn it off as you cook and you're left with just the flavors."

"Delicious, hon," Stuart said. "Really, this is outstanding."

Gilley blushed and swished his head from side to side, clearly loving the compliment and it was adorable.

We ate in companionable silence for the next a

few minutes—the food was simply too good to pause for conversation, but soon we'd polished off our meals and Stuart sat back and patted his stomach. "Well, now that I've been properly nourished, I need to get to the warehouse and check on the team's progress. We've still got several gowns to finish and I want to keep our momentum going."

"Are you behind schedule?" I asked.

Stuart had a little glint in his eye when he answered. "No, dear. We're several days *ahead.* I like running a tight ship and bringing it in early, just in case there are any last minute emergencies."

"Smart," I said. I used to run my own business the exact same way.

Once Stuart had left, I helped Gilley with the dishes and then we both sat back with a cup of ginger tea and some of his homemade cookies.

Gilley's phone pinged and he glanced at the screen and once again that blush and perfectly smitten expression took over his complexion.

"Text from Stuart?" I asked.

"Yep," Gilley said, typing a quick reply before setting his phone facedown again.

I grinned and shook my head. "How amazing is it that, just three weeks ago, you were so heartbroken over your divorce, and now you look more radiant than I've ever seen you."

Gilley bounced in his chair. "Cat," he whispered. "*I'm in love*!"

"Duh," I said. "When did this happen, though, Gilley? I mean, I remember you two being quite taken with each other by the time we all left Paris, but I didn't expect it to bloom this fully in such a short period of time."

"The whole time we were in Europe, Cat, Stuart and I had been texting, talking, and Zooming like crazy. I just didn't tell you because, well . . . you know how you are."

"How I am?" I said defensively. "How *am* I, Gilley?"

He smirked. "Cat Cooper the professional life coach just can't help but offer unsolicited advice. If I told you how quickly Stuart and I were progressing you'd sit me down like one of your clients and start telling me how I should be all *reasonable* and *cautious* and *take it slow.* And the irony is that you're as bad as I am at navigating relationships."

My jaw dropped. Did he actually just say that? "I'm bad at navigating relationships? Really? Gilley, I was married for fifteen years and I've been in a three-year relationship with a terrific man. If anyone could give you sage advice when it comes to building a successful relationship, it'd be me."

Gilley's mouth flattened into a skeptical expression. "So, I must be mistaken, or did you *not* just flee town the moment the man you've been dating for those three years in that very successful relationship took the *obvious* next step and asked you to marry him."

I frowned. "That's different."

Gilley dropped his chin and stared up at me. "Really?"

"Yes."

"How exactly?"

My eyes searched the countertop for a moment, as if I could find the answer within the swirls of the marble. "I have children," I said at last. "Their opinions have to factor into whatever answer I give Shepherd."

Gilley picked up a cookie and took a bite. "Your children don't even live with you, Cat. *And*, I seem to recall a couple of barbecue dinners, days at the beach, and nights out at the movies that included you, Shepherd, *and* the boys and there were no reports afterward of any animosity between the boys and Shep. In fact, when I asked Mike about your man, he told me he actually thought Shepherd was pretty cool, so don't try playing that card with me, sugar."

Of course Gilley was right—my twin sons, Matt and Mike spent the school year away at boarding school—which they'd chosen to attend four years ago when my ex-husband and I filed for divorce. The boys hadn't wanted to live with either one of us, and frankly, that had really hurt my feelings, but I'd agreed to their request, knowing divorce can be very hard on young men their age and only wanting them to be as happy as possible given the drama of our contentious divorce.

Since then the boys had been thriving at school, but they also spent half the summers with me and half the summers with Tom—my ex. He had already remarried, and I'd found happiness with Shepherd, whom, the boys had taken in stride. So Gilley was also right to call my bluff.

"Gilley," I said while he eyed me judgmentally. "My divorce from Tom was excruciating. I don't ever want to go through that again."

Gilley nodded almost casually. "Anyone who's ever been through a divorce isn't anxious to do it again, but what's the other option when you meet someone wonderful who wants that kind of stability in their life?"

I pointed at him. "That. That right there is my conundrum. I don't want to lose Shepherd. I love him. In fact, I'm madly in love with him, but marriage wasn't something I gave much thought to until we discovered the ring in his blazer pocket three weeks ago."

"And you've had three weeks to think about it," Gilley said. "Your heart wants to say yes, correct?"

I nodded.

"But your fear is keeping you from taking the next step."

I nodded again.

"So, I gotta ask you, Cat," he said. "Why are you allowing fear of what *might* happen stop you from doing something you know you want to do?"

"Do I though?" I asked. "Do I *know* I want to be married again?"

"No, that's not what I meant. I meant, you know Shepherd's the guy for you right?"

"He is," I said immediately. God help me, but I loved that man with the whole of my heart.

"Then what's the problem? I mean, it's just a piece of paper, Cat. A marriage license is really all that's standing between you and making Shepherd feel safe and secure in your relationship. Isn't that something worth giving to the man you love?"

I took a long moment to consider what he was saying. As usual, Gilley had nailed it. "I'm okay with signing a marriage certificate," I told him. "I'm not okay signing another set of divorce papers."

Gilley rolled his eyes and sighed. "Cat," he said. "You're only considering a hypothetical and not considering the reality of the past three years with Shepherd."

"What do you mean?"

Gilley got up to fetch the teapot on the counter near the stove. Bringing it back, he topped off both my cup and his. "You and Shep have been through a *lot* together, right?"

"Yes," I said. We had. There had been some very dramatic—sometimes deadly—moments in my life over the previous three years and Shepherd had been involved in all of them in one way or another.

"And your track record for getting through those very difficult times with your relationship still intact has been one-hundred percent, correct?"

The corner of my mouth quirked in the hint of a grin. I understood exactly what he was getting at. "It has."

"Could your relationship with Tom have endured all the things you've been through over the course of these past three years?"

I took another minute to think that through.

Gilley allowed me the time and busied himself with downing another cookie.

"No," I said at last. "Tom and I wouldn't have survived everything that's happened these past three years."

Gilley nodded. "You and Shep are far better poised to handle the rough spots in a marriage than you and Tom—who were happily married for over a decade, correct?"

"Yes. Until he had an affair, yes, we were happily married. Or, at least I *thought* we were."

"I think you can assume you and Tom were both happy for a large part of that decade, but my point is that if your relationship with Shepherd can endure so much chaos, murder, and mayhem, what the hell are you worried about? You already know how to work through the most difficult situations life could throw at you. Marriage would be a cakewalk for the two of you."

I sipped my tea and continued to think through all Gilley was saying. "Thank you for the advice, Gilley," I said after a bit.

"You're welcome, Cat. And if you want to scamper off to your room and call Shepherd, I won't mind."

The hand holding my teacup stopped midway to my mouth. It was an involuntary reaction, and that was troubling.

Gilley sighed, noting my body language. "What now?" he said with a groan.

I set the cup down. "I . . . I don't really know, Gilley. But I think I need to think this through a little more before I can talk to Shep. I don't want to mislead him, or give him a false sense of either hope or denial. I just need a few days to consider if marrying him is the best thing for both of us."

"Okay, sugar," Gilley said, letting the matter drop.

I smiled at him but that quickly turned into a huge yawn. "Oh my," I said, widening my eyes to try to wake up a bit. "I think I'm a bit more tired than I thought."

"Cat," he said, getting up from his chair to grab

both of our teacups. "You're exhausted. Go to bed. I got this."

I sighed wearily. He was right. I hadn't slept a wink on the flight from Europe and obviously I hadn't slept on the flight from New York to Texas, which meant I'd been up almost thirty-six hours and I was weary to the bone. "Thank you," I said, leaning in to kiss him on the cheek. "I appreciate you more than you know, Mr. Gillespie."

"Gurl, you better," he chuckled, wrapping me in a big hug before letting go and pivoting me around toward the hallway. "Now shoo!"

I made my way to the guest bedroom and smiled when I walked into the lovely space. The room was decorated in shades of apple green, light pink, and bright white. It was feminine and elegant and the vintage four-poster bed was a nice touch. Off the bedroom there was a small seating area with big bay windows that overlooked the well curated garden. The bathroom held a fabulous garden tub with whirlpool jets and I very much wanted to relax in that tub but factoring how long it would take to fill up and how exhausted I was I opted for a quick shower instead.

Once I'd washed off all the day's stress and worry, I climbed into that four poster, delighting in the Egyptian cotton sheets and I was asleep thirty seconds after my head hit the pillow.

I woke with a start some hours later. The room was dark, given that I'd drawn the blinds, so I didn't know what time it was until I reached for my phone.

Swiping to activate it I immediately noted that Shepherd had called. Twice.

I bit my lip and checked to see if there was a voicemail

There wasn't. I tossed the phone on the bed and laid back to stare up at the ceiling. I owed the man an explanation at the very least, but what explanation could I give that would satisfy his hurt feelings?

So I lay there wide awake for a good half hour trying to work up the courage to call him back. And I would've sat there even longer if Gilley hadn't knocked on my door. "Cat?" he called softly.

"Come on in," I said.

Gilley opened the door, took one look at me and came right to my side to give me a hug. "Oh, shug," he said, that southern lilt to his voice kicking in. "Did you talk to Shep?"

I leaned against him and sighed sadly. "No. But he did call."

Gilley pulled his head back to look at me. "And you didn't answer?"

"Slept through it. I only woke up a half hour ago."

"When did he call?"

I lifted the phone to look. "About three hours ago."

"Voicemail?"

I shook my head.

"And you haven't called him back?"

"No," I said softly.

"So you mean to tell me you left that poor man wondering where you were, what happened between you two to make you run off like that, and if you two are even still a couple?"

I gulped. "I know, I know!" I said, getting up out of bed to stand in front of Gilley. "I should've called him the minute I was on the plane to Texas."

"Definitely."

"And when I didn't, I should've called him the minute I got here."

"For sure."

I took a few steps to my right, then retraced them, then went back again because pacing felt better than sitting or standing still. "And I one-hundred-percent should've called him back the minute I woke up and saw that he'd called me. Twice."

Gilley winced at the word "twice" but he also added a "Hear, hear!"

I paced back and forth a few more times, staring at the pattern in the carpet as I went, acutely aware that I was a) still holding my phone which had Shepherd's number already cued up and b) that, by sitting causally on the bed with his lips pressed into a thin, judgmental line, Gilley was basically double-dog-daring me to find an excuse as to why I wasn't even now hitting that speed dial.

"Grrrrahh!" I growled and threw the phone onto the far side of the bed. "I can't, Gilley, okay? I just can't!"

"Can't what, love?"

I stopped pacing to stand and face him. "I *can't* break his heart. And calling him right now feeling as pressured as I am to say yes to something that I haven't thoroughly thought through would *defi-*

nitely make me want to turn him down, just to make a point!"

"How about a text?" he offered.

I stood there for several seconds staring at him with wide eyes. "And what would I say in a text?"

Gilley crossed his legs and pretended to study his nails. "Maybe something along the lines of; I'm truly sorry, Shep, but I need some time to work this through. I love you. I don't want to lose you and I promise I'll call you soon."

I bit the inside of my cheek for a few moments while I considered that. "Okay, so *that's* perfect."

Gilley stretched his arm out to grab my phone and he tossed it back toward me. "Let me know if you need me to repeat any of that."

I caught the phone and immediately began to type. "I got it," I told him. "Or the gist of it at least."

After crafting the text I held my finger over the Send button for another long moment.

"Oh for Petrov's sake," Gilley said, getting up he took a step toward me and tapped the arrow send button for me.

"I was getting there!" I scolded.

He gave me a pat on the head. "Sure you were, shug. Sure you were."

I glared at him but it did no good. He didn't look one bit guilty. "Shall we?" he asked, offering me his arm.

"What?" I asked.

"Head to the kitchen for breakfast. I've rustled up some french press coffee and just took out from the oven an apricot coffee cake this morning that'll make you fall even more in love with me."

I sighed out a small laugh softening my irritation with him. “Let me grab my robe,” I said. “I’ll be out in a minute.”

Gilley took my chin between his thumb and forefinger and said, “And brush your teeth. Maybe use a little mouthwash while you’re at it.”

My cheeks seared with heat and I quickly covered my mouth with my hand.

Gilley laughed. “Kidding,” he sang as he sashayed out the door.

“Brat!” I yelled after him.

I moved to the bathroom and gave my teeth a good scrub, then dug through my suitcase for my silver silk robe with blue trim, donned it and head to the kitchen. Once there I found Gil seated at the counter, sipping on some coffee with a big piece of coffee cake parked on a plate in front of him.

“That looks delicious,” I said, pointing to the morning pastry.

“Wait till you try it. I made a cream cheese frosting that takes it to the next level.”

My mouth watered just thinking about it. I took a seat next to Gil while he poured me a cup of Joe and cut me a slice of coffee cake. “Where’s Stuart?” I asked.

“Getting ready to head to the warehouse.”

“Does he really work out of a warehouse?”

Gilley nodded. “It’s a sleek looking warehouse as they go. About three thousand square feet and Stuart has use of all of it for his crew—not that he needs all that space, but it’s there for him if he wants it.”

“Are they building the floats there too?” I knew

only enough about the festival to remember that the queen and her court rode the parade route atop lavishly decorated floats.

"No. That crew is at an even bigger warehouse closer to the high school. There are a lot of kids that volunteer to work on the floats and the school encourages students to get involved. It's good for the community, I mean, half a million people come into town for this event and spend *lots* of money at local businesses, hotels, and restaurants so a community wide effort is just part of the town's civic duty."

I nodded and switched topics. "What're your plans for the day, Gilley?"

"I'm going to help Stuart at the—"

Gilley's voice was cut short when a loud, panicked cry sounded from the second floor. Both of us shot off our chairs and raced out of the kitchen toward the stairs. There, we saw Stuart, flying down the steps, his face ashen, his expression, panicked.

"What? What?" Gilley cried.

Stuart came the rest of the way down to us, and reached out to grip our hands. "It's Broderick!" he gasped.

I snapped my gaze to Gilley. I had no idea who Broderick was.

Sensing my confusion, Gilley muttered, "Broderick Carmichael—Stuart's top assistant designer."

Stuart nodded, and opened his mouth to speak again, but no words formed.

"What?" I asked, squeezing his hand and fearing the worst. "Stuart, what's happened?"

"He's dead," Stuart said at last.

"*What?*" Gilley and I said in unison.

"I . . . I just got the phone call," Stuart continued, his breathing erratic and his gaze swiveling to look back up the stairs where he'd no doubt left his phone.

"What happened?" I asked.

Stuart shook his head. "I don't know," he admitted. "Imani called. She's a wreck. She kept repeating, 'He's dead! He's dead!' and I asked her if she meant Broderick and she said, 'Yes.' That's all I could get out of her before the police were at her door and she had to hang up."

Gilley pulled Stuart forward and wrapped his arms around him. "Oh, love," he said gently. "I'm so sorry!"

I didn't know who Imani was, but I wasn't about to intrude on the moment with Gilley comforting Stuart by asking. Instead, I stood there and rubbed Stuart's back, feeling the moment when the shock wore off and the grief came. He shook as he cried on Gilley's shoulder. One glance at Gil told me his own eyes were misting as well as my own.

I didn't know these people at all, but Stuart's grief was so palpable, it simply gutted me to bear witness to it.

After a while, Stuart's sobs lessened, and he pulled back from Gilley to wipe at his eyes and sniffle. I hurried to the restroom right next to the stairs and grabbed a few tissues to bring to him. He took them gratefully and said, "I have to go. I have to get downtown. Imani needs me."

"Of course," Gilley said. "I'll drive. Cat can sit with you in the back if you'd like."

I nodded to show Stuart I was available for that duty and he smiled so sadly, tears still glistening on his cheeks. "Thank you. Let me just change and retrieve my phone and we'll go, okay?"

Once Stuart had hurried up the stairs to grab his cell, I turned to Gilley and said, "What do you think happened?"

"I have no idea," Gil said. "We spent a lot of yesterday with Broderick and his sister, Imani—she's a very talented maker, and nothing seemed amiss."

"Maker?"

"Dress maker."

"Ah," I said, then asked, "Was Broderick old?"

Gilley shook his head. "No. Younger than us, actually."

"Sick?" I asked next.

Again Gilley shook his head. "Peak of health."

I hesitated a moment, then whispered, "Suicide?"

Again, Gilley shook his head. "I can't see it, Cat. Like I said, we were with Broderick and Imani for most of the day yesterday. The man is—was lovely. He didn't seem at all depressed. Stressed, for sure, but not anything that had Stuart worried about his mental health."

"Car accident?" I whispered next.

Gilley bit his lip. "He's a true New Yorker. He doesn't have a driver's license. He and Imani Uber everywhere they go down here."

I stared at Gilley and he stared back, his expression mirroring my concern. *Murder?* I mouthed.

Gilley bit his lip, shook his head, then bit his lip again, and I knew that the feeling of doom in the pit of my stomach matched his own.

The odds that he and I would be embroiled in yet *another* murder mystery had to be astronomical. And yet . . . my gut was suggesting that this was the start of something ominous.

Gilley reached out and grabbed my hand, squeezing it tight. “Let’s hope not,” he said. “I mean, it’d be nice to go longer than six months without another murder to solve.”

I nodded and tried to smile but I knew that it failed to reach my eyes.

And, as it turned out, we wouldn’t make it even one month. But in that moment I could still hope that, although tragic, Broderick’s death wasn’t something that would sweep Gilley and me up in a web of danger, lies, and murder.

Ignorance is only blissful until the truth comes out and smacks you in the face.